MW00416051

FIRST COMES LOVE

EMILY GOODWIN

First Comes Love
Copyright © 2015 by Emily Goodwin
Photography by Kelsey Keeton
All rights reserved. This book or any portion thereof may
not be reproduced or used in any manner whatsoever without
the written permission of the publisher except for the use of
brief quotations in a book review.
This is a work of fiction. Names, characters, businesses, places,
events, and incidents are either the products of the author's
imagination or used in a fictitious manner. Any resemblance to
actual persons, living or dead, or actual events or places is purely
coincidental.

To anyone who's life hasn't gone according to plan

Other Books by Emily Goodwin

Contagious
Deathly Contagious
Contagious Chaos
The Truth is Contagious

Unbound
Reaper
Moonlight

Beyond the Sea

Stay
All I Need

Never Say Never

Outside the Lines

First Comes Love
Then Comes Marriage

One of Many

ACKNOWLEDGMENTS

While this book was a joy to write, the writing came at the most inconvenient time and putting the finishing touches on this book did not come easy. A huge thank you needs to go out to Erin Hayes, and Christine Stanley for keeping me calm and encourage, to the gals in my street team for being excited with me, the amazing writers in the BIC group for support an encouragement, and of course my family for everything.

NOAH
Then...

I CURL MY fingers into my palm, making a fist.

Clench.

Unclench.

I look at the boy on the floor, the one who just seconds ago threw the first punch. It was a punch I easily caught and deflected, which was embarrassing enough for him as it is. He thought he would win this fight. I twisted his arm and hit him back, popping him square in the nose. Blood is dripping down his face and he's scrambling away.

The small crowd that gathered around to watch the fight erupts into cheers. I smile, soaking it all in. I've been at this school a few weeks and already took down some mega-douche bully. I think. Maybe? I don't care. This guy—I don't even take the time to learn his name— wanted to fight.

And so did I.

"Fucking awesome," Colin Winters says as I turn and walk away. He's the first friend I made in this new town. "Josh deserved that. Hell, he's deserved that for years."

"Glad to be of assistance." I shrug like it's no big deal. And it's not, not really. I've been in my fair share of fights

… which is the reason I got expelled and am "starting over fresh," as Mom calls it, in this new town in Michigan.

"Come on, let's get out of here before Coach Cook catches you. We fucking need you for the game next week."

I nod, actually excited to be part of the football team. That's the best part of this fresh start so far. We go down the hall, joining a few other guys on the team.

"Noah Wilson!" a teacher calls out. Dammit. I roll my eyes and turn. "Principal's office. Now."

"I'll meet up with you later," I say to Colin and head to the office. Mrs. Jefferson's door is closed, so I sit on a cushioned chair across from the secretary's desk. I cross my arms and lean back, hoping I won't be too late for practice.

Finally, Mrs. Jefferson emerges from her office. I already know the drill. She calls my mom—who doesn't always show up—and we have a meeting to discuss my behavior and what I can do to fix it.

Wash. Rinse. Repeat.

It was this kind of shit that got me expelled from my old high school.

"We meet again, Mr. Wilson."

"It's your favorite part of the day, admit it," I say with a grin.

Mrs. Jefferson raises an eyebrow and sighs. "Humor isn't going to save you in the real world."

I just shrug. It's been six weeks at this new school and I've been to the principal's office, uh … I've actually lost count. Fighting, talking out in class, not doing homework, the usual. I just don't give a fuck.

They label me defiant, a troublemaker, the *bad boy*.

4

I can live with that.

But no one sees that it's hard to give a fuck when no one gives a fuck about you. It's been six weeks in this new town and I can count the number of times Mom's had dinner with me on one hand.

Whatever. It is what it is and it's been that way since Dad left. I'm used to it. Hell, I like it. I can do whatever I want, and she leaves me plenty of cash to get into trouble with.

Mrs. Jefferson looks at her watch—again—and then flicks her eyes to the door. Don't hold your breath, lady. Mom's going to be late … if she shows up at all. She got held up at work and missed the last meeting with the principal. There's something sympathetic in Mrs. Jefferson's eyes, and a small part of me wants to confess how lonely I am.

"She's going to take her sweet time," I huff. "Might as well get some of your other work done while you wait."

Mrs. Jefferson gives me a tiny nod and disappears into her office. I lean back in the chair, cross my arms, and debate on closing my eyes and napping. Sleep isn't something I'm doing much of lately. Not when I've been invited to party after party.

I'm sitting in front of the secretary's desk, with a clear view of the front doors of the high school. A black SUV slows and my heart actually skips a beat. Mom's here? She actually showed up within a reasonable amount of time?

The SUV rolls on and I catch the back bumper sticker that says the driver has a kid on the honor roll. Nope. That's not my mother. I sigh and let my eyes close. A minute later the office door opens and closes. Someone walks in, gait slowing as they draw near me.

"Is this seat taken?"

I look up, breath catching when I see her. Fuck, she's beautiful. It's my first thought.

Beautiful.

Not hot or sexy, but beautiful. Her eyes are kind and gentle, like eyes I could stare into for hours while talking about anything and everything. She nervously bites her lip as she waits for my reply, warm eyes widening just a bit.

They're the kind of eyes that can fill with lust in an instant, flicking up to me as I nail her.

I want to nail her.

I want to feel her, all of her. Now. I can't help it.

"No, it's not," I finally say and move my books out of the way. She sets her stuff down and gracefully perches on the chair. "I haven't seen you in here before," I blurt, heart lurching as she takes a seat next to me.

What the fuck is wrong with me?

Maybe the better question is, what the fuck is wrong with her? Why is she making me nervous, turning me on just by sitting in the goddamn chair next to me?

"I'm not in trouble," she says, then looks embarrassed. She's not in trouble, but I am. Six weeks and I have that reputation already. And she knows it. She knows who I am.

Why does that excite me?

"Why are you here then?" I ask.

Her sea-green eyes run over me with a bit of familiarity that throws me off-guard. It's not fair. She's looking like she knows me by more than my rep. Yet I have no idea who she is. I don't even know her name.

"I'm protesting."

I don't mean to laugh, but I do. She pushes her

perfectly full lips into a pout. "Sorry," I say, curbing my laughter. "You don't look like someone who would throw a public fit."

One of her eyebrows goes up and she pushes thick brown hair over her shoulder. "You don't have to cause a scene to make a statement."

"Yeah, true. What are you protesting?"

"The cats AP biology dissects," she starts.

"Let me guess," I interrupt, grinning, needing to say something because I had no idea advanced bio sliced up cats and the shock on my face doesn't jive with the bad boy image I've decided to roll with. "You think it's awful and want to put a stop to it?"

"Yes and no. I think it's important to learn about the body, but I don't think it should be a requirement. The less students who dissect cats, the less that have to die for the name of science."

"That's actually a really good point."

"Thanks." She smiles. "I hope Mrs. Jefferson thinks so too."

"She might." My mind races with something else to say, something intelligible that will make this girl want to keep talking to me. I should ask her name. I should tell her mine. I should say something, yet all I can do is stare at her beautiful face, unable to form a logical thought.

She.

Is.

So.

Distracting.

And I don't know why. I don't know why I'm reacting to her the way I am. This isn't me. I don't get tongue tied around chicks. I don't worry what they think of me.

7

Because I don't care.

So why do I have this weird yearning for this girl to like me? And why am I worried I'm not good enough for this stranger. This attractive stranger.

She pulls a notebook from her bag and flips through the pages. Doing my best to not be obvious, I look over her should and read her notes. She's written out what she's going to say to Mrs. Jefferson, like a script. It's cute, in a total OCD way.

"What side of the fence do you fall on?" I ask her. "Do you want to dissect the cat or no?"

She wrinkles her nose, distaste for cutting into a dead animal obvious. "I want to be a vet, so I should do it. Though at the same time, I'd rather wait until vet school. I don't see how this will benefit me now."

"Good idea. And being a vet would be cool." I'm internally wincing. Could I be more lame?

"I think so. Half the time I like animals more than people."

I chuckle. "I agree with you there. Animals don't let you down."

"Exactly!" she exclaims and turns toward me. Her hand lands on the armrest of the chair, fingers brushing my skin. It's the most innocent gesture, one she didn't even mean, yet leaves me craving her touch. "They don't judge you either."

"That's always a plus."

"I hate being judged," she says quietly. "And I try not to judge others." Color rushes to her cheeks and she looks away, head dropping and a shock of that gorgeous hair falling over her face. "I think if we were more like dogs the world would be a better place."

8

I refrain from a joke about sniffing asses and agree. "I like dogs. Never had one, but they're cool." And I'm wincing at myself again. Fuck. I just want this girl to like me.

"That's kind of sad," she tells me. "We have a dog. And two cats."

"Lucky." Suddenly I want to go get a dog just to have a reason to invite this girl over.

Mrs. Jefferson emerges from her office. "Oh, Lauren, you're early."

Lauren.

Right now, that's the best name in the entire world. *Lauren.* I repeat it in my head a few more times.

"It seems my prior meeting isn't going to happen, so come on in," Mrs. Jefferson says. "You're not off the hook yet, mister," she tells me. "Stay put, Noah."

I roll my eyes and lean back again, watching Lauren get up. She's wearing a pink and white dress, nothing out of the ordinary but nothing tight and revealing like so many of the other chicks in this school do. I admire her full ass as she walks into Mrs. Jefferson's office, wondering how I've never seen her before. She has to be a freshman. I've never seen this girl before in my sophomore class. Maybe? She didn't look that much younger than me.

It shouldn't matter, and she probably has a boyfriend anyway. For now. Someday, she'll be mine.

Someday Lauren will love me.

*

"Dude, what the hell is wrong with you today?" Colin tosses the football into the air and catches it.

9

"Nothing," I retort and drain my bottle of water. The sun is beating down on us during football practice today. It's late in the fall and we got hit with a week of unusually warm weather.

"You're a fucking liar, but I don't care as long as you get it together by the game tomorrow."

I roll my eyes and make up an excuse of fucking some college girl at a party last night for being distracted today. Colin doesn't press even though he knows it's another lie.

I'm not one to give a damn about labels, but I consider Colin my best friend. We have a lot in common and just get along great. I can't bullshit him, and he knows I wasn't at a party last night. Yet he doesn't push the issue. He knows when to stop and give me space. I respect the hell out of him for that.

The real reason for my distraction is Lauren, the girl from the principal's office protesting about dead cats. I haven't seen her since—and I looked.

But she's here today.

Sitting in the bleachers, at the top and by herself, away from the small crowd of girls who always watch us practice. Lauren hasn't looked away from the book she's reading. Not once.

I try to catch her eye the rest of practice but she's buried in that fucking book.

"You guys want to go to Pete's?" Josh asks Colin and me as practice concludes. Pete's Diner has cheap food and doesn't always card when you order beer. It's the popular hangout.

"I'm in," I say.

Colin grumbles, "I have to take my sister to the library."

"Bring her with," Josh suggests. "She's hot."

Colin shoots daggers at him. "Shut the fuck up."

"I'm just saying it like it is. Why are you driving Katie?" Josh asks. "She has a car."

I look over my shoulder at Lauren. She closed her book and is coming toward us. My heart and my dick jump. Fuck, she's beautiful.

"Not Katie," Colin says. "Lauren." *Lauren.* Funny he said her name the same time she makes eye contact with me. Colin turns around and sighs. "Speak of the devil."

Wait, what? I look from him to Lauren, the girl I'm going to make mine someday.

No.

No, no, no. Lauren is his sister. His *baby* sister.

She will never be mine.

CHAPTER ONE

LAUREN
Now...

I CHECK THE time on my phone and bite my lip, contemplating what to do. I take a deep breath and look around the restaurant, trying my hardest not to feel self-conscious about sitting alone—and about already finishing one glass of wine.

I shouldn't be alone, though. But for the last fifteen minutes, I've sat here solo, stomach grumbling from the wonderful smell of Italian food being served around me, waiting for my date to show up. It's not technically a blind date, since I've seen Gavin's pictures before, but we've yet to meet in person. I met him on one of those dating apps, and I think I can recognize him from his photos. Well, if he ever gets here.

To be fair, I got here early. I get everywhere early. If I don't, I panic. And yeah, I know the world won't end if I show up late to dinner, but being late opens the door to a lot of other bad stuff, like people thinking I'm rude, losing my table … making others wait on me. Serious shit like that. I know, I need to lighten up a bit. I try. Really, I do.

But life is easier when things go as planned, when I can stick to a schedule. Life is hard enough as is. Why make it even more chaotic?

My stomach grumbles again and I'm tempted to pull the fancy white-cloth napkin off the basket of bread that's been set on the center of the table. I inhale and lean back in my chair, feeling a bit woozy from the wine. I don't drink very often because I don't like the taste of alcohol, but a sweet bubbly wine like the one in front of me is too good to resist, and I agree to another glass when the waiter comes around.

I unlock my phone and text my sister, Katie, to tell her that my date hasn't arrived and is officially ten minutes late. I'll give him another ten then I'm paying for my wine and leaving.

And that it's all her fault. She set up the dating app and made my account. She's been with the same guy for seven years and is living vicariously through me, though the few dates she's set me up on never amount to anything but an awkward goodbye.

Five minutes later, I'm scrolling through Pinterest to keep myself busy and I feel someone stand near the table. I flick my gaze up and see Gavin. And he does look like his photos, thank God. I take a quick second to take it in: he's tall with broad shoulders, has a bit of gray peppered in his dark hair, and is well dressed. He's attractive in a non-obvious way. I can handle this.

"Lauren," he says with a smile.

"Yeah, hi," I say back and stand. Should I shake his hand? Or go in for a hug? We've talked on the phone and via private message, but I'm far from being comfortable around him.

He decides for me and leans in, wrapping his arms around me. He squeezes me tight and I almost choke on the smell of cigarette smoke on his clothes. I internally sigh. I hadn't thought to ask about that. Such a turn off.

"How are you?" he asks and releases me.

"I'm good," I say. "Hungry. You?"

He laughs softly. "Hungry too. And sorry I'm late. The temperature dropped and I had to change my socks. It's not cold enough for the wool ones yet, but cotton wasn't cutting it."

I take a step back toward my chair. "Uh, okay." Socks. What?

He lifts up his leg a bit so show me his feet, which are covered in bright-red fuzzy socks.

"Cold feet run in my family. So do hot feet, which leads to sweaty feet. So I have to find the right balance with sock thickness."

I just smile and nod. Yeah, that's weird. Too weird? Weird enough to bail out the bathroom window? I sit down and tuck my brown hair behind my ear. It's thick and doesn't hold a curl very well, so I left it naturally wavy, with some hair product help, of course.

The waiter comes over to take Gavin's drink order and to give us menus.

"Dinner is on me," he says. "Order whatever you want."

"Oh, thanks," I say and feel a little awkward. I didn't want to assume he was paying this whole time, but kind of thought he would since this was our first date and all. Fuck these social rules when it comes to dating. Why make an already awkward thing more awkward?

My phone buzzes on the table. It's Katie asking if my date showed up. I pull my phone into my lap and smile at Gavin. We put in our order for dinner, and I get up to use the bathroom, texting Katie as soon as I'm out of eye sight.

Me: *He went home to change his socks...because his feet were cold.*

Katie: *That's why he was late?*

Me: *Yes. He's wearing fuzzy socks. Fuzzy. Socks. What should I do?*

Katie: *Run. Probably has a foot fetish*

Me: *He's paying for dinner. I think I'll stay for free food lol. PS if he kills me and cuts off my feet, my death is on your shoulders. No big deal or anything.*

She sends me a kissy face emoji. *I only find the best for you, sis!*

I smile and shake my head, tuck my phone into my cleavage, and use the toilet. I wash my hands, give myself a quick onceover in the mirror, and go back to the table.

"So, how was your day?" Gavin asks when I sit down. He's gotten into the bread, thankfully. I grab a slice and butter it.

"It was pretty good. I worked, though. But I like my job."

"And you're a veterinarian?"

"I'm a vet tech."

"Oh, right. Like a nurse to animals."

"Yes, you can say that."

He smiles. "I love animals."

I smile back. That's one of the reasons I agreed to meet him on a date. His profile said he's animal lover. "Me too. Sometimes more than people."

He laughs, flashing me a broad smile. Gavin isn't a bad-looking man, not at all. "And you have a dog?"

"Two right now," I tell him. "My German Shepherd is a permanent resident and I foster when I can."

"That's just great," he says. "We had a dog when I was a kid. He was my best friend. He got hit by a car though, and Mom's allergic so I can't get another. But I still have Rufus."

"You live with your mom?" I ask, before the tail end of his statement hits me. His profile said he was twenty-nine. Several years older than me, but the age gap didn't seem like a big deal. And living with a parent wasn't a big deal either. A lot of people live with their parents after college. I did for a year and a half until I had enough saved up to move out and not be strapped for cash. "Wait, you still have the dog? He's still alive?"

"Oh no. He's been dead for years. He's stuffed."

"That's, uh, interesting."

Gavin eagerly nods. "Taxidermy is a bit of a hobby. You could say Rufus got me into it. I wasn't willing to let him go."

"Mh-hm," I say and squirm in my seat. A lot of people like taxidermy animals. They decorate their house with them, showing off game they caught and killed. A lot people might like that stuff, but I'm not one of them.

Thanks for this one, Katie.

"So," I say. "What else do you do?"

"I like to build stuff."

Building stuff is good. Manly. With tools. "What kind of stuff?"

"Right now I'm putting the finishing touches on an ice cream parlor to complete my village."

I raise an eyebrow and reach for my wine. I have a feeling I'm going to need another glass—or two—to get through this date.

"It's a dollhouse village," he says with a laugh. "I've

16

got three houses and a school completed."

"Oh, uh, interesting." Fuck a glass. I'm going to need a whole bottle. Nothing says serial killer like a foot fetish and hobbies that include posing dead things and dollhouses. I see it now: appearing on an MSNBC special, talking about my date with one of America's Most Wanted, saying he appeared normal and I had no idea he was capable of murder.

Except I did, because I'm thinking that now.

I'm deleting the dating app the moment I get home. Katie, you were right, as usual. I should have run when I had the chance.

*

"It's all right," I soothe and run my hand over a growling cat's head. "You'll feel better once we're done, I promise."

The tabby is tightly wrapped in a towel as Julie, one of my co-workers, carefully extracts ticks from her front legs. The cat hisses at me in response and tries to get away. I hold her tighter against me.

"So the date was a bust?" Julie asks.

"Total bust." I shiver at the thought. "He looked so normal online."

"Honey," Julie says and takes her eyes off the cat for a second to look at me. "You need to meet these men face to face. I didn't meet my husband on an app."

"Apps probably weren't invented when you got married."

"Hey now," she says but smiles. "It's only been ten years."

I laugh. "I agree, and it was my sister's idea," I remind her. I'm twenty-two and in no rush to get married, but ever since my brother celebrated his one-year anniversary a few months ago, everyone else is in a rush to find me a husband. I'm the youngest of the three Winters children, and incredibly picky, according to my mother, who has set me up with countless different men, all sons of her church friends.

I'm selective when it comes to dating. I don't want to settle, and I don't see the point in seeing someone more than once if I don't think it will lead anywhere. Yeah, I know what I want is probably unrealistic, but I blame Disney for putting the idea of Prince Charming in my head when I was a little girl.

But that's what I want. Not an actual prince, but someone who treats me like a princess. And by that I mean someone who loves and respects me, someone romantic and reliable, who would go through hell and back to fight for my heart. Because I'd do the same for them. I want an epic love, one that can stand the test of time and a villain or two, and come out stronger in the end.

So while I wait for my knight in shining armor to come galloping in on a white horse, I'm focusing on my career, and waiting to hear back from the vet school I applied to, which doesn't leave much time for love. And, right now, I'm okay with that.

"I think I'll just avoid men for a while," I say as Julie pulls another tick. "Or just find someone to have fun with for one night."

Julie straightens up only to double over with laughter. A few other techs look at us, wondering what is so funny.

"Oh please, girl," Julie says and lets out a breath.

18

"You, have a one-night stand? Let me know when that happens because I don't think I'll live to see the day!"

"I'll send you pictures."

"Mhh-hmm," she says and moves back to the cat. "Please do. I'll need proof."

"Oh come on, it's not that hard to believe."

Julie just laughs again. I shake my head and try to soothe the growling cat. I'm no prude, but I learned the hard way giving it up on the first date doesn't lead to what I wanted for a second date. I want a relationship, not meaningless sex. Although, I do enjoy sex. Meaningless or not.

I don't leave the clinic until nearly eight PM. The early March air is past chilly and back to cold. Frost glistens on the windows of my Jeep. Every spring, I wonder why the hell I still live in Michigan. I'm sick of the cold by now. I dig into my pockets for gloves, start the SUV, then start scraping away at the ice. We had a random few days of warm weather last week.

What a tease.

But that's the weather near Lake Michigan for you. I check my phone while I wait for the car to warm up. I have a text from Jenny, my sister-in-law, asking if we are still on for a wine and canvas art event tomorrow. Katie, Jenny, and I try to do stuff monthly, and it's actually really nice to have "sister night" every now and then, even more so now since Rachel, my childhood friend, moved to Dallas with her fiancé last summer. I have no one else to hang out with.

I reply "yes" to my sisters, test the heat in the Jeep to make sure it's not blasting cold air, and head home. I live in an old, small house in quiet part of town. I have a living

room, an eat-in kitchen, one bathroom, and two
bedrooms. It's tiny, but it's all I need.

"Hey, guys!" I say when I unlock the backdoor and
the dogs come running over, tails wagging so hard their
whole bodies shake. "Sorry I got home so late. We had an
emergency that I couldn't leave."

I drop to my knees, petting Vader and Sasha, the
rescue. She's not good around people, hence the fostering.
I've had many dogs come in and out of the house over the
last year, but there is something different about the
stubborn mutt that made me keep her.

I let the dogs out into my small, fenced-in yard and
start my after-work routine. I eat dinner, and take the dogs
for a walk. We make it one block before I'm too cold so
we turn around. Then I come in, shower, make a lunch for
tomorrow, and watch my recorded shows until it's time for
bed.
Yeah, okay, my life isn't super exciting. But it's steady, and
I like knowing what to expect. It's safe that way.

*

"Just to warn you, you won't have a brother much
longer." Jenny pours wine into three plastic cups and gives
one to me and another to Katie. We are sitting in an art
studio, waiting for the Wine and Canvas event to start.

"What did he do now?" Katie asks, bringing her cup
to her lips.

Jenny reaches up, twisting her red hair into a bun, then
secures with a clip. "He wants to get a motorcycle again."
She rolls her eyes. "It took me two years to get him to sell
his old one. If he thinks he's getting a new one, he's got

another thing coming."

"Sounds more like someone has been hanging around with Noah," Katie says with a smirk.

"Ugh, don't get me started on him." Jenny lets out a breath.

I arrange my paint brushes in a row in front of me, mind flashing to my brother's best friend. They met sometime in high school and Noah was trouble from the start. After getting expelled at his old high school, he came to ours and hit the ground running, quickly earning the reputation of the bad boy your mother warned you about, a reputation he still carries with him today.

And my mother *did* warn me about him. She warned me to stay far, far away from boys like Noah. And even farther away from men like him.

He spent high school in and out of trouble, getting more detentions than anyone I knew, yet somehow remained the star of the football team. His track record isn't as spotted now, but I don't think it's from learning his lesson, but instead by learning how to not get caught.

I haven't seen him in a while, but he hasn't changed much over the years. Except he gets better looking every damn time I lay eyes on him. Tall, with thick brown hair, sky-blue eyes, a stubble-covered face, tattoos, muscles, and a motorcycle ... Men like him should come with a warning label.

Men like Noah Wilson are nothing but trouble.

I may or may not have had a secret crush on Noah since I was fifteen and saw his gorgeous face for the first time. Between my father outright forbidding Katie or me to so much as flirt with a boy like Noah, and Colin promising to make my life hell if I crushed on his friends—and do the same to them if they crushed on me—I watched Noah from the sidelines, dreaming about a day when the popular boy would take notice of the shy underclassman. Obviously that never happened, and I've let go of the idea of Noah wanting me.

"They've been going to the gym together every morning," Jenny says. "Which is fine, Colin can stand to get in better shape, but why does it have to be with him, ya know?"

I smile and shake my head. "Good luck with that. I never knew what Colin saw in him. Well, other than being friends with the popular kid."

"Just lay down the law," Katie says. "No sex if he gets a motorcycle."

Jenny diverts her eyes. "I thought about that, but that's not an option."

"Why?" Katie and I ask at the same time, our minds on a similar wavelength.

"We've been kind of trying for a baby," Jenny says with a smile her on face.

Katie and I burst into excitement, then start bickering over who will be the best aunt.

"It'll totally be me," I say. "Kids love animals, and I always have animals. Plus I own every Disney movie and like wearing costumes."

"But I'm the fun aunt," Katie says. "I do fun shit all the time."

"Your fun shit isn't kid appropriate," I tell her with a laugh.

"Guys," Jenny says, still smiling. "Don't get too excited. I have a few issues that might make it difficult anyway. Colin and I don't want to get too excited just to be disappointed."

"What kind of issues?" Katie asks.

"I have cysts on my ovaries and have never had a regular cycle," Jenny says, her smile fading. "I've been on birth control to regulate things, but the doctor warned me it will make things difficult, though not impossible. I stopped taking the birth control, and we're just seeing if it happens on its own." The smile creeps back on her face.

"I think that's reason enough to *not* get a motorcycle," I say. "Just guilt Colin into leaving you widowed and pregnant."

Jenny laughs. "Good thinking." She shakes her head. "I'm really trying not to stress about it, since stress makes it worse. And," she picks up her wine, "I'm going to enjoy this while I can. Anyway, how was your date last weekend?"

I raise an eyebrow then glare at Katie, who snickers. "There will not be a second one, I'll leave it at that."

"So you're open to another date this Friday?"

"I think I'm done with the dates for a while." Really, I'm done with the setups. Because I keep getting set up with people totally incompatible with me, and it's starting to feel like there is something wrong with me personally when date after date after date ends with a big fat nothing.

"Then this is perfect! Just something fun, no pressure."

"If he buys me dinner, maybe." There is no denying I like a free meal.

Katie laughs. "You can almost always bribe Lauren with food, you know."

"I'm starting to figure that out," Jenny says. "But seriously. One of my co-worker's friends just got out of a

23

serious relationship and wants to get back into the dating world."

"That doesn't make me want to go out with him," I confess. "I'm not a rebound type of person." I consider it. "Or maybe I am."

"It's just dinner," Jenny says. "I met him once. He's tall, handsome, and just got hired at some big law firm. And I hear he's great in bed."

"Fine," I sigh. "But I don't hook up after one date."

"But you'll go to dinner with him?"

"Yeah, dinner."

"Great!" Jenny takes out her phone and texts someone, presumably her friend to tell her I'm agreeing to go out with this guy.

"Then no more after this," I say, talking to Katie, who enjoys playing matchmaker as much as she enjoys a good Netflix and chill.

"It hasn't hurt anything," Katie says back. "And you've gotten to go to some pretty swanky restaurants because of it."

"That is true. And it gives me a reason to buy fancy shoes. I like fancy shoes."

"See?" Katie finishes her wine and leans back in her chair.

"Dinner and a movie Friday at seven?" Jenny asks me. Wow, that was a fast response. Is the guy that desperate? "You can pick the movie."

"I do want to see *The Last Ride*," I say. "You know I have a huge celeb crush on Aiden Shepherd."

"Probably don't bring that up," Katie says.

"Oh please," I say with a wave of my hand. "Like I'd even have a chance. Celebrities don't date regular people."

"Aiden Shepherd does," Jenny says. She follows all that celebrity gossip. "He's engaged and getting married this summer to some girl who's not famous."

"That's not fair," I grumble. Though I just like the characters played by the actor. I'm a sucker for a villain turned hero in fantasy series. "So tell me more about this guy I'm going out with Friday night."

CHAPTER TWO

NOAH

"WE'VE GOT TO stop meeting like this." I smile as Officer Reilly uncuffs me. I bring my hands around to the front of my body and rub the sore skin. Asshole tightens them on purpose.

"I won't hold my breath," the cop sighs. "Live and learn doesn't apply to you. Especially when that old man refuses to press charges." He casts his gaze at Joey, the owner of The Roadhouse. He's been like a father to me over the years and never presses charges. "One of these days you won't get so lucky," he warns me.

"Yeah, yeah." Deep down I know it's true. Another bar fight turned drunk and disorderly, leading to property destruction. Basically, I got pissed at someone for something that's not important enough to remember and used a window to break his face.

Or something like that.

The guy was drunker than me and took a swing at Officer Reilly, diverting the attention away from me. I got lucky.

And luck runs out.

I'm willing to push it a little bit farther tonight and go back into the bar, staying for another couple hours before heading home to my apartment. It's been home for the last two-and-a-half years and has more space than I actually need, with a huge kitchen I never use filled with brand-new appliances and shiny, granite countertops.

I pull my keys from my pocket the same time the woman across the hall opens her door. Our eyes meet and I smile, tipping my head toward my door. She returns the smile and crosses the hall.

"Just getting in?" Melody asks, reaching for me. "Late night."

I put my arm around her slim waist and pull her in. "It's about to get later."

"I like the sound of that," she says and we move inside, clothing coming off instantly. Melody isn't beautiful, but she's hot by anyone's standards. She's tall, fit, and tan. Her hair is dyed blonde, usually done up, as well as her makeup. Her tits are as fake as her new nose, but what the hell? You're only young once. She told me her goal in life was to look like a blonde Kardashian, whatever the hell that means.

We fumble our way into my bedroom and fuck on top of my unmade bed. I collapse next to her when we're done, and she rolls over, running her fingers through my hair like she did the last time we fucked.

"Noah," she pants.

"Melody," I say back.

She pushes up, large breasts smashed against my chest. Melody moved in across the hall three months ago, and we've hooked up several times. It's been a good arrangement. She makes up some excuse to come over, then another to take off at least one item of clothing, then we end up in here, naked and tangled together.

Or sometimes I bang her in the kitchen.

Or against the large, floor-to-ceiling windows in the living room.

She hangs around for a while then leaves. The rules have been unspoken, but she knows I'm not one to date. What we have—or don't have, really—is working out great.

"I've been thinking," she starts, speaking slowly as she traces a tattoo on my chest with her finger. I flick my gaze to her face. Fuck. She has that look in her eye. I should have known better than to shit where I eat.

Or in this case, fuck who lives across the hall from me.

"Oh yeah?"

"We should go out sometime."

I flip her over on top of me and smack her ass. "Why should we do that when we have so much fun in here?"

She laughs, but it's not enough. Fuck me. "I'd love to introduce you to my girlfriends."

"Some other time, babe," I say, not wanting to cross her off just yet. This is what my life is about.

No strings. Nothing to hold me back, to slow me down. Fucking, drinking, and raising hell might catch up with me someday, but not today.

"I gotta get ready for work," I tell her.

She sighs and gets up, putting her clothes back on. "I'll see you again?" she asks.

"Sure thing. We live in the same building."

She gives me a "that's not what I meant" look that I ignore. Just take the hint so I don't have to tell you. I'm don't deliberately break hearts. Just accidentally.

I'm not against a relationship. Having a steady girlfriend, someone to come home to … someone to love. But I won't settle. I'll keep looking for that one woman I can't live without, the one who completes me in a lame Hallmark card sort of way. Though really, I don't have to search hard. I know exactly where that woman is, where she's been all these years.

Problem is, she'll never love me.

CHAPTER
THREE

LAUREN

I TAP MY nails along the pink case of my phone, watching TV while checking the time every thirty freaking seconds. My date is five minutes late, and every minute that ticks by tells me this is a horrible idea.

And I think I'm being stood up.

Which bothers me and doesn't at the same time. This guy doesn't know me, so I can't take it personally (but I do.) Because what if Jenny showed him my picture and that was enough of a turn off? I'm not bad looking, but I'm nothing spectacular.

Vader and Sasha lay by my feet, both chewing on various dried cow parts. I take my attention back to the TV, watching Ariel swim through the ocean, longing for a man she can't have. I love when the Disney Channel plays the classics on the weekend. Though, it's not like I don't own every single one of them on DVD.

Ten minutes later, I stand up to change. I catch a glimpse of myself in the mirror above the couch and sigh. I went all out tonight. Attempted to curl my hair, heavy eye makeup that even included my eyebrows. According to the millions of beauty pins I went through on Pinterest, that's a must. It took three tries, but I was able to contour my face.

I'm wearing my best pushup bra, giving my average-sized breasts the biggest boost possible. Over that went a pink dress that showed off my cleavage and hugged my curves. I have on my favorite charm bracelet (all the charms came from childhood vacations to Disney world) and Cinderella earrings. Yeah. I like Disney. A lot.

I'm dressed to the nines with nowhere to go. What a waste of time. I make it into my bedroom when the dogs bark. Is my date finally here? I quickly fluff my hair and pad my way through the living room, standing in the tiny foyer, if you can even call it that.

A car is in front of my house, but no one has gotten out yet. I spy through the living room window. The guy— Luke is his name—looks like he's on the phone. A few more minutes tick by before he kills the engine and gets out.

Twenty minutes late.

It might be stupid, but I'm insulted. Yeah, this is a blind date but have some freaking respect. And yeah, I'm taking it personally again. *Dammit.* I hurry into the kitchen, grab a handful of dog treats, and toss them as far as I can when the doorbell rings. I step into tall heels, grab my purse, and slip on my coat, then sneak onto the porch.

"Hi," I say, closing the door before Vader can rush out. He's protective like that. "Sorry, it's just easier to keep the dogs inside."

Luke, who is tall, dark, and handsome like Jenny promised, smiles. "Sounds like it."

I hold out my hand. "I'm Lauren, nice to meet you."

Luke takes a second to look me over before shaking my hand. Does that mean I met his approval?

"Luke. Shall we get going?"

31

"Yeah," I say and snap my mouth shut. *I will not comment on how late he is ... I will not comment on how late he is.* "Where are we going?"

"La Cantina," he says and walks ahead of me to his black BMW. "My buddy's working the bar tonight and can get us free margaritas."

"Sounds fun," I say. I've never heard of that restaurant, but I do like Mexican food. And watermelon margaritas. Though if I get one, I need to drink it slow. Tequila and I don't mix. Or maybe we do mix, and mix too well? It doesn't take much to get me shit-faced and blacked out when it comes to drinking tequila. Been there, done that in college.

I get in the car and settle onto the leather seat. It smells new, and everything is impeccably clean. Luke plops into the driver's side and starts the car. Rap music blasts from the speakers. We make it down two blocks before he turns the volume to a level where we can speak.

"So, your sister-in-law tells me you're a vet?"

I mentally roll my eyes. Why do people always think I'm a veterinarian? Do they not know what a tech is?

"I'm a vet tech. Very much like an animal nurse."

"Ah, so you want to be a vet then."

I do, but am able to pull apart the subtle insult in his statement. Do all nurses want to be doctors? Nope. Do all techs want to be vets? You bet your ass not.

"Yes. I just applied to vet school. I'm waiting on the reply now."

"I'm a lawyer," he says without me having to ask. "And I just got in at the Harrison firm. You've heard of them, I'm sure."

"Uh, probably. Do they have a commercial with a

cheesy yet catchy song?" I ask and turn to him, smiling.

"No," he says, void of any humor. "The Harrison firm doesn't need commercials." I raise my eyebrows and nod. He tells me about his hot-shot firm the rest of the way, talking himself up the entire time.

Maybe he's nervous and trying to impress me … or maybe this guy is just an asshole and that's why his girlfriend left him.

La Cantina is on the outskirts of town, bordering the line between where I feel safe and where I'd never dare go alone at night. Or during the day. It's just a part of town I'd avoid unless I had a sword-wielding Prince Charming at my side. And by sword I mean guns, because I'm pretty sure this is where the high school kids come to buy drugs.

We wait for a table in the busy restaurant, then get seated near the bar. Luke leaves me to talk to his bartender friend, and after ten minutes, I look around and see him talking it up with a pretty blonde behind the counter. So that's his "buddy." Interesting.

He comes back with two drinks in hand. I take a sip of mine and recoil. It's so strong.

"So, Lauren," he starts. "Tell me more about yourself. What do you do for fun?"

I dip a chip into salsa and look at Luke. Fun. My definition of fun probably isn't his. "I like to read and watch TV. I'm a sucker for fantasy shows. And I foster dogs, so I spend a lot of time training them. I love anything Disney and have been getting into online computer games a bit lately. One of my friends raves about *League of Legends*."

He keeps looking at me, and I realize he's waiting for me to continue and tell him something he can agree is "fun." But that's what I like to do. I like to hang out at home with a good book or a good show. I like to cuddle with my dogs and pretend I'm going to go off on an adventure where I battle villains and meet Prince Charming.

"Do you work out or anything?"

I nod. "I jog with the dogs. I'm not really a fan of running. I mostly do it in case I find a wardrobe or something that takes me to a magical land. I want to be ready for an epic battle."

Luke looks at me like I'm a circus freak. He's never heard of Narnia? He's the circus freak.

"What about you?" I say and eat the chip I've been holding.

"I hang with friends. Work out. Play video games on the weekend when I'm not playing football with the guys."

I mentally sigh. He doesn't need to go on to explain. He's basic; one of those people who likes mainstream stuff just to be mainstream, and anyone who doesn't blindly float down the river of social norms is labeled, and not in a good way. People like him still apply the middle school caste system, and he's a jock and I'm a nerd.

Well, fuck you, Luke, and your high-paying job and good looks. I sit back and smile, covering up how crappy I'm feeling inside. If he doesn't like me, his loss … blah, blah, blah, I know. But still … no one likes to be given *that* look.

We make awkward small talk until our food comes, and then he starts telling me about a case he's working on. He knows his client is guilty of discriminating against pregnant women, and "can see why." And now I just can't with him.

"But that's illegal," I say. "And you're supposed to uphold the law, right?"

He waves his hand in the air. "That's what cops do." He leans in. "And, honey, I make hell of a lot more than a damn cop."

I almost choke on my taco. So he's saying he doesn't have to uphold the law as long as he gets paid, right? Wow. This guy is a winner. I have no idea why his long-term relationship ended. I roll my eyes, not even attempting to hide it.

"Hiring a pregnant lady cost my client's company. Filling her position during leave takes away too. And when they have one, they tend to have more. Having a baby makes women all whack-a-do crazy with hormones and shit."

I scoop up the last of my rice and beans, using my fork to push it onto my chip. I finish chewing, swallow, and take a big sip of my margarita. Then I grab my purse and coat.

"I need to use the bathroom," I say. I get up and walk right out the door. I call Katie as I walk, and get her voicemail. She's probably out with her friends and can't hear her phone right now, and most likely isn't in the position to drive anyway.

I step onto the covered patio, getting an instant chill. Misty rain is falling around me, and the air is thick with the threat of a storm. I put my coat on and call Jenny. She doesn't answer either. She's probably working and won't be off until later. I try my brother next; still no answer. I sigh. I could call my mom, but I don't want to make her drive all this way. Julie is another option, but it's late and she has her kids.

I need to get away from Luke before I throw a drink in his face or stab him with my fork. He makes my skin crawl, and the thought of getting in the car alone with him is quite frightening. I look around the dimly lit street. There is a bar not far from here, definitely within walking distance.

It's called The Roadhouse and ninety percent of the parking lot is filled with motorcycles, despite the chilly air and the threat of heavy rain. If anything, I can go in, order a drink, and wait for one of my family members to answer. Jenny owes me; after all, she set this disaster of a date up. It's getting late, so she should be off soon, and I'm not that far from the hospital for her to come pick me up. I try Katie one more time then push off the side of the building, walking toward the glow of the neon sign.

CHAPTER

NOAH

THE BAR IS busy, packed like usual on a Friday night. The crowd is rough and loud, the music even louder, the smell of cigarettes, booze, and leather filling the air. I bartended here for years, and paid my way through college on tips. It holds a special place in my heart. I used my first fake ID to get in here. I got in my first bar fight at this place. And it was my first place of legit employment.

Joey, the owner, isn't getting younger, and he's filling in for a call-off tonight and playing second bartender. I came here with the intention to bring someone home with me, but when I see the old man struggle, I hop behind the bar and take a few orders. I was one hell of a bartender back in the day. You don't lose those skills.

I'm taking in orders, grabbing my tips, and serving drinks at record speed all while talking to the regulars and hitting on women. Time flies by and a weird sense of nostalgia takes over, like I'm back in college and working my ass off to get an art degree. No one but Joey knew how much it meant to me to actually graduate. I wanted to come home with that fucking degree if it was the last thing I did.

The mad rush slows down, and I'm about to hit the floor again. I've already set my eye on who I'm going to take home with me tonight. I have it all planned out, and am ready to cut through the crowd to get to the chick in the tight leather pants. Yet I just happen to look up the door opens.

And *she* walks in.

My heart does a weird skip-a-beat thing. Just like it did the first time I saw her. I freeze, and run my eyes over Lauren Winters. She's wearing a low-cut pink dress that showcases her tits and hugs all her curves. Her dark hair is swept up and away from her face, and her makeup is done, simple yet elegant.

She's beautiful.

Just like the first time I saw her all those years ago when we were just teens. I wanted her then, back in high school, before I found out she was my best friend's sister. Being off-limits only made me want her more, and I've never been able to fully get her out of my head.

Over the years I got to know her. She's a little neurotic, which is adorable in a weird way, and one of the kindest people I've ever met, one of those people who'd do anything for anyone. She poured her heart and soul into helping animals, and is quiet, kind of a book nerd, keeps to herself, and stays out of trouble.

She's my exact opposite.

And right now, she's looking upset. I go around the bar to get to her. When I look for Lauren again, she's gone, hidden behind the many bodies that crowd the bar.

I go from curious to concerned. This isn't the type of bar someone like Lauren Winters should be at alone, or, really, at all. The crowd here is rough, and no one comes in wearing a classy dress, expensive heels, and gets out with no trouble.

Why the fuck is she here?

I wipe my hands on my pants and hurry through the crowd, pushing past dancers. I need to find Lauren.

Finally, I spot her in the back, leaning against the wall. She looks frightened and keeps her head down, quickly typing on her phone. Right before I get to her, Neil, one of the regulars, blocks my path. Oh fuck no. I know Neil, and know he's a pushy asshole when it comes to women. I might not have room to talk, but I'm never pushy. I never have to force myself on a woman to get her to sleep with me. Not like Neil does. I've had to escort him out more than once for getting too up close and personal with the ladies.

"Lauren," I call in a loud, deep voice.

Her head snaps up and she has to look around Neil's large frame to find me. She smiles and relief brightens her face. I don't think she's ever looked relieved to see me.

"Noah," she says and Neil turns. He doesn't particularly like me. I have thrown a few punches to put him in his place. He huffs and leaves, acting like he was walking somewhere else anyway.

"What are you doing here?" I ask when I get closer. I notice her hair is damp. So is her jacket. It's been raining on and off all evening.

She lets out a breath and shakes her head. "Long story."

I raise an eyebrow and cross my arms. She's a several inches shorter than me, even in heels. It takes everything I have not to stare down her dress. She has a rocking body, one I'd love to touch and have on me, under me, pressed against me in any way, but she never shows it off.

Conservative, that's how she's always been.

"You're at a biker bar dressed like you just left the fucking opera. I need to hear this story."

"Jenny set me up with someone for a date and it did not go well."

"That's not a long story."

"That's a summary."

I smile. "What happened?"

"What?" she calls over the thumping base.

I lean in closer, putting my hand on her waist. She moves away but backs into the wall. She can't get any farther from me. "What happened on this date?"

She purses her lips and shakes her head. Then she sighs and moves her face closer to mine, putting her lips by my ear. Her breath on my skin makes me shiver.

There is not a single woman in the world I've wanted more than Lauren Winters.

Not a single woman in the world is more off-limits than her.

And there has never been a single incident where she has indicated any sort of attraction to me. Not once, and I've thrown a few moves at her from time to time. It's frustrating, a bit of an ego blow, and really, just makes me want her more. She's a challenge, but it's so much more than that.

Lauren is everything I'm not, everything I don't deserve. I respect her as much as I want her.

"The guy was a total sexist pig. So I left."

"You just walked out?"

She nods. "I said I was going to the bathroom. I think he got the hint when I took my coat and purse."

I lean away just enough to look into her eyes. "Sorry you had a date that bad."

"I got a free dinner out of it, at least. But Jenny's probably going to get an earful. It was a friend of a friend sort of thing."

"But how did you end up here?"

"We were at that Mexican restaurant down the street. He drove, and I'm not getting in a car with him. I called Katie, Colin, and Jenny, but no one picked up. So I walked here to get out of the rain and to hide from the asshole. And I can really use a drink right now."

"I think you need one after that kind of night. Come to the bar, it's on me."

"Thanks," she says. I extend my hand and she looks at it for a moment, considering taking it. She looks around the crowded bar and pulls her shoulders in. She knows she's out of place here. After the longest few seconds, she puts her hand in mine and lets me lead her through the crowd.

I kick another regular out of his spot at the bar so Lauren can take a seat. She pulls her jacket closer to her body and smiles at me again. The gesture is cordial at best, and I know she's just waiting for someone to come get her and take her away from this place.

It shouldn't bother me. So why the fuck am I taking it personally?

"What do you want to drink?" I ask her.

She wrinkles her nose just a bit, and I find it adorable. "I don't know. I don't really like the way booze tastes, unless it's wine."

I laugh. "You can't get wine here. Want a beer? I can get you one of those sissy lime-flavored ones."

"I don't like beer either."

"You're killing me."

"Sorry," she offers. "Make me something that tastes good?"

"I can do that." I quickly make her a Cherry Vodka Sour then get flagged to fill another order. Joey is struggling, and Lauren is hunched over, busy texting, so I mix up another few drinks before I go back to her.

In the few minutes it takes me to get everyone around the bar what they ordered, Lauren has finished her drink.

"Can I have another?" she asks and leans back a bit. Her body begins to relax, starting with her shoulders. She's always been a bit uptight. "That kind of tastes like lemonade. It's good."

"Sure," I say and mix up another. She sips it slowly and diverts her eyes to her phone.

"Find a ride?" I ask, leaning on the bar so she can hear me.

"Not yet."

"I can take you home," I tell her.

"But you're working."

"Actually, I'm not. Just helping out."

"Oh," she says, looking confused. Is she drunk already? "Okay."

I go back behind the bar to get my leather jacket, talking down my cock. Lauren is my best friend's sister. I've known her for years. She should feel like my sister. I should not be thinking about rolling the straps of that tight dress off her shoulders, watching it fall to the floor. I should not be wondering what she tastes like, what it would feel like to stick my dick inside her.

"Ready?" she asks me when I get to her side.

"Yeah, come on."

She follows me outside, heels wobbling on the gravel

drive. The rain has stopped and the night is cool. I zip up my jacket and tell Lauren to do the same.

"Why?" she asks and pops buttons into place. "Does the heat not work in your car?"

"Oh it works just fine," I say and fish the keys from my pocket. "But I didn't drive my car tonight."

She slows, tipping her head as she tries to make sense of what I said. I stop next to my bike.

"Oh hell no!" she exclaims. "I can't ride that! I'm in a dress!"

I give her a crooked grin. "That's never stopped anyone before. Hop on, baby."

She arches an eyebrow. "Don't call me baby. And you said nothing about riding that *thing* when you said you'd take me home. I'm in a dress and heels and it's cold."

"Then go back inside and wait for a ride, princess." I don't start the bike, don't make a move to get on. I'm not going to leave her here, no way. Not dressed like that, and not drunk. Not ever. Because I never want to do anything that doesn't make Lauren happy.

"Maybe I will," she says. "And I'll find someone with a car to take me home."

"Really? Be my guest then," I say flatly with a shake of my head. She might be drunk, but she's not shit-faced enough to think that's actually a good idea.

She lets out a breath. "Just take me home."

I fire up the engine and laugh. "You know," I say and turn back to Lauren. "I've never had an issue getting a chick on the bike before."

"Sure," she says and rolls her eyes.

"Really. They dig it."

She slowly runs her gaze over me and then looks at

the bike. "I suppose some people might find getting on the back of a motorcycle with a leather-clad tattooed man sexy."

Was that a compliment? Does she find me sexy? Fuck, I need to distance myself. "Of course they do. Have you seen me?" I smile so she's knows I'm joking, though really, this works.

"Try it on me."

"On you ... on ... what?"

"Your lines. That these women supposedly 'can't resist' and go home with you." She even adds air quotes when she's talking.

"I can't just say it. It has to happen naturally."

"Mhh-hmm. So pretend you already put the moves on me. We're out in the parking lot after all."

I shrug. "Then I'd say something like get on, come home with me, then I'll get you off." I lower my voice as I speak and give Lauren the best eye fuck I can.

It always works.

But not this time, and she doubles over laughing. "Sorry," she says, gasping for air. She straightens up, wipes her eyes, and laughs again. "That actually works?"

My jaw is set. "Every time."

"If you say so."

I swing my leg over the bike. "Get on."

She comes up behind me and puts her hands on my waist. I can't think about it. I can't acknowledge her gentle touch. "Then you can get me off," she says in a deep voice, imitating me. And now she's laughing again. Maybe she's drunker than I thought.

We're halfway to her house when it starts to rain. We are both soaked and freezing by the time we get there.

Lauren opens the garage door and there is just enough room to squeeze the bike in. I hate when my baby gets rained on.

"Come in," she says through chattering teeth. "You can hang out until the rain stops."

For as long as I've known Lauren, walking into her house doesn't feel strange. What feels strange is taking someone home from the bar and not getting any.

She's Colin's baby sister. I can't do this.

Her dogs bark at me, and I almost run back into the rain when a large German Shepherd lunges for me. I've actually met the dog before, having gone to a few family get-togethers at the Winters' house.

"Hey, Vader," I say to him.

He barks and flashes his teeth. "It's okay," Lauren says, holding him back. How the hell is she not falling over? That dog has to weigh close to what she does. It takes several minutes of talking to the dog to get him to let me in the house.

When Lauren lets him go and stands, she closes her eyes and shakes her head. "I'm a bit dizzy."

I reach out, steadying her. "How about you take those heels off?"

"Good idea." She kicks them off and disappears into her room, returning in a minute in her pajamas. "I don't have any guy clothes for you to wear."

I take off my jacket and peel my wet black T-shirt over my head. "Do you have a dryer?"

Her eyes widen when I undo my belt and pull down the zipper of my jeans. "I ... uhh ... I." She blinks a few times. "Yes. I do." She holds out her hand for my wet clothes, shaking her head as she walks away. I smirk, somewhat surprised I got that kind of reaction out of her.

Fuck. Stop it. I can't. She's off-limits. My best friend's sister.

I follow her as she walks through the living room and into the kitchen, disappearing into the laundry room. I open the fridge and look for something to eat. I'm hungry, and Lauren probably is too. Her fridge is full, but it's all ingredients, all healthy stuff. I don't want to make anything. I close the fridge and open the freezer.

There is one frozen pizza, buried underneath more healthy crap ... and a bottle of tequila. I pull it out, grinning.

"For someone who claims not to drink," I start when she comes back into the kitchen. "This is an awfully big bottle of booze."

She waves her hand in the air. "I didn't say I don't drink, I just don't like the way alcohol tastes. And it's from a sex toy party. Months ago."

My eyebrows go up. "You had a sex toy party?"

"Yeah, why is that so surprising."

I step back and let the freezer door close. "You just don't seem like the type who would."

"You're typing me?"

"It's hard not to, after knowing you for so long."

She crosses the kitchen and leans against the counter next to me. Her arms cross and she tips her head. "So, tell me what type I am."

I give her a good look over. Her wet hair is brushed and pulled into a ponytail. She removed her rain-smeared makeup and is comfortably dressed in a tank top and pajama pants ... which I think are patterned with Disney princesses. She took off her bra and I can just make out the outline of her nipples.

No, stop it. Off-limits, remember?

"You're a bit uptight. Maybe a little prude-ish. Definitely not the type who'd have sex toy parties … or even buy sex toys. You don't like to get in trouble or do anything you think is wrong. And really, that means what you think others think." I set the bottle of tequila down. "Actually, that's your whole issue."

"Oh, I have issues now?"

I nod. "Yeah. You're so worried about what other people think of you, you forget to live your own life."

Her eyes narrow. "My own life is fine, thank you very much. I'm happy, I work hard, and I'm headed in the right direction."

"And you give that answer to everyone, right? You don't have to be perfect all the time, you know."

She gives me a what-the-fuck-are-you-smoking look, then laughs. "I'm far from perfect. I'd think you of all people would know that."

She's perfect to me.

"Yeah, you're right. You're not that great." I shrug and put my hand on the fridge. "Got anything good to eat?"

"You're not that great either," she snaps. "And yes, I do. What do you want?" Her tone hasn't changed and I'm not sure if she's serious. Then she steps in close. "Is a sandwich okay?"

Well, I guess she is. "Yeah, that's fine."

I sit at a table under a window, watching the rain come down while Lauren pulls out what she needs to make us both sandwiches. Suddenly, she turns to me.

"I'm not a prude. And I do have sex toys. That I use. And enjoy."

47

I try not to think about that, try to keep the image of her pleasuring herself out of my head.

I fail.

"And there is nothing wrong with being good and staying out of trouble. Maybe *your* issue is seeing others not fuck up their lives makes you feel guilty."

I slowly shake my head. "Nope. No guilt. I do what I want and don't care what others think. I'm just as happy as you are."

"I don't care what others think either. And that's good for you," she says and puts four pieces of bread on the counter with more force than necessary. I watch her open a bag of lunch meat and cheese, all the while glaring at the food. "And I'm not a prude!" she finally exclaims. "I can have fun. I can be spontaneous. Wild, even."

"Uh-huh, sure you can." Pushing her buttons is pushing mine. I need to stop.

She glares at me then snatches the bottle of tequila from the counter, gets two shot glasses, and fills them both. She puts one in front of me and holds hers up.

"See?" she says after she takes it.

"That doesn't make you wild."

She takes another shot. "Whatever."

I smile when she turns her back, drinking my shot slowly. Nothing is said while she finishes making our food. She comes to the table with both plates, and the bottle of tequila. She takes another shot.

"You might want to slow down," I warn her. She ignores me. I eat half the sandwich before speaking again. "Thanks. For this and for letting me wait out the rain."

"Don't worry about it," she says and her words slur. In a few minutes, that last shot will hit her and she'll be fucked. Then I'm tucking her into bed and parking my ass on the couch until morning. "I wouldn't make you ride in the rain. Seems dangerous."

"Nah, I'd be fine." I take another bite, chew, and swallow. "So being called a prude really does bother you?"

"It's an insult," she says. "And is kind of sexist. I'm a prude for not sleeping around. But I'm a slut if I do sleep around. I just can't win."

"I prefer sluts over prudes."

She wrinkles her nose. "You're a pig."

"I just know what I like."

She shakes her head. "Aren't you a little old for that?"

"I'm not much older than you."

"I'm twenty-two and think I'm too old for that. We're not in college anymore. The time for partying is over."

"Hence why you're a prude."

"And hence why you're a dick."

I laugh. She gets a bit of a devilish glint in her eyes when she's pissed off. It's sexy as hell.

"Well this *dick* gets a lot, lives it up, and has fun. I enjoy life, not resent it."

"I don't resent life, not at all."

"I live every day like it could be my last. Enjoy every second I have. I don't waste time worrying over unimportant details."

She looks up, face softening. "There's a right and wrong way to do that."

"How the hell is there a wrong way to live each day like it's your last?"

"Because tomorrow probably *isn't* going to be your last. Yes, enjoy it metaphorically, but be responsible."

I shake my head. "Prude."

"Asshole."

I lean forward over the table and take her hand in mine, slowly running my fingers up the soft flesh on her wrist. She shivers and licks her lips. "Why haven't we ever hooked up?"

She yanks her arm back. "Because you repulse me."

"I don't believe that."

She closes her eyes in a long blink and takes another shot. "Better start believing. I know your habits. I know your ethics. I know *you*, Noah."

Her words sting, as much as I hate admitting it to myself. I don't give a shit what other think about me, but Lauren is something else. Someone else, and I can't deny the feelings I've had for her since we were teenagers. If I sought anyone's approval, it was hers.

I slide the bottle of tequila over and take another shot. I need it right now. "Maybe you're wrong about me," I say quietly.

"Hah, I'll believe it when I see it." She stands only to sit back down. "I think I drank too much."

I chuckle. "No shit."

She glares at me for the millionth time tonight. "Walk me to the couch?" I take her hand and help her. She sinks onto the cushions and takes a breath. "I feel better. Thanks."

Thunder rolls overhead. Vader jumps onto the couch, burying his head between the cushions. "He's afraid of thunder?"

"Terrified," she slurs and bends over to hug him. "But he'll be fine."

I pet him. "It's okay, big guy," I say softly.

Lauren watches me. "I didn't know you liked dogs."

"There's a lot about me you don't know, Lauren." I look up, eyes meeting hers when I say her name.

She parts her lips, inhales, then looks down. "Tell me."

"Fine," I say, and really, I'd love to sit down and talk to Lauren. I trust her. Maybe I shouldn't, but I do. I've never just opened up before, not to the counselor I was forced to see after my parents' divorce, or the many parole officers I had after getting out of juvie. I've never opened up to anyone before. I can't do it. I need something else, some sort of excuse to sit here and pour my fucking heart out. "But let's make it a game."

"What kind of a game?"

I stand, going to get the bottle of tequila. "Have you ever heard of Never Have I Ever?"

"I have, and I've played it before."

"Then this will be easy. Just, uh, take half shots or sips or something. I don't want to clean vomit tonight."

"I won't throw up, but fine."

I'm glad she's an agreeable drunk. People seem to fall on either side of the spectrum and it's either irritating as fuck or amusing. I fill the shot glasses. "This isn't going to really work with just two people, you know."

She shrugs. "We'll make it work. Say something you've never done. Then I'll say the same."

"Okay. Want to go first?"

"I've never had a one-night stand," she says. I take my shot. "Knew it."

I refill the glass.

"I've dated more than one person at the same time," she says.

"You don't get to go twice in a row."

"Yes, I do. I got the last question right."

"We're not playing fucking *Uno*. You don't get to go until someone gets it wrong," I chuckle. "But..." I take the shot to let her know I have done that. We keep asking questions, and it turns out there isn't a lot I haven't done. She's taken half a shot by the time I'm drunk. My mind is spinning and I can't filter my thoughts.

Or my actions.

"You've really never had a one-night stand?" I ask, spilling tequila on the coffee table as I try to fill the shot glass. I give up and drink straight from the bottle.

She shakes her head, eyes bloodshot. "I'm like ... I just ... how? Because that person might be yucky."

I laugh like it's the most hilarious thing in the world, because everything is the most hilarious thing in the world when you're wasted. And fuck. Lauren is the most beautiful thing in the world no matter what.

"It's just one night."

She shakes her head and almost falls off the couch. I grab her, then we both go tumbling, hitting the floor in a fit of laughter. I pull her onto my chest and push her hair back.

"One night," she says softly and looks into my eyes.

"One little, harmless night."

I don't know what I'm doing, but suddenly I'm kissing her. And she's kissing me back.

"Fuck," she says and pulls away after a few seconds. "No. Can't ... can't do that."

"Right. You're my friend's sister." Each word comes out slowly. My mind is too drunk to think logically, and for the first time, my heart rules over my head. I reach for her, bringing her closer.

"I liked that," she slurs.

And then we are kissing again. I hold onto her, pulling her to me. I'm drunk and I'm desperate and deep down I know I've wanted to feel her, to taste her for such a long time that there is no stopping once I get started.

Right now, I don't care.

"No," Lauren says and moves off of me.

I just move my head up and down, trying to convince myself that I agree with her, that I'm not going to go back to her. I put the bottle to my lips and take a swig. I make a promise to myself. I'm not going to do anything inappropriate with Lauren. She's off-limits.

I stand and extend a hand to help her up. She stumbles, and I catch her. Laughing, she looks up, slowly moving her face closer to mine. I should move away, turn my head, tell her no.

But I can't

She bites her lip and moves in. She kisses me.

Lauren Winters.

Kissed.

Me.

Holy fuck. I know I'm going to break that promise.

CHAPTER FIVE

LAUREN

I'M PRETTY SURE I'm dying. Or maybe I'm already dead. My entire body hurts, my head pounds, and my mouth is drier than the Sahara. The contents of my stomach slosh around like acid and I need to use the bathroom *now*, but I can't seem to get my arms and legs to work.

And I don't know why.

I force my eyes open, knowing I'm just seconds away from peeing myself. I'm in my room, tucked under the fluffy down comforter in my bed. It's warm yet hardly weighs anything, though right now it feels like a lead blanket trapping me against the mattress. Me and my very angry bladder that is screaming it can't wait much longer.

My vision is fuzzy and I have to blink several times to look at the clock. It's eleven thirty. At night? I yank my foot out from under Vader, who sleeps on my legs almost every night, and blink again. No, it's the day.

What the hell? I'm too confused to think about it, and right now all I can think of is running to the glorious toilet. I swing my feet over the bed, realize I'm naked, then feel a wave of nausea come on. I cover my mouth and wait for it to pass. I let my eyes close, the light too much to take in. My feet hit the cold hardwood and I shuffle my way to the bathroom, tripping over something. I catch myself and look down, expecting to see a dog toy or my clothes.

I'm not expecting to see a motorcycle boot. My blood runs cold. I know that boot. I know the foot that goes in it, the leg that foot is connected to, and the body that owns them both.

Holy shit.

I know that body very well after last night. I'm suddenly dizzy, and the fear of passing out then waking up in my own urine is the only thing that keeps me from turning and looking in my bed.

But I don't have to. I know *he's* still there.

I don't allow myself to think. I don't want to recall what happened, what we did to each other—with each other—last night. I barely make it to the toilet on time. The relief I feel from taking the longest pee in the history of pees does nothing to settle my already upset stomach. My hands shake and my head is spinning.

I slept with Noah Wilson.

I don't know why. I don't know how. Well, the *how* is self-explanatory … and also explains the rug burns on my knees. I put my head in my heads and try to think back. What happened last night?

Do I want to remember what happened? I stand and turn on the shower. I went on a date, a date Jenny set up. A date that went horribly wrong. And then I went to that trashy bar and Noah took me home, and … oh god. I recall the rain and sitting on the couch with Noah. I remember his lips pressing into mine, then it's black from there. I get into the shower, and images of flesh and lust flash before me.

I can still feel him between my legs, and I know he

55

must have a huge cock or we did it many times. Hell—probably both. And I don't have carpet in my room to get the rug burn on my knees.

I'm alone in the shower yet I'm embarrassed. What the hell was I thinking?

Noah. Fucking. Wilson.

If I was to hook up with anyone in the world, why did it have to be him? I shake my head. No one can know about this. I turn my face up into the water. No one has to, actually.

My heart stops racing. Noah won't tell Colin he slept with his little sister. He might not give a shit about his reputation, but he wouldn't ruin their friendship. And I won't tell anyone. As far as I'm concerned, Noah took me home, I went into my room, closed the door, and slept through the night in my own bed—alone—while Noah snoozed on the couch.

They don't even have to know he stayed. He could have dropped me off at home and left.

Yes, that's a better lie. He dropped me off, I went to bed, and that's that.

I go about washing myself, trying not to panic. It was one night. One time. It meant nothing, though I probably won't be able to look Noah in the eye anytime soon.

As stupid as it sounds, I have a little ball of dread that I sucked in bed. I'm no virgin, but it's been a while. Though, if Noah was as drunk as me, maybe he has no idea.

Oh! Maybe I can get dressed and tell him nothing happened! Yes, I'll give it a try. Now to convince myself nothing happened ... yeah right. March 11th will be tainted forever as the night I had sex with Noah Wilson.

"Stop," I say out loud. I'm an adult. I can sleep with who I want, when I want. I have every right to do this.

So why do I feel so guilty?

I get out of the shower, towel off, and put on my bathrobe. I tip-toe into my room and close my eyes. I don't want to look at him. I don't want to see those rippling muscles and tattoos.

I don't want to feel attracted to him.

Because I am. And I have been for a while ... just like I've wondered about him. Of course I've thought about Noah as more than my brother's friend. More than once. More than twice, if I'm being honest. It's like someone putting a plate of chocolate-covered strawberries in front of you and not thinking about eating one. Wondering how fast the chocolate will melt in your mouth. Wanting to know how sweet and juicy the strawberry is, how good it will feel as it pushes past your lips and hits your tongue.

He may not be the ideal hookup, but he's attractive and he knows it, and I always assumed he knows his way around a woman's body. And, of course, I had a chance to see just how good he is and I can't remember a fucking thing.

I let out a breath and flick my eyes to the bed. Noah is still sleeping. He's on his back and is naked, with the blanket barely covering his junk, which is disappointing. I hoped to check out the equipment used to rail me last night. He has one arm above his head, and the other is wrapped around Sasha, who's snuggled up with her head on his chest.

Even I have to admit that's adorable. Vader has taken over my spot, sprawled out and comfy. Waking up to this—a hot guy cuddled in my bed with my dogs—is something I can get used to.

If only that hot guy wasn't Noah.

I creep to the other side of my room and get clean underwear, leggings, and a sweatshirt. I go into the hall to get dressed, then sneak into the living room.

My pajama pants are on the couch. So are Noah's boxers. Well, I guess that answers where I got the rug burns. The bottle of tequila is on its side, and it's empty. My stomach churns just looking at it.

The shot glasses are on the floor, and there is a stain on the coffee table from spilled booze. I grab the bottle, glasses, and my pants. I find my shirt when I go into the kitchen. The shock is leaving and I'm feeling like complete and total shit from being hungover as fuck.

I force myself to drink an entire glass of water before I fire up the coffee pot. I need to eat something, and I'm starving and nauseous at the same time. I drink another glass of water, have to pee again already, then finally pour a cup of coffee.

I bring it to my face and inhale, the aroma instantly soothing my nerves. There is almost nothing a good cup of coffee can't solve.

Almost.

I mix in just a bit of creamer and grab the bag of bread that was left out on the counter from last night. I think I made sandwiches. Knowing I should eat something, I put two pieces of bread in the toaster and get out the butter. That seems safe, and will put something other than bile and leftover tequila in my stomach.

I feed the dogs, get my toast, then sit at the table carefully eating, still unable to remember exactly went down last night, other than Noah. On me. Because that's how I've imagined it.

I squeeze my eyes shut. No. That wasn't a tiny bit of desire that tingled my lady bits when I imagine his bearded face between my thighs, skin getting red from the burn of his facial hair.

Gah, no, just no!

I take another sip of coffee and let out a steadying breath. I might not remember what happened, but I'm sure I enjoyed it.

And I'm allowed to.

I lean back in the chair and take a few more sips of coffee, reminding myself what I did was more than okay, and I'm actually feeling a bit empowered. Everything is fine. It was one night. We never have to think about this again.

And I'm definitely no prude.

"Hey, baby," Noah says, his voice thick with sleep. I turn, almost having forgotten he's here, and quickly close my eyes. He's naked, standing in the threshold of the kitchen. His hair is a rumpled mess, and there are pillow creases on his face.

He does not look adorable. I am not feeling turned on by the sight of his bare skin. I do not want to gaze at his glorious body, tattoos and muscles and that stupid V that guides my eyes to his perfect cock.

"I'm not your baby," I say and stand to let the dogs out.

"Well you were last night."

My hand freezes on the doorknob. Dammit. He remembers. "Well, I, uh…" I stumble over my words. Vader paws at the door. I shake myself and let both dogs out, then turn to face Noah.

Shit, I looked right at his package. And shit, it looks nice. Even now when it's just hanging in front of him. I hold up my hand.

"Put some clothes on," I say and Noah laughs. "I'm serious, Noah."

"Fine, fine. It's not like you haven't seen it before."

I force myself to look into his eyes. "We shouldn't have done ... whatever it is we did."

"Ah, shit, you don't remember either?" He walks through the kitchen—still bare-ass naked—and sits at my seat, eating my leftover toast. "I was hoping you'd at least tell me I rocked your world."

I cross my arms. I'm able to look at him now. I can pretend he has pants on.

"No, I don't remember. And let's keep it that way, okay?"

He laughs again, then shakes his head like it hits him all at once. "Fuck."

"You can say that again."

"Fuck." He's looking a little sick now. Is the thought of sleeping with me that repulsive? I know I haven't shaved my bikini line in a few, uh, days? Weeks? Hell if I know. Nobody else was supposed to see it but me. "Seriously. Fuck. I *fucked* you."

Then I know exactly what he's thinking. He slept with his best friend's little sister.

"This never happened," I say.

Noah nods and picks up my coffee. Oh hell no. I rush over and take it from him, sloshing some down the side. "Get your own cup."

I regret my words as soon as he gets up and turns around, and I'm looking right at his tight ass. That ass I

60

probably gripped while he thrusted in and out of me.

Maybe?

Oh my god. I let out a breath and bring the cup of coffee to my lips.

"I don't recall exactly what happened," Noah says and opens cabinets in search of a coffee cup. I can't stop staring at his butt.

What is wrong with me?

"Neither do I. And that's fine. Probably better that way. As far as I'm concerned, you took me home and crashed on the couch while you waited out the rain," I say.

"Sounds good to me. And don't go getting attached. I don't do relationships."

"You're a pig." I finish my coffee and feel sick. Ugh. I'm never drinking again. "And don't worry. This wouldn't have happened if you hadn't gotten me drunk."

"Like you could resist this," Noah says, wiggling his eyebrows and shaking his hips. I look away. I've resisted *that* since I've known him, since I was fifteen years old, thinking he was the most gorgeous boy in the world. Over the years, the boy turned into man, and still held a spot in my mind as one of the best-looking males out there.

"I can. Easily. Now get dressed and get out. I have, uh, a lot to do today."

"Yeah, me too." He locates a mug and fills it with coffee, then sits back down. So much for leaving. "You're not going to tell your brother, are you?"

I widen my eyes. "No! He would probably kill you."

"Meh, he can try."

I shake my head. *It was one night. One night. One. Night.* Noah will leave, soon hopefully, and this awkward moment will be over with and we can move on with our lives.

And I'll never have to think about it again.

CHAPTER SIX

LAUREN
Six weeks later...

I AM DRAGGING. Completely and totally dragging ass and no amount of coffee can wake me up today. I shouldn't have stayed up past my bedtime reading, but I *had* to find out what happened to Edie Harker, the vampire hunter. Had to. And one more chapter led to finishing the damn book

I'm paying for it now.

Though, truth is I've been feeling run down for a week now. I'm not sick, don't have a fever, yet something is … off.

"Late night?" Julie asks me sit down for lunch.

"Too late," I say, and poke at the beans and rice that came with my tacos. There's a little hole-in-the wall Mexican restaurant close to the clinic and is my go-to when I'm too lazy to pack a lunch. I get the same thing every time and love it, but today, Lunch Combination #12 isn't appealing.

She laughs. "Don't tell me you had another 'one night stand' with some mystery man again."

I glare at her. "It's possible, and it really did happen."

She just laughs again. "Sure it did. Sweet little Lauren went home with someone she didn't know, and never got a name."

I purse my lips and shake my head. I hadn't told a single soul—not even my best friend Rachel—about Noah. But I couldn't keep the entire situation a secret. I can't keep secrets to save my life. So my friends know I had naughty dirty sex with some hot guy I met at a bar. But that's all I tell them, and really, that's all I *can* tell them.

I assume the sex I had with Noah was naughty and dirty. And probably sloppy and wobbly; since I was too drunk to remember it, I was too drunk to do, well, anything remotely sexy. In all honestly, I probably got the rug burns on my knees from falling, and then I passed out under Noah as soon as we both finished.

"I live on the edge, duh," I say with a smile and set my fork down, unable to eat anything in front of me, and drink my lemonade. I can't get enough of that.

Soon enough, I'm busy rewrapping bandages, inserting an IV for the *eleventh time* into the leg of a beagle that somehow manages to pull it out as soon as our backs are turned, and prepping for surgeries.

Finally the day is over. I'm exhausted, and my back hurts from hoisting heavy dogs up and down the surgery table all day. I yawn the whole way home, stopping for takeout so I don't have to cook.

"Sorry, guys," I say to the dogs. "I'm too pooped to take you for a walk."

Vader cocks his head at the word "walk," and I feel guilty. It's a nice night, with a clear sky and warm air. But I just can't.

"You had plenty of play time today, and I have a short shift tomorrow. You'll be fine for one night." I pat my leg and head to the kitchen. "Come on, I'll give you an extra treat, okay?"

If there a better word than "walk," it's "treat." He trots ahead of me. Sasha follows, and I toss them both a handful of treats before getting myself a drink and falling onto the couch. I watch a re-run of *Once Upon a Time* while I eat.

I'm so drained from staying up late last night, I shower and get into bed as soon as I'm done eating with the intent of reading a new book, but I'm asleep before I know it, waking when my alarm goes off the next morning.

Despite over eight hours of sleep, I'm still drained in the morning. What the hell? I must be getting sick. And I'm cramping like crazy. Come on, Aunt Flo. Just show up so I can get this over with and feel better. Stupid hormones.

But she doesn't show up the next day, or the day after that. I go to bed Thursday night feeling like shit. Cramps, no appetite, and I'm super tired. Just one more day to get through and I can spend two full days doing nothing but sleeping and watching Disney movies.

Getting out of bed Friday morning is one of the hardest things I've ever done. If Vader hadn't come and licked me after I turned off the alarm, I never would have gotten up.

I fire up the Keurig while I take care of the dogs, stick my favorite Ariel mug in place, and push the button to fill it. As soon as the coffee pours from the Keurig, my stomach flip flops.

What the hell?

The scent is so strong, filling the air, and making me sick. It's like the smell of coffee is day-old roadkill in July, left out to bake on black pavement in the afternoon sun.

I want to throw up.

I cover my nose with my hand and press the power button, shutting off the machine before it has the chance to fill my mug. I dump it down the drain and leave the kitchen.

Okay. This isn't right. I'm one of those people who can't function without coffee. This has to be a PMS thing, right?

Deep down, I know it's not.

A little over a month ago, I hooked up with Noah.

And I don't remember a thing.

I don't remember if he used a condom. I don't remember if he pulled out. And right now, I don't know what to do.

My hands are shaking and I feel like I'm going to pass out. It was one time. The odds are against me, and the stress of life is probably what's delaying my period.

It was one night. One time.

And I know it's entirely possible.

*

I slow as I walk down the aisle. The plastic handles of the shopping basket slide under my sweating palms. My heart is racing and I don't think I can do this. I should go home and order from Amazon. I can even get next-day shipping, though since it's getting late, next day will actually be the next, next day.

And I can't wait that long.

I let out a breath, set my basket down, and flip up my hood. I look like I'm about to rob the fucking place, but I don't want to risk getting seen. That would be worse than robbery.

I hunch my shoulders and look at the white boxes. Why the hell are there so many different options? I drop my gaze to the price tags. Twenty bucks for a pregnancy test? Really?

Fuck, it doesn't matter, not really. I'll pay anything for the peace of mind I'm going to get once this sucker pops up with a big fat negative. Because I'm not pregnant. I do *not* have Noah's child growing inside of me, sucking my energy and making me hate my favorite foods.

I. Am. Not. Pregnant.

Jenny and Colin have been trying for a few months and nothing has come about yet. She told me you only have like a twenty percent chance of getting knocked up each cycle, which means I have an eighty percent chance that I haven't been knocked the fuck up.

By Noah.

Oh my God. I just ... can't. I literally cannot.

I grab a box of the Target-brand pregnancy tests, saving myself a few bucks, and quickly hide them under the random items I didn't need but had to have from the dollar bins at the store front.

I practically jog to the registers, thankful now more than ever for the self-checkout. I pay for my items, put the basket away, and stop. My heart is still hammering, hands still shaking. I turn, looking at the big red sign that says "restrooms." I chugged two bottles of water before I came, thinking it wouldn't hit me until I got home. But since I got nervous and put off walking down the pregnancy test aisle and instead spent thirty minutes looking at Disney toys—yes, the ones for little girls—my bladder is winning. I have a twenty-minute drive home and

I honestly do not know if I will be able to make it that long.

Since I'm an adult who is perfectly capable of *not* peeing my pants, I go into the bathroom. I lock myself in a stall and rip open the test, read the instructions, then sit on the toilet. I stick the test between my legs and … now I can't go. Nerves are stopping me up and someone else just walked in.

I close my eyes. They don't know what I'm doing, but I better hurry up or they will think I'm pooping, which embarrasses me for some reason but at the same time shouldn't matter at all. Everyone poops.

Finally, I'm able to go, and I count to five then pull the test out, recapping it and watching the little white screen darken. The instructions say to wait three minutes before looking at the test. I count to ten and look.

The blue test line pops up right away. There is nothing next to it. I relax. I'm not pregnant, see? I knew it and now I can go home and stop worrying. In fact, I'm sure my period will start tomorrow and I'll laugh at myself for all this anxiety.

I'm about to throw the test in the little metal trash when I look at it one more time.

Holy fucking shit balls. Is that a second line?

No. No, no, no.

I bring the test closer to my face. I see a faint shadow. But it's not a line. So I'm not pregnant, right? I close my eyes and count to thirty again. It hasn't quite been three minutes, but I look again anyway.

There is definitely something there, making a little plus sign. If I am pregnant, the line would be bright like the rest line, right? Crap. I don't know these things.

There is one more test in the box. I'm about ready to rip it open and take it when I remember that I just went pee. Double crap. I've never wanted to have to pee more in my life than I do right now.

But I need to know.

I stash the possibly positive test in my purse and leave the bathroom, going into the little cafe. I order a blue Slushy and a big pretzel. Both actually sound good, and the smell of butter and salt makes me hungry. I nibble on the pretzel, so nervous I can hardly eat.

I do a bit of online research while I gulp down the Slushy. It seems that tests with blue lines can have an "evaporation line" that gives the illusion of a positive test. Pink line tests are a bit more reliable, and the digital ones are fool proof. Also, chugging something like I'm doing now can dilute the pregnancy hormone and give you a false negative. I should test again in the morning.

Though, there is no fucking way I can wait that long.

I finish my pretzel and drink, and get up. I take my bag to the car, then go back inside, praying I don't run into anyone I know. I don't waste any time. I get another basket and head to the personal hygiene aisle.

I end up spending seventy dollars on pregnancy tests. I clutch the white shopping bag to my chest as I walk to my Jeep, heart in my throat. The drive home stretches forever, and I'm crawling out of my skin when I get stuck by a train. I'm such a wreck that I don't even listen to music.

Finally, I get into the house, let the dogs out, and put the boxes of tests on the counter. Each came with two, oh—this one has a bonus so three!—and I take one out for now, saving the other for the morning.

I take the used test from my purse, lay it on a napkin,

and scrutinize it. Like any sane person would do, I take a picture with my phone then play with the color contrast to see if that's a line or just as shadow of where a line *could* be.

I come up undecided.

There is nothing to do but wait and test again. I try to do my normal routine, play with the dogs, shower, make a lunch for tomorrow, that sort of thing, but I keep going back and looking at the one test like it might change. Not knowing if it's actually positive or negative is driving me up the fucking wall.

About an hour and a half later, I'm staring at a counter full of tests. I flipped them all upside down, not wanting to look at them until the full amount of time has passed. On some level I know this is crazy, taking so many tests. I can't believe I spent so much on them all. I should have gotten the expensive digital one from the start and would have known one way or the other without analyzing every little shade of blue.

I'm sure I'm not the only one, and I know there have been countless women on both sides of the fence desperately wanting to know if there is a tiny life force inside of them or not. But I have to know. One way or the other, I'm finding out. I check the time. Five minutes have passed. I stand and slowly walk the two feet from the edge of the tub to the sink, feeling like it's D-Day.

I want to call Katie and have her come over, holding my hand as I flip the tests. I hate doing stressful stuff like this on my own, though if the tests turn out all negative, then I'll have gotten her all riled up for nothing, and she'll never let me live it down.

Because I'm Lauren Winters. The responsible one. The one always prepared, always early and on time. I'm not crazy or spontaneous. I like to stay home and watch Disney movies, play video games online, and chat with my friends via Facebook PM rather than face to face. I'm the last one you'd expect to worry about an accidental pregnancy.

Things like this don't happen to me.

I reach out, hands shaking as I flip over the tests.

I'm Lauren Winters. The responsible one. The last one you'd ever expect this to happen to.

And I'm fucking pregnant.

CHAPTER SEVEN

LAUREN

I LOOK AT my name on the clipboard, my handwriting nearly unreadable because I can't stop shaking. I took the remaining tests this morning and all came back positive, of course. I called the OB/GYN office on my way to work and was able to get in for an ultrasound this afternoon. I wasn't expecting visual confirmation that quickly, but since I wasn't sure exactly how far along I could be the doctor ordered an early ultrasound. I was hoping I could live in denial for a little longer, though the million positive tests were making that hard to do.

The receptionist smiles at me and hands me a packet of papers to fill out. There are a slew of questions concerning this pregnancy. Checking "yes" or "no" is making it seem more and more real.

I'm close to a full panic attack.

I've told no one about the positive tests yet. Of course, I did more internet research online and found that a positive test doesn't *always* mean there is a living baby inside of you.

I focus on answering each question, guessing on the date of my last period. I turn in the info, then wait. I had to leave work an hour early to make it here on time, and I knew it raised questions when I slipped out the door. I told my boss I had a doctor appointment and that was it. Still, I felt like I was walking out of the clinic with a big letter P on my face.

P for Pregnant with my brother's best friend's baby.

Oh. My. God.

I flip through a *Parents* magazine as I wait, just looking at the pictures. I'm too nervous to concentrate on words. Fifteen minutes go by and I relax just a bit. Then the door opens and a young woman in gray scrubs calls my name.

I stand, holding my purse for dear life, and move one foot in front of the other. I feel like I'm trekking to Mordor as I cross the waiting room, and my fate lies ahead of me. I want to tell myself I'm being dramatic, but I'm not.

"Hi, Lauren," the ultrasound tech says. "How are you?"

"Nervous," I admit. I follow her into the room and hop up on the table. She reviews my paperwork, gives me a minute to prepare, then comes back and starts the ultrasound.

"Try to relax," she tells me and moves the transducer around. There is a TV screen mounted high on the wall in front of me. I hold my breath and will my stiff muscles to loosen. The screen is just a blur of black and white, and I have a slight idea of what I'm looking at from doing ultrasounds on pregnant animals at the clinic.

Then she stops moving the transducer and hits some buttons on the computer in front of her. There is a shrimp-shaped blob in the middle of a dark lopsided circle. Something flickers inside the blob. I know what it is before she says it.

The little blob is my baby and the flicker is the heart beating. Tears prick the corners of my eyes. I feel a connection to the little thing, and at the same time I'm panicking.

The tech types "HI MOM" onto the screen and takes a picture. It prints out. Then she turns up the volume and lets me listen to the heart beating away. I can't think, can't form a logical thought as she finishes the ultrasound, taking measurements and more pictures.

"All right," she says and hands me three black-and-white images. "Baby is measuring eight weeks and two days, making your due date December third. Are you seeing the doctor after this?"

I shake my head, not trusting myself to speak. I have an appointment Monday with the doctor. I have days to agonize over everything. Again.

"Okay. I got all the images I need, so you're good to go. Congrats!"

"Thanks," I squeak out. I barely make it out to my car in time before I burst into tears. The ultrasound pictures and the little card with the date of my next appointment are clutched in my right hand. I'm so confused, so conflicted, and I don't know what to do.

I don't want to get rid of this baby by any means, but I don't want to raise a child on my own. I can't. I work full time, and I'm going to go back to school eventually. If not, I wouldn't even be able to support a child on my income alone. I didn't become a vet tech for the paycheck, that's for sure.

I inhale and force myself to stop crying, carefully folding the ultrasound pictures and putting them in my purse. I wipe my eyes, back out of the parking space, and head home. Katie calls me when I pull onto my street. I don't answer. I don't want to tell her.

But I have to eventually. She's bound to notice when I start getting a baby bump … and when I show up to family holidays with a crying kid in my arms. I can't put it off forever.

I wait until I'm in my garage to call her back.

"Hey, lady," she says, cheerful as ever. "Want to do something tonight? Wes got mandated at work and I'm bored and alone. Disney movies and booze at my place?"

"Katie," I start, voice flat.

"Yeah?"

"Can you come over instead? I … I need to talk to you."

"Way to sound ominous, sis. Don't be so lame about staying out and leaving your dogs. They are dogs. They'll be fine."

"It's not that," I say and it takes all I have not to start sobbing again. "Please, Katie?"

"You're freaking me out now, Lauren. What's going on?"

"I'll tell you when you get here, okay?" My voice is high pitched and trembling.

"Okay. I'll be right over. Do you need anything?"

Oh lord, do I. "No, just to talk to you."

"Okay." She's shaken up, I can tell. At least she won't waste time getting here. I go inside and change out of my Tinkerbell scrubs, putting on PJs. Katie lives fifteen minutes away, and she walks through my door not even twenty minutes after we hung up.

"Lauren?" she calls from the small foyer. "Where are you?"

I'm in the kitchen, and I'm scared to go to her, to tell her the truth. Should I tell Noah before I tell my sister? This child is half of me and half of him. Does that make him entitled to know first?

"Lauren?" Katie calls again. "You're freaking me out! Where are you?"

"In the kitchen," I say. "Letting the dogs in."

I open the back door and both dogs come in running, wildly greeting my sister. I meekly follow behind them.

"What the hell?" Katie asks when she sees me. My eyes are still red and puffy from crying. I hold my hand behind my back, keeping the ultrasound pictures out of sight. "What happened?"

I swallow the lump in my throat. I just need to come out and say it. Then my big sis can hug me and tell me that things are going to be all right.

"Sit down," I say and look at the couch.

Katie steps out of her purple Toms and unzips her jacket. "Okay, tell me right now, because you're seriously scaring me."

"I'm scared," I say, not meaning to put fuel on the fire. Tears fill my eyes and I take a few steps back and plop onto the couch. Katie rushes over.

"What is it, Lauren? Do you have cancer or something?" Her eyes mist over. It wasn't that long ago that our mom had a cancer scare. We're all sensitive to it.

"No, I don't."

"Then what the hell is wrong?"

Fat tears roll down my cheeks. "I messed up," I start, choking up. "I ... I ... It was one night."

"Lauren!" Katie puts her hand on mine. I close my eyes, feeling like I'm getting sucked backwards into a vortex of darkness. "Tell me what is wrong!"

I make myself open my eyes. "I'm pregnant," I whisper.

"No, you're not," Katie says right away. "Because you have to have sex to get pregnant and you don't have a boyfriend, and you don't sleep around."

"I know. But I did. Just once." I carefully unfold the ultrasound pictures and hand them to her. I watch her face go from confusion to horror then back to confusion.

She leans back on the couch, looking straight ahead. "When—how? You ... no. This is a joke, right?"

"I wish it was." My eyes are filled with more tears, and I'm trembling. Katie turns to me, face as white as a ghost. Then she bursts out laughing.

"Sorry," she says, covering her mouth. "Just you ... Everyone thought I'd be the one to get knocked up before marriage. No one ever expected *you* to be the family slut!" She's doubled over laughing.

"This isn't funny, Katie! I'm not a slut. It was one night, one time, one mistake!"

The laughter dies in Katie's throat. "Oh my God." The seriousness has hit her. "This is from your drunken one-night stand none of us believed."

My eyebrows push together. "Why is it so hard to believe that I—never mind. But yes. That's when it happened because that's the only time *anything* happened in a very long time."

"What are you going to do? I assume you've considered all your options."

"I'm keeping it. Once I saw the heart beating ... I don't know. I just know I have to keep it."

"Okay, that's good if it's what you want. So you don't

know who the father is?"

My lack of response tells her everything.

"You have to tell me who, Lauren."

I put my head in my hands. "No, I don't. It's bad, Katie. Really bad."

"You're already pregnant, Lauren. It can't get much worse than this. Even if this guy turns out to be nothing more than a sperm donor, we can make him pay child support or something. Just tell me who you hooked up with and I'll help, okay?"

"Okay." I look up, meeting her eyes, feeling sick again. His name is on the tip of my tongue, yet I can't make myself say it. I close my eyes and let out a breath. Fuck it. "Noah."

Katie doesn't say anything for a good thirty seconds. Then she blinks several times and pushes her eyebrows together. "Colin's friend Noah?"

I put my head in my hands. "Yes," I say, voice muffled.

"Are you sure it's his?"

"Positive. Like you said, I don't sleep around. He's the only possible one."

She holds up a hand. "I need a minute to process this." Her eyes close. "So you got drunk, slept with Noah, and now you're pregnant with his child."

"It sounds worse when you say it out loud."

"It sounds pretty bad in my head too. Does he know?"

I shake my head. "I thought about telling him, but I actually don't know his number, or where he lives."

"I'll get the info for you."

"Do I have to tell him? I mean, Noah ... he's not exactly father material."

78

"He has the right to know. Colin is going to beat his ass. You know that, right?"

My stomach flip-flops. "I haven't even thought about telling anyone else. Oh my god—Mom!"

"She's going to beat *your* ass, once you push that baby out, that is."

I take a sharp breath in but get no air. I take another, and another.

"Lauren, calm down!" Katie says. "Do not hyperventilate on me."

"I ... I ... can't." My hands are trembling. I haven't thought about pushing or labor or anything either. "I don't know what to do," I say and start crying. Katie's arms go around me.

"It's okay, Lauren. We'll figure this out. I won't say anything to anyone until you're ready."

I nod, unable to say anything while sobbing into her shoulder. She rubs my back for a minute then moves away. "Dry your eyes. Crying doesn't solve anything, and I'm only allowing this because you're probably hormonal and shit."

"Probably," I hiccup. "At least now I know why I've been so tired." I wipe away tears, smearing mascara down my face. I don't care. "What am I going to do, Katie?"

"Nothing I can say will make you feel better," she replies slowly. "But we'll figure this out, and you know I'm here."

"Thank you."

"Don't thank me. This is what sisters are for. That and it automatically gives me 'best aunt' status."

Aunts. Babies. It's all too much. "I wish I could drink right now."

Katie laughs. "Hell, I think I need a drink. I can only imagine what you're feeling." She puts her arm around me. "For now, take a deep breath. I think no matter what, no matter who you're with or where you are in life, expecting a baby causes everyone to freak out on some level."

"I'm sure. So where do I go from here?"

Katie takes a breath. "You've already decided to keep the baby, so ... in a perfect world, what happens next?"

I raise an eyebrow. "In a perfect world this wouldn't have happened."

"Well, it did," she says pointedly. "But from here. What would happen next?"

I rub my eyes, feeling a headache coming on. "By some miracle, Noah and I would end up together. I want this child to have a mom *and* a dad. But that's not—"

"Stop," Katie says gently. "We've known Noah for a long time, but do you really *know* him?"

I start to move my head up and down then stop. "Not on a personal level. But I know him enough to know having a baby and getting married is the last thing he wants."

Katie pushes her brunette hair back. It's the same shade as mine, only she's added blue and purple highlights. "Sometimes things like this change people. Remember my friend Erica?"

"The drunk? Yeah, what about her?"

"She got knocked up two years ago. She's in nursing school now, and doesn't party anymore. From the moment she peed on that stick and found out she was pregnant, she turned her life around. So it is possible. And you'll never know if you don't tell Noah and give him a chance. And if anything else, you will find out if you need to cross that hope off your list and move on. Plus figure out child support and custody and all that other legal shit I know nothing about."

"Can I just call him? Or text. Texting is better."

"Lauren," Katie starts. "I know you prefer to not talk to or see people when you can help it, but this needs to be said in person. Call him, say you need to talk, and go somewhere private, like have him come back here. And if you want me to be there, I can be."

I raise an eyebrow. "You just want to see how he reacts to this, don't you?"

"I'd be lying if I said I didn't. But really, I want to support you. I don't get to be the older sister that often, since you're the responsible one. I mean, how many times in high school did you help me not get caught drinking, or sneaking out, or sneaking a boy in? You're my sister, and I love you. And regardless of who the father is, that baby is my niece or nephew. *We* are family."

"I love you," I say and rest my head on her shoulder.

"Ditto, sis." She gives me one more hug. "Let me do some digging and make some calls and I can get Noah's number for you."

"Do I have to tell him?"

She moves her head up and down. "If there is a chance he steps up, then yes."

A chance. Hah, yeah the fuck right. I've known Noah for years, and have had a secret crush on him most of that time. I've watched him. I know the type of women he dates. I know he's a regular heartbreaker. I've seen countless women fall for his charm, believe his lies, and think they can change him, that they can tame his wild heart and make him theirs.

81

And it never works.

So why would it work for me? I'm just Lauren, his best friend's kid sister who just happened to get drunk and horny when he was stuck at my house waiting out the rain. I'm not the type of girl a man like Noah seeks out. Is having his baby enough to change him forever?

I lean back on the couch and look at the ultrasound photos again. Katie is right. It doesn't matter who the father is. This is my child, my family.

"Got it," Katie says.

"That was fast."

She shrugs. "I might have a friend with a friend who's hooked up with him."

"Whatever. It is what it is."

"Ready to call him?"

"I'm never going to be ready."

She takes my phone and dials the number. Her finger hovers over the green call button. My heart skips a beat. She holds out the phone and presses "call." I take the phone and put it to my ear.

Please get his voicemail. Please get his voicemail.

"Hello?"

Dammit.

"Uh, hi, Noah. It's Lauren. Lauren Winters. Listen, Noah … we need to talk."

*

Crap. Maybe Katie should have stayed, because I'm not prepared for how incredibly attractive Noah is when I answer the door half an hour later. It's been over a month since we've seen each other, and the stubble on his face has grown into a beard, and damn, he looks good with it.

Fuck. Me.

Wait, no. Fucking me is what got us into this mess.

"Lauren," he says, my name rolling off his tongue like silk. "Is everything okay?"

I stare into his blue eyes, heart racing so fast it might burst out of my chest and shatter into a million pieces onto the floor.

"In theory, yes."

He raises an eyebrow. "That's not convincing."

I shuffle back, taking the dogs with me so Noah can get in and through the door. I just shake my head and go into the living room. The ultrasound pictures are on the coffee table, flipped upside down. I plop onto the couch. Vader jumps up next to me, standing and wagging his long tail as Noah draws near. He sits on the opposite side, laughing when the big dog licks his face.

"What's going on?"

I inhale and wait until Vader settles down in Noah's lap. The dog might weigh in at a little over a hundred pounds, but he thinks he's a lap dog.

Just say it.

"Well, I, uh, I'm…" My cheeks start to flush and I want to throw up or cry. Probably both. I take a steadying breath, close my eyes, and try to mentally prepare myself. I open my eyes and look at Noah, taken aback by how worried he looks.

It's a look I've rarely seen on him. A little line forms between his eyes and that cocky, panty-melting smile is gone from his attractive face.

"Lauren?"

Fuck. Now or never.

"I'm pregnant."

He looks ... relieved?

"Fuck," he says. "I'm sorry."

I wait for him to say something else, to have the news sink in and the panic hit. Vader jumps off the couch to get a toy. Noah scoots closer.

"I can see how that's upsetting," he starts, keeping his gaze locked with mine. "But, uh, why are you telling me?"

I blink once. Twice. Three times. "Seriously?"

"Yeah," he says and confusion takes over his face. He really has no idea. He hasn't put two and two together. "I don't get what this has to do with me."

It's like I have no control over my body. My right hand comes up and swings, flat palm hitting him in the face. The slap stings, and causes Noah to jump back in surprise.

"What the fuck?"

"I'm pregnant and you are the father," I say slowly through gritted teeth.

If I thought Noah looked surprised before, I was mistaken. The color drains from his face. Then he shakes his head.

"No, I'm not."

"We hooked up. And now I'm pregnant. You are the father."

His eyes dart around the room. "But that was over a month ago."

"Yeah, these things take some time."

He runs a hand over his face. "Fuck. Fuck, fuck, fuck." Then he looks up at me. "Are you sure it's mine?"

I raise my arm to slap him again but Noah catches my wrist. "Yes, I'm sure. There are no other possibilities. I've only been with you in the last six months."

"You've had sex *once* in half a—never mind. Are you sure?"

My eyes fill with the tears I've been battling. "Positive."

Noah slides his hand up my wrist and laces our fingers. The tears roll down my cheeks. He pulls me to him, wrapping me in a hug that I didn't know I desperately needed.

"It'll be okay," he says. "I don't have a fucking clue how, but it'll be okay."

I slide my arms around his muscular torso, inhaling slowly to calm myself. Noah smells intoxicating, like soap and cologne, mixing with the scent of leather from his motorcycle jacket. My heart pounds in my chest, pressed against his, and it's beating just as hard.

His lips sweep against my neck, so soft I almost don't feel it.

Almost.

I shiver, and fight against the warmth that tingles inside of me.

I lose.

"You're pro-choice, right?" he starts.

"Do you want me to slap you again?" I ask, yanking my hands from his.

"But you are, right?"

"Yes, I am, and *my* choice is to keep this baby."

Noah swallows and moves his head up and down. "Just making sure. Because I want you to keep it."

"Oh," I say, having expected a different response from him. Silence falls between us, broken by the loud squeaks of Vader chomping on a rubber ball. "What do you want to do?"

"I'll do whatever you want," he answers without skipping a beat.

"And why would you do that?"

He looks away. "No reason ... well, no reason other than my child is growing inside of you. I ... I want to try, Lauren. So, what do *you* want?"

I shake my head. "I don't even know. Do you think you'll, uh, be involved, help me raise the kid, be there during the birth ... that sort of thing?" I quickly look into his eyes, afraid of what I'll see. "I don't know what else goes into this. I'm going off of movies I've seen."

"Yeah," he says. "I think so." He rubs his forehead. "You're sure it's mine?"

I tip my head up, jaw trembling. "Yes. You can get a fucking DNA test if you want. But I promise you it's yours. I haven't had sex, or even gotten past first base, with anyone but you in a very long time."

He nods, considering my words. "I want to be there for all of it. If it's mine, I mean, *since* it's mine, I want to do whatever I can." He takes my hand again and turns to me, blue eyes clouding over. "My father was never there for me. I don't want this kid to go through that."

A tear escapes and rolls down my cheek. Noah catches it and brushes it away. He pulls me in and kisses my forehead, then puts one hand over my stomach.

"I want to be here for both of you."

"I want you be here too," I say softly, and it hits me just how much I want things to work out. But we only have nine months to figure this out, to see if we're not only compatible with each other, but capable of loving each other enough to commit and raise our child together.

86

"Did you tell Colin yet?"

I shake my head. "Only Katie." My voice quakes and I realize I'm trembling head to toe. "I have to tell my parents soon. Holy shit, they're going to freak."

Noah moves closer. His thigh presses against mine and he puts an arm around my shoulders.

"I'm sorry, Lauren."

"Thanks," I say. "It takes two, ya know. And neither one of us were thinking straight that night, so I don't blame you entirely."

"Not entirely? So partially?"

"Oh of course. You got me drunk then took me on that oh-so romantic motorcycle ride in the rain. I was pretty much a goner from the start."

He laughs and the knot in my chest loosens. "I told you I'm irresistible."

"Hardly." I rest my head against his shoulder, blaming pregnancy hormones for finding him so fucking hot right now.

I reach out and grab the ultrasound picture. "That's the baby," I say, pointing to the little blob. "I'm eight weeks and got to see the heart beating today too."

Noah takes the pictures from me, bringing it close to his face. His expression is neutral.

"Fuck," he finally says.

"I agree," I say with a sigh.

"We had sex six weeks ago, and you're eight weeks along ... Am I missing something?"

"You start out at two weeks. It's confusing, I know. I'm eight weeks along but the baby is only six weeks old ... if that makes sense."

"It doesn't." He hands me the images. "This is ass

backwards, but let me take you on a first date?"

My first inclination is to tell him no, that it's not worth it. Because I don't have faith in him, that I know better. Because a first date with Noah isn't going to lead to a second. A first date isn't going to change him, isn't going to make him flip a switch and settle down...as much as I wish it could.

But I need to give him a chance—a chance to prove that he isn't up for this, that he's not going to stand by me and this child in any way other than helping pay for food and clothing. I need to witness it first hand, hell, maybe even get my heart broken so I can scratch this off forever and move on, raising this child the best that I can.

In the end, that's all that matters.

And in order to do that, I need to let him take me on that first date.

"Deal," I say.

"This Friday night?"

"I get off work at seven."

"So I'll pick you up at eight?"

"Eight thirty. Give me some time to get ready."

Noah rests his hand on my thigh. "So this means I can fuck you again, right? It's not like I can knock you up twice."

I turn, raising an eyebrow. "It takes at least three dates and some good food to get into my pants."

"I already proved that wrong. Don't be a prude."

I sigh. Yep. This first date is totally going to show me how much Noah isn't ready to be a father.

CHAPTER EIGHT

NOAH

I HAVE GOT to clean up my act.

No more drinking. No more getting arrested. And no more one-night stands. Fuck. What am I going to do with my time? And I can drink ... just not in excess like I had been. I can do this. For her. For *them.*

Lauren is having a baby. My baby. I'm going to be a dad.

I'm also going to throw up.

Is this really happening? The ultrasound pictures don't lie, and neither does Lauren. We are having a baby.

Together.

It would be a damn lie if I said there's a part of me that isn't happy about this. Because there is. Knocking Lauren Winters up is the last thing I wanted to do, but knocking her up means I get a chance to make her fall in love with me.

A chance to make her mine.

It's the chance I never got so many years ago. And now that it's right in front of me, I'm fucking terrified. Add in the baby and it's just about enough to make me lose it completely.

I lean back in my leather chair at my desk, unable to concentrate on doing any sort of work. I run my hands over my face and log onto the internet to do some research about babies and pregnancy. Looking up info does nothing to soothe my nerves, but only reminds me of how little I know, and makes me feel guilty for everything Lauren is going through.

I've never held a baby. Never changed a diaper or given a bottle. The leather chair crunches under me as I lean back, running my hands over my beard. We'll figure this out. And maybe, by some extreme miracle, I can pull off this Daddy thing.

The thing is, I want to be a good dad. I want to be there for Lauren and for the baby. But, how? The only father figure I had in my life was a pathetic excuse for a man. Can I step up to the plate and not repeat his errors?

I left Lauren's house with nothing set between us. We're going slow, going to give being together a try. She needs it. She needs time to fall for me.

And she will. I won't give up until her heart is mine.

But for now, we're taking things slow, one day at a time. We're not a couple, not even dating. Can I even call her my friend? We've never hung out one on one, and my interactions with her before were less than genuine since I was hiding how I felt.

I better not fuck this up.

My heart is beating fast, making me anxious. I stand and grab the keys to my motorcycle, intending to speed off to The Roadhouse and toss a few back to calm my nerves.

"Fuck," I say to myself when I put my hand on the door to leave. I don't want to be that guy who runs away to a bar to get drunk when shit hits the fan.

I don't want to be my father.

And I won't.

The only rule we have set is no sex. Obviously, that was Lauren's idea. She said sex got us into this situation and she doesn't want to complicate things further, not when she's trying to see where things could go. Other than that, there's nothing set up, but I've already decided to treat her like my one and only. Because she is. And it won't be hard, since I haven't hooked up with anyone since I slept with her. Though I can't remember the details, I haven't been able to get her out of my head. She's been there for years, after all.

My phone buzzes in my pocket and I grab it, smiling as soon as I see Lauren's name.

"Hey, baby," I answer.

"Don't call me that," she retorts.

"Fine, fine. You're calling because you miss me and changed the no-sex rule, right?"

"Hardly." She lets out a breath. "My mom called."

Oh fuck. "Did you tell her?"

"Not yet, but she invited me over for dinner tomorrow. We have family dinners on Sundays ... Not sure if you remember."

"I do." Dinner at the Winters' was the only time I got to sit around with others as I ate. Mom couldn't be bothered to eat a meal with me.

"I thought we could go together and tell everyone."

Tell my best friend I not only slept with his little sister, who's been off limits since we met, but knocked her up. My best friend, who's bailed me out of jail more times than I care to remember, who knows me and my wicked ways ... who's going to hate my fucking guts after we tell him. Yeah, sounds like a party.

"Noah?"

I blink. "Yeah. Tomorrow. Better to get it over with, right?"

*

Sunday dinners at the Winters' house was always a safe haven. Colin and I would play video games during the day, eat dinner, then resume whatever game we were currently addicted to. I'd stay until Mrs. Winters kicked me out, or my probation officer came to get me, because that was the case more than once during my teen years.

But pulling into the driveway that leads to the two-story brick house is making me sweat like a whore in church. I don't want to fucking do this. Lauren's face is white. She doesn't want to either. I wonder if she'd be okay with turning around and not coming back until our kid was in college. I cut the engine, nerves at an all-time high, and reach over Lauren to grab a flask from the glove box.

"Seriously?" she asks when I unscrews the lid and takes a drink.

"Hey, I need this. You know everyone in there is going to hate me."

"You better take another shot," she grumbles. "Then pour it out, because you can't have open containers in your car. The last thing I need is a baby daddy in prison."

"I won't go to jail over this," I say and roll my eyes.

"You might. Don't you have a record?"

"Hey now," I start. I haven't for years, and it hurts—just a bit—that she only remembers me as the hell raiser I was in our youth. "Nothing recent."

Lauren closes her eyes and puts her hand on her chest,

no doubt feeling her heart race. Mine is going a million miles an hour. I take her hand, gently threading my fingers through hers.

"You can do this. We can, I mean."

She opens her eyes and looks right into mine, causing my heart to swell in my chest with longer. I want her to look at me like that every day for the rest of our lives.

"Thank you, Noah. For doing this with me."

Again, her words hurt. What do I need to do to prove to her this matters to me? "It's my kid too. From now on, it's not just you and just me, it's us."

She squeezes my hand and leans in, lips parting. I can't help it. There is something about Lauren that makes me lose control.

I kiss her.

And she lets me.

Soft lips crash against mine, tasting like strawberry lipgloss. I twist in my seat and cup her face in my hands. I. Cannot. Stop. Kissing. Her.

"Sorry," I pant when I stop for air, pressing my forehead against hers.

"Don't be," she says softly and doesn't move away. Gently, she places her hands over mine and brings my face to hers, kissing me again. "We should go in." She makes no attempt to leave. "Before someone comes out and sees us."

I nod and run my hands through her hair, afraid if I let go I'll never get to kiss her again. We kiss again. I'm not physically able to stop.

"Noah," she moans. "We." Kiss. "Need." Kiss. "To stop." More kissing. Finally she turns her head, wiping her mouth with the back of her hand. "Fuck," she whispers.

"You're rethinking the no-sex rule, aren't you?" I give her a grin.

"Actually, yes." She's grinning right back. "But no. Come on, let's get this over with."

Lauren's family is already seated in the dining room when we walk in the house. I can hear them talking and smell dinner, which is no doubt on the table. I'm a bit surprised no one has called Lauren asking where she is; it's unlike her to be late for anything. We purposely arrived after the others. Me walking in hand in hand with Lauren is going to be a shock on its own.

Lauren takes a deep breath and pulls the ultrasound pictures from her purse. She keeps a tight hold on my hand as we walk through the house.

"Finally," Mrs. Winters says when she sees Lauren. The table is already set. Chicken, corn on the cob, mashed potatoes, and roasted vegetables are waiting for us, all served family-style. "I was about to ca—" She cuts off, eyes darting to me.

"Hey!" Colin says, greeting me like usual. "What are you..." He trails off, looking at his sister's hand in mine. "What are you two doing? Trying to be funny, right?" A line forms between his eyes as he looks back and forth from Lauren to me. I wince, feeling like I betrayed nearly ten years of friendship.

"I wish," Lauren says softly, looking at her sister, Katie, who gives her an encouraging nod. Oh right, she already knows. Mr. Winters glares at me, and I'm glad looks can't kill, while the others, Jenny, Lauren's mom, and Wes, Katie's fiancé, try to figure out what the hell is going on.

Colin stands up so fast his chair almost tips over. "No.

No way, man. You and … no."

Mrs. Winters gasps. "Lauren!"

I look down at the table. I'm fucking dying; I can only imagine how Lauren feels.

"The surprises don't end there," Lauren says and gives my hand a tug. We take our spots at the table. Colin sits back down, a bit too shocked to be pissed at me just yet. Lauren is shaking. I put my hand on her thigh and she puts her hand on mine, curling her fingers under my palm. She looks at her parents. "Mom, Dad … you're going to be grandparents."

Mrs. Winters flicks her eyes to Colin and Jenny, but when they mirror her confusion, she sucks in air and stares at Lauren. "What are you talking about?"

"I'm pregnant," Lauren says. "Noah and I are having a baby."

CHAPTER NINE

LAUREN

MOM'S FACE IS as pale as a ghost. "You're pregnant?"

I just nod.

"You're having a baby?"

"That's what being pregnant means, Mom," Katie says.

"You're not serious, right?"

I put the ultrasound pictures down. "I figured you'd think that, so I brought proof." Mom takes them, mouth open as she processes this.

Colin has already gotten it. He jumps up again, coming at Noah. Wes is sitting between us, strategically placed by Katie, I'm sure, and pops up just in time to stop Colin from throwing the first punch.

I turn to Dad, sure he'd be hightailing it to the coat closet to get his shotgun, but he's sitting there, looking too stunned to breathe. *Please don't have a heart attack.*

"My sister!" Colin says, batting at Noah, who stands. He's shielding me, keeping me from becoming part of the scuffle. "Why would you do this to my sister?"

"It's not like I had no say in this," I snap, surprised at how defensive I feel over Noah. "It takes two, you know."

Wes gives Colin a bit of a shove and he backs off,

sitting back down. He's staring at his best friend with a mixture of hate and shock. Jenny has her head turned down, and I think she might cry.

Oh my God.

How could I have forgotten? She's been wanting a baby for months and hasn't been able to get pregnant. And here I am, knocked up after one night. I should feel horribly guilty, right?

"Everyone just calm down, please," I say, tears coming to my eyes. Yes, I feel horribly guilty. Terribly guilty.

Mom looks at me, stricken. "How could you let this happen?"

"I didn't mean to," I start, unable to look my mother in the eye.

"I would hope not," Dad says. "We raised you better than this, Lauren. And you." He glares at Noah, at a loss for words.

Mom's hand is resting on her chest, feeling her rapid heartbeat. "You're so young, Lauren. You have your whole life ahead of you and … and now…" she trails off, tears springing to her eyes.

"I know, Mom. I know." Great, and now I'm crying. Noah flips his hand over, lacing our fingers. "But it happened and now … and now…"

"Now we're dealing with it the best we can," Noah says.

I wipe my eyes, glad I decided to forego any eye makeup today. "Please don't be mad at me."

"We're not mad," Dad tells me. "We're disappointed." Ouch. That's even worse. "I didn't expect this from you. Him on the other hand…"

"Mom, Dad, please!" Tears fall freely from my face.

Katie gives me a sympathetic smile. Colin is staring daggers, and Jenny's eyes are on the table. Wes looks a bit entertained, and I know Katie told her fiancé beforehand what's going on. "I know this is the last thing any of us wanted, but it happened, and I need your support. I'm really scared."

Mom's face softens and she gets up, coming around the table to hug me. "I'm here for you, honey. I always am."

I press my head against her shoulder to muffle a sob. Mom pats my back, holding me for a minute. I didn't realize how much I needed my own mom until I discovered I'm going to become one.

"Shhh," Mom soothes. "It's okay, Lauren. We'll figure this out." I nod and sniffle. Mom takes my hands in hers. "It'll be okay in the end." She kisses my forehead then takes the ultrasound pictures off the table.

"When are you due?"

"December third."

She looks back at the ultrasound for a full minute, processing everything, then smiles. "I'll have a grandchild in time for the holidays!" She turns to my dad, who is as still as a statue. "We're going to be grandparents, Riley!"

Dad blinks, then takes the ultrasound images. "I assumed your brother or sister would be the first to provide some grandkids," he starts, still staring at the pictures. "This is incredibly unexpected, Lauren."

"Trust me, I know," I sigh. Should I apologize?

"But every child is a blessing."

I sink back in my chair, relieved. I can tell my parents are less than thrilled, but they're not going to yell at me. Not now, at least, when everyone else is around.

"How are you feeling?" Mom asks. "And when did you find out? How long have you kept this from me?"

"I'm really tired, but other than that, totally fine. And I just found out a few days ago. I wanted to tell everyone at the same time, ya know. To get it over with."

Her eyes go to Noah, who barely uttered a word since we got here. "And you two have been dating in secret for a while?"

"Uh, well, not that long," I say. *Or at all.*

Mom's still looking at Noah. He's always been polite to her, never causing a scene at any sort of family get together he's tagged alone with Colin to, but she still didn't like them being friends. Noah was the wild child, dragging Colin into trouble right along with him.

"Well," Mom finally says. "It could be worse."

"Mom!" I say and feel embarrassed.

"What?" She shakes her head. "So you're eight weeks already?"

"Yeah."

"Have you picked out names?"

I turn to meet eyes with Noah. That hasn't even come up. "Not yet."

"What about called insurance or asked about leave at work?"

My blood pressure rises. "Not yet either."

"You can't wait on these things, Lauren," Dad says and I'm suddenly feeling like a bad mother already and totally overwhelmed.

"It's been a shock," Noah says. "And we're still wrapping our heads around this, but we will get everything figured out."

"Are you going to be involved?" Mom asks, point

blank.

"I am," Noah says, deep voice steady. "I care a lot about Lauren. I have for years, actually."

I turn to him and our eyes meet. Something unspoken is said between us, and it's genuine. My heart does a little flutter thing and I feel some sort of connection to Noah.

"I'm sorry to spring this on you all," I say, thinking I need some sort of closure. "But it is what it is, and there's no going back. Noah and I are going to do the best we can to make this work, and I really need your support."

"Treat her and my future granddaughter right," Dad says, tone threatening. "And you won't give me a reason to castrate you in the shed behind the house."

Noah swallows. "I think I can do that. And if Lauren wants another kid someday, I'll need my balls."

I kick him under the table. *Just agree and shut the hell up, please?*

"Dad, you don't know it's a girl," I say.

"Yes I do," he says. "Intuition."

My stomach grumbles in warning, telling me I need to eat or risk feeling sick. I reach out and start filling my plate. No one speaks, but some of the tension leaves the air.

Thank fucking goodness.

Noah serves himself and we both start eating. The others take our cue and do the same. Then Mom starts a string of questions asking about cravings and saying she's helping me decorate the nursery. I can't bring myself to look at Jenny. Just as I start sharing in Mom's excitement, I accidentally turn my head and see just how crushed she looks. I don't want her to be mad at me, but at the same time, I can't blame her. Though nothing was done on purpose or to beat her to the punch. *She* should be having this conversation with my mother. *She* should be giving them their first grandchild.

Not me.

After dinner, things move along normally. The guys go into the family room to watch TV, and the girls stay in the kitchen, drinking wine and cleaning. If Noah and I make things work he is so helping me clean the kitchen after meals.

"How did this happen, Lauren?" Mom asks.

I raise an eyebrow. "After three kids, I'd assume you'd know how someone gets pregnant."

Mom makes a face. "That's not what I meant. You and Noah ... I never saw that coming. You're a smart girl. Noah is, well, Noah. I thought I raised you better but apparently didn't."

"Mom," Katie says. "Stop with the guilt. She already has enough to worry about."

Mom waves her hand, dismissing Katie's comment. But Mom's been like that, always has, always will. She's great at a good guilt trip and half the time doesn't even realize it.

I choose my words carefully. A lot of alcohol is how this happened, but I don't want Mom to know her first grandchild was conceived during a night of blackout drunk sex neither of us remember.

Not yet, at least.

"I don't really know. It just did. We got to talking, one thing led to another, and—"

"That's all I need to know," Mom interrupts.

I roll my eyes. "You asked." I take a breath, feeling emotional again. "Are you really disappointed in me?"

She puts a pan away and comes around the island counter to hug me again. "Yes and no."

"That's not what I want to hear."

"And this news from you isn't what I want to hear," she counters.

"I thought you wanted grandchildren."

"I do," Mom promises. "And I hoped you would have kids someday ... just someday when you were a bit more ready. I love you and will love this grandchild. You know I support you no matter what, and I'm proud you owned up to keep this child. I worry about your future, but I have faith in *you* to raise this baby right."

But she doesn't have faith in Noah. And honestly, as of right now, neither do I.

"She's not a teen," Katie says.

Mom smiles. "Silver lining this didn't happen in high school. Or college." She gives me another hug. "Whatever you need, you let me know."

"Thank you," I say and hug her back. I can see the heartbreak in Jenny's eyes, so I change the subject to work.

Later, when Noah and I are ready to leave—yep, I'm tired already and it's only eight—Colin pulls me aside.

"You let me know if he puts one toe out of line," my brother whispers. "He's my best friend and all, but I know him, and I know he's not, uh, ready for something like this."

"I will, and thanks. I'm beginning to see what you've been saying for years though. He's not that bad of a guy."

"Underneath it all, he's not." Colin lets out a breath. "I'm still pissed at him, and you—there's a rule against hooking up with your brother's friends, you know. But having my best friend be the father of my niece or nephew is kinda cool."

"I'm so glad you are the level-headed one," I say with a smile. I consider telling him I'm sorry for upsetting Jenny, even though I didn't mean to, but decide against it. He doesn't know I know, and I don't want to risk upsetting him even more. He's taking this better than I thought he would at the moment. "And really, he's trying. He said he wants to be involved, and I believe him. For now. Go easy on him. He won't admit it, but he's worried you'll hate him. It's not just his fault this happened."

Colin's nose wrinkles in disgust. "I don't want to think about it. Noah has told me stories, and nope. Can't do it. Can't go there." He holds his hands in front of him, blocking me from sight.

I laugh. "I'll spare you the details then."

"Are *you* okay?" he asks. "This definitely isn't on your list."

"I'm coming to terms," I say honestly. "It's a lot to process. Having Noah with me is helping a lot."

Colin nods. "Just let me know if I need to put him in his place."

"I will. So far so good … though we haven't even gone on our first date yet."

"First date?" Colin shakes his head. "This is so messed up."

I sigh and put my hand over my stomach. "You're telling me."

*

I stand in front of the bathroom mirror, smoothing my dress over my stomach. I'm a little bloated, but I don't look pregnant yet. My hair is up in hot rollers, and I've done up my makeup. Eyes lined in black, dark shadow on my eyelids, and red lipstick. I rarely put this much effort into my appearance, and I almost regret that I did tonight.

Because this first date isn't going to lead to anything.

And yet I want to look good.

Why? It's not because Noah Wilson looks like a fucking bearded Norse god or anything. Nope, that's not why at all.

I take out the curlers, finger-brush my hair, then spray it with hairspray. I can use hairspray, right? It's not toxic to the baby or anything? I put away my hair and makeup supplies then go into my bedroom to Google hairspray and pregnancy. I'm ready to go, and Noah isn't supposed to be here for fifteen more minutes.

I'm surprised when the doorbell rings five minutes later. The dogs run, barking again, and I close the computer (yes, hairspray is fine) and grab my shoes.

"Lauren," Noah says, deep voice rumbling as he says my name. Dammit knees. Why are you getting weak? "You look … beautiful."

"You sound surprised," I say and give him a quick up and down with my eyes.

"Not surprised," he says. "But I rarely see you like this."

"You rarely see me at all," I say with a smile. "And thanks. You look good too." He does. In dark jeans and a light-gray button-up shirt, he looks effortlessly put together. His dark hair is styled in a way that makes it look like he woke up like that, which is as sexy as it is unfair.

Nobody wants to see me when I just woke up. I look like a creature from the black lagoon, not a model from a

Calvin Klein shoot. Damn him.

"Should we get going?" I ask, turning to grab my purse and my coat. "You made reservations, right?"

"Yeah. You only reminded me to a dozen times."

"Sorry," I say with a shrug. "It just doesn't make sense not to, ya know?"

"I guess." He extends his hand for me to take.

"Where are we going?"

"Zazzios."

"Really?"

"You sound surprised."

"That's a pretty fancy place." Fancy, and expensive. It opened last year and got very popular after some reality TV star was seen dining there with her boyfriend.

"I don't do first dates often," he starts and holds out his hand for me to take. "But when I do, I do them right."

I just smile, not sure how I should feel that my perspective on things has already changed. I love getting dressed up and going somewhere fancy—it doesn't happen that often—and this is an ideal first date. But it feels ... weird.

This date isn't going to end with sexy time and the hope for a second date. I already know Noah and I will be getting together again for pretty much the rest of our lives. The nature of those meetings is still to be determined, but it takes the fun out of this dating thing.

Noah pays for valet parking, takes my coat, and pulls out my chair when we get to the table. He's playing the part of the perfect gentleman perfectly, and I worry that's all he's doing.

Playing.

Not taking this seriously. I look across the table at

him, and find it hard not to feel like I'm back in high school, longingly staring across the hall at my brother's best friend, wishing he would take notice in me … and then realizing that if Noah and I ever did hook up, I don't know who would murder me first: my parents or Colin.

I don't know much about Noah, and that needs to change. He might not be the trouble-making bad boy he used to be. Fuck, I hope not. If he is, there is no way this can work between us.

"Would you like to start the evening off with a glass of wine?" the waiter asks as he hands us our menus.

Noah orders two glasses, then realizes what he did right after the waiter walks away. "Fuck, I forgot."

"It's okay. You can have it." I look over the menu. There aren't even prices listed out. Wow.

The waiter brings us the wine, along with bread and salad. My mouth waters at the sight of lettuce and tomatoes. At least I have healthy cravings, right?

"So," I start after I order some sort of fancy pasta. I'm not entirely sure what all went into it (why are fancy dishes so confusing?), but it has cheese and noodles and a cool name. Plus it probably cost more than what I make per hour, so it should be good. "Do you still work at the Roadhouse Bar?"

Noah laughs. "You don't know?"

"No, I don't. I told you, Noah, I don't know you anymore."

"You will soon enough," he says, eyes meeting mine. Damn you, Noah. Only you are able to make ordinary words in an ordinary sentence borderline orgasmic.

"So, what do you do?"

"I'm a photographer."

"Really?" I might have leaned back with surprise. "Like a real one?"

He laughs again. "As opposed to what, a fake one?"

"Or one that takes pictures of naked women in their basement and calls them models."

"I don't have a basement," he says. "I live in an apartment in the city. And yeah, I'll call myself a real one. I did get a degree in art."

I knew he and Colin went to the same college. My brother got a degree in marketing, and I kind of assumed Noah just floated along, posing as a TA to get in girls' pants. And now I'm starting to feel guilty for assuming anything about him.

"Why photography?"

He shrugs. "Being honest ... I had to pick a major. Photography seemed easy and was a good excuse to take those basement photos you were referring to, which led to hookups in college. Then I got my first photography job and realized I could make a decent living doing something that had no set hours. Plus I'm good at it, I guess. Win for me."

"What kind of photos do you take?"

"Whatever I get hired to do, really. I worked for a magazine for a while before starting my own business. I can show you sometime."

"So do you have a studio?"

"I do. On Washington street."

I know exactly where that is. It's the historic district of this town, located near the heart of the business center. It's a busy place, ideal for any sort of shop or store, and rent isn't cheap on that street. He must do pretty well.

"And you work at...?"

"Banfield Animal Hospital. I'm a vet tech."

"You like it?"

"Oh, I love it. It's what always wanted to do."

"I remember. It was one of the first things you ever told me," he says then looks almost embarrassed. "In Mrs. Jefferson's office."

I have to think back for a second. "Oh right. You were in trouble or something. Why?"

He shrugs. "I don't even remember."

Curls fall over my shoulder when I shake my head. "I never would have thought we'd be here, in this situation."

"Yeah … things have gone off course of what I expected too." He reaches across the table, fingertips touching mine. "It doesn't mean it's bad, though."

He locks eyes with me, holding steady as if looking away would be the death of him. My heart flutters and suddenly I'm looking at a whole new Noah, one that holds a promise of a future.

Maybe this can work after all.

"So," I say and pull my hand back, afraid of how intense my feelings are becoming. "If this was a normal first date, what would we do after dinner?"

"I'd take you back to my apartment and we'd have sex."

"You're very certain about that."

He gives me that smartass smirk I remember from years back. "I am. It's almost a shame you don't remember anything from that night."

"Almost. So, then what? You part ways and that's that?"

"Yes, I wasn't interested in dating anyone. But that was then."

I smile back. That was then.
And this is now.

CHAPTER TEN

NOAH

I LOOK AT Lauren, who fell asleep while we were watching Harry Potter after our first date, and feel something I haven't felt in a long time. Is that my heart swelling … with happiness? The movie ends and Lauren is still sleeping. Carefully, I move away and make sure she's comfortable, covering her with a blanket. Should I leave? I don't want to, as odd as that is.

The recliner chair is good enough for the night. TV goes off, I sit, and close my eyes, not falling deep asleep but dozing off. Around midnight, Lauren wakes up.

"I didn't mean to fall asleep," she says groggily. Her eyes meet mine and I can't help but smile.

"It's okay. I can only assume you're tired. You're growing a person and all."

"Yeah, no big deal, just creating life." She sits up. "You didn't have to stay."

"I didn't want to leave you," I blurt. "I can't lock the door behind me. That's not safe."

"Oh, right. Thanks. Do you want to stay the night?"

Stay the night? With her? Hells yes. "I thought you said no sex."

"I did, and I didn't mean it that way. It's late, and you're here…" She looks into my eyes again.

110

"Then yeah."

She leads the way to her bedroom. "I have an extra toothbrush. I'll set it out for you."

"Thanks," I tell her and get ready for bed, striping down to just my boxers. Lauren is in bed when I come into her room. Her eyes widen as she looks at me, eyes slowly trailing over my body. Then she closes her eyes and looks away. Trying to resist temptation, is she?

I won't tempt her—because really I'd be tempting myself. She's tired and needs extra rest, right? Shit.

Before I know it, I'm in bed with Lauren Winters. Again. Though, this time nothing is going to happen. My leg touches Lauren's as I try to get comfortable. Her skin is soft and warm and instantly turns me on. I want to feel more of it, to run my hand up that smooth calf, past her thigh and—stop. Dealing with an erection while next to Lauren in bed isn't something I want to do right now. With a huff, I roll over, moving as far away from Lauren as I can without falling off the bed.

Lauren stretches her arm, fingers brushing my bicep. I tense. There is no way I can sleep like this when all I can think about is parting Lauren's legs and diving in between.

"Can you, uh, move over?" I ask.

"It's okay if you touch me," she says. "But not like that," she adds before I can make a pass. There is no middle ground. If I'm touching Lauren, it's leading to something. I bring my arms close to my body, figuring I'll just stay like that until I fall asleep. Lauren laughs. "You've never literally just slept in bed with someone before, have you?"

"Nope," I tell her. "I've never stayed the night with someone like this either. Especially someone I'm attracted

111

to. This is weird."

Lauren laughs again and moves her pillow, scooting closer to me. "Here," she says and rests her head on my chest. I swallow hard, feeling something rise inside me, something other than desire.

"I don't like to cuddle," I say out loud. "But this is nice." It feels right. Holding Lauren like this, innocently, softly, brings me a sense of content I never thought I'd feel. "Your no-sex rules includes blowjobs, doesn't it?" I ask, joking. Though I wouldn't turn one down.

"Sorry to disappoint, but yeah, those are out."

"That's what I thought. Just checking." My eyes close and I rest my head against hers. "Have you told anyone else?"

"No. I want to wait until the first trimester is over. Which is only about a month away now."

"Fuck, that sounds scary. I thought we had more time to figure this parent shit out."

She chuckles. "I don't know if I ever will."

"You'll be a good mom."

"I hope so."

She doesn't return it with a "you'll be a good dad." Because she doesn't know. I want to be angry with her, but I share her doubt.

"There's a lot I don't know," she says.

"I don't think anyone is fully ready. We'll get it. Together."

She holds me tighter. "Together. I like that."

Oh, Lauren … if only you knew how much I've wanted to be together, what I would have given to make you mine.

*

My arms are still around Lauren when I wake up. Her dogs have joined us in bed, and we're all crammed together like one big happy family. I'm uncomfortable, and the arm Lauren is laying on is all pins and needles, but I don't dare move.

I kind of love this.

"Morning," I say to Lauren when she opens her eyes. Her hair is a mess and there are pillow crease along her cheek. I reach over and brush her hair out of her face.

"Morning," she says back and runs her hand up my arm. "This is a different kind of waking up together."

"Very different. Is that bad?"

She smiles. "Not at all."

I kiss her forehead. "Good."

We stay wrapped up together for a few more minutes, then Lauren gets up to use the bathroom. After, she lets the dogs out and offers to make breakfast. I go into the kitchen with her, and together we make pancakes and eggs.

"This is new to you too, isn't it?" she asks when we sit at the table.

"Eating breakfast with someone? Yeah, it is. But it's nice. I would say I should have done this years ago, but I probably wouldn't have had it with you."

She smiles and a bit of color rushes to her cheeks. "Are you busy today?"

I shake my head. "I usually go to the gym with Colin in the morning on the weekend, but I've been avoiding him."

Lauren chuckles. "He won't stay mad at you forever."

"We'll see. Are you busy the rest of today?"

"No."

"Do you want to do something together?"

Her smile returns. "I would like that. Any ideas?"

"I don't care as long as it's with you."

*

"This counts as our second date, right?" I ask Lauren. We dropped her dogs off at the dog park—doggie day care is a real thing and Lauren utilizes it all the time—and stopped for lunch at a small diner. "It should, and then I'll only have to take you out one more time until I get some."

Lauren laughs, grabbing a French fry. "I change it to three formal dates then."

"What, this isn't fancy enough for you? Come on, I'll take you to Taco Bell tonight. Bam. Three dates done and over with and we can make another baby."

She laughs again and shakes her head. "That's not funny. And don't tempt me, Noah."

I wiggle my eyebrows. "So you're thinking about it."

"I'm thinking about tacos, not *it*."

"Liar."

She purses her lips. "Fine. I might be thinking about it, but only because of hormones."

I lean back and run my hands over my chest. "You want this."

"Stop it!" she laughs and looks around. "People can see you!"

"Right, right. I don't want to tempt those old ladies over there."

"Hey, I hear they give pretty good blowjobs when they take out their dentures."

114

I wrinkle my nose. "Gross."

She reaches for her lemonade, laughing. I like this, the laid-back time together, talking and laughing and just being ourselves. I don't have to put on a show for Lauren. I'm just me. I've never been this comfortable around anyone.

The rest of the day is just as easy going, and we spend the evening watching movies. Halfway through the second Harry Potter movie—and, yes, these movies are fucking awesome—Lauren rests her head on my shoulder. I wrap my arms around her and pull her close, stretching out on the couch so that we are both laying down.

"You can lay on your stomach, right?" I ask, suddenly worried she's going to hurt our baby.

Fuck, that sounds weird. *Our baby.*

"Yeah. I can for a while. And the baby is like the size of a grape right now. Very small."

"Oh, good. When can you feel it move?"

"From what I read, about halfway through."

"It's like a little alien inside you."

"Hah, it feels like it sometimes. Well, not the movement parts obviously, but the part where it's sucking all my energy."

I've had so much fun with Lauren all day, enjoying her company, that I didn't think about the reason we were together. Now that I'm thinking about babies again, my head is spinning. I hold tighter onto Lauren, anchoring myself. "Do you want a girl or a boy?"

"I don't care as long as it's healthy. What about you?"

"I don't know care either, though I think it's a girl."

Lauren lifts her head off my chest and looks into my eyes. "I wonder who he or she will look like."

"This is so weird," I blurt. What's even weirder is my

imagination getting ahead of me, and I'm seeing this play out like it was planned, like Lauren loves me as much as I've loved her, and we're ready and excited to embark on this stage of life together.

What the fuck is wrong with me?

"It is." Lauren lays her head back down and turns her attention back to the movie. I run my hands up and down her arms, bare skin under my fingers. Goosebumps break out along her flesh, so I sit up to grab the blanket that's on the back of the couch. We resituate close together, blanket draped over us both.

Lauren turns, probably to say something to me, but I don't give her the chance. I move in, putting my lips to hers. Time stops and it's just us, just this kiss.

I can't get close enough.

I can't stop kissing her.

It's like I'm that sixteen-year-old boy, feeling the effects of teenage love at first sight all over again, ten years later.

Only this time, she's feeling it too.

Lauren moves into my lap, straddling me. We kiss with fury, and soon I'm laying her down on the couch, moving between her legs. She rakes her nails down my back and grabs the hem of my shirt, yanking it up halfway then stopping.

"Noah," she groans. "We … we … oh fuck."

My lips are on her neck, and she likes it. Really likes it. Her legs widen and wrap around me.

"Noah," she starts again and puts her hands on either side of my head. "We shouldn't do this."

I let out a breath and nod. "Okay, if that's what you want."

"It's what I need," she whispers. "I want you."

Worst possible words, Lauren. Thanks for that. With great control, I move off of her, and we cuddle together again. If Lauren wants three dates, I'll wait. Hell, I'll wait if she wants thirty dates. I'll do whatever it takes.

CHAPTER ELEVEN

LAUREN

"IT'S BEEN MORE than three dates," Noah reminds me as we sit down at dinner after seeing a movie. I ate pretty much the entire bucket of popcorn and I'm fucking starving again.

"I know," I say, picking up the menu. I want my freaking hamburger. Now. And salty French fries and strawberry lemonade.

"So, that means I get some tonight, right?"

I look up into Noah's blue eyes, falling under the spell of his sexy grin. The word "yes" wants to roll off my tongue. Actually, I want my tongue all over him.

"You said it takes good food to get into your pants," he continues. "And I think we should fuck a few times before you get a baby belly. That'll be a little awkward."

I raise an eyebrow. "I'm only twelve weeks. It'll be a while before I get a bump that big. And you're making it really easy to say no." I'm lying through my teeth. With hormones raging through me and all the time we've spent together the last three weeks, I'm horny as fuck and want nothing more than to feel him on top of me, kissing me as he drives his big cock in and out, rocking me into oblivion.

"Prude," he says with a hint of a smile. "Come on,

throw me a bone."

"You have hands, don't you?"

"Yeah, but Rosie and her four sisters don't compare."

Should I give him credit? We've been dating for about a month now and I cut him off after several minutes into a makeout session, like a teenager afraid of getting caught by her parents. He hasn't complained too much, and never once pushed me. Actually, every time he begrudgingly moves off me, I feel deeper for him. I know this is the longest he's gone without sex since only God knows when, yet he's still here, still with me. He's trying. He cares. He wants to make this work.

And so do I.

We've spent a lot of time together over the last few weeks, and I feel like I'm seeing the real Noah. There's more to him than tattoos and motorcycles, but I'm still working to find out why he puts up that front.

He sighs. "I think sleeping together is a good way to see if we're really compatible. People in relationships do fuck, you know."

I roll my eyes and look back at the menu. Do I want bacon on my hamburger? What the fuck? Why am I even asking myself that? Of course I want bacon. Maybe extra bacon. Yes, definitely extra bacon.

"Sex complicates things."

Noah lets out a deep laugh. "I think we're past that."

"Shut up," I say with a smile, shaking my head. I don't want to tell him that I'm scared sleeping with him will mess with my head. I've seen him naked and know he's a man I can easily get physically addicted to. I want my heart and soul to be addicted to him too.

I think they're getting close.

"You are a prude," he says with a hint of a smile. He's teasing but also means it.

"Is that the way you're going to talk to the mother of your unborn child?"

He twitches and exhales. "You're making me."

"Oh yeah, *forcing* you."

"I wouldn't have to ask if you put out."

"I'm not that type of girl."

He laughs. "Says the mother of my unborn child."

"You're insulting yourself by insulting me."

"Dammit, you're right." He picks up his Coke and takes a drink. "Though I don't really care. I am that type of guy. *Was* that type of guy. I've been good. I think I deserve a reward, like maybe let me touch your butt."

I laugh, finding it harder to resist him. There is something so sexy about a man who can make you laugh. And Noah does, pretty much every time we are together. I like being with him. A lot. A whole fucking lot.

"Do you want to spend the night at my place?" he asks. "And I don't expect anything," he adds. "I just want to be with you. I like having you next to me at night even if all your fun parts are off-limits."

"I do want to." I have yet to stay overnight at his apartment, actually. "But it's hard to leave the dogs overnight."

"Bring them with," he says.

"Can you even have dogs at your apartment? I don't want to get yelled at."

"I honestly don't know and don't care. If someone gets their panties in a wad about it, they can deal with me. No one is going to fuck with you, I promise."

Yeah, that makes me smile. And realize that if we

FIRST COMES LOVE

really do have a girl, she's going to have one overprotective daddy.

We stop at my house after dinner. Noah plays with the dogs while I pack a bag. I grab my go-to Harry Potter PJs, and hesitate, Noah's words echoing in my head. I want to look good for him. I might not sleep with him tonight, but my hand is gravitating to the back of my drawer, and I'm pulling out a rarely worn black silk and lace nightie. It has delicate thin straps and lace around the hems. It ends just below my ass cheeks. If I wear this, along with matching black lace undies of course, it's because I want Noah to see me in it, which really means I want him to see me *out* of it.

And I must, because I shaved and shit.

I was a little afraid all the hair would clog the drain in the shower, but hey, if there is even a slight possibility of getting some, I don't want to look like a wooly mammoth.

It *has* been several weeks of dating . And Noah is looking very fine tonight in distressed jeans, and a white T-shirt under his black leather jacket. Plus he smells good, and what the hell, I'm already pregnant.

Shut up, vagina.

You shall not rule here. Brain, quick, take over before I'm throwing myself at Noah in the living room. I grumble at myself and throw the sexy nighttime clothing in my bag anyway. I can decide what to do later.

Noah grabs my bag. "Ready?"

"Yeah. Just need the dogs." We each take one, loading them into the car. I've only been to Noah's a few times, since I'm a homebody and have dogs to take care of. Pulling into the parking lot tonight impresses me just as much as the first time. It's three stories, dark red brick, and upscale. I'm starting to think I've been wrong about Noah for a long time. Though I can't help but see the rough-and-tough bad boy when I look into his eyes. Only now he's grown up a bit, and apparently has money.

Which makes him all the more dangerous.

He leads the way to his apartment, unlocks the door, and turns on the light, then steps aside to let me in first.

"Movie, shower, dessert, bed?" Noah asks as he takes off his shoes and coat. "And feel free to add sexy time anywhere in between those."

I smile and shake my head. His cocky jokes are starting to seem charming. Dammit, Noah. What are you doing to me?

"What movie?" I ask, trying to ignore the warmth and longing that go through me, making their way from my heart to my lady bits.

"We'll see what's on."

We take a few minutes to make popcorn and get the dogs settled down, then sit together on his leather couch. Noah flips through movie options, and settles for *The Avengers*.

"I love this one," I say and bend my knees, tucking my feet under myself. It's chilly in here and there are no blankets on the couch, like a typical bachelor pad.

"Really? I thought you only liked fru-fru Disney shit."

"Disney isn't shit, and I do like that, but I like other stuff too. Superheroes or princesses, they're all about good overcoming evil, and most end happily. That's what I like. I'm a sucker for a happily ever after."

He turns to me, and when our eyes meet, that same feeling goes through me. Like we're on the same wavelength. Like we're connected on an emotional level. He holds my gaze, and I'm moving closer on my own accord. He reaches out and pushes my hair back. I shiver.

"Cold?"

"A little," I say, feeling breathless.

"Hang on," he says and gets up, returning with a blanket. He pulls me into his lap, encircling in his arms. I rest my head against his firm chest and he kisses my forehead.

I let out a breath and close my eyes. Noah runs his fingers up and down my arm. My heart thumps in my chest yet at the same time I'm perfectly content.

"Are you tired?" Noah asks me.

"I'm okay. But if you keep doing that, I'll fall asleep. It feels good."

He tips his head down and nuzzles my neck. "I can do something that feels better."

His lips meet my skin, sending a jolt through me. He kisses my neck and it's everything a kiss should be. Gentle. Wet. Warm. I want his mouth all over me.

Now.

"Noah," I groan. "We ... we shouldn't." He doesn't stop kissing my throat. "Plus I've been super constipated and bloated the last few days."

He pulls away, raising an eyebrow. "I could have lived my whole life without knowing that."

I smile and turn around to look at him. "It's a symptom of carrying our baby. You get to know all the nitty-gritties I'm experiencing."

"Our baby," he says softly. "Sorry she's making you feel like shit."

"You don't know it's a girl. And it's okay. I haven't felt that bad, really." I take a deep breath. "I kinda killed the mood, didn't I?"

"Just a bit. But I'll still have sex with you if you want."

I shake my head, laughing. "Oh, thanks. I want to," I add, afraid Noah is going to take my abstinence personally. "I just…"

"What are you afraid of?" he asks. "You're obviously not a virgin."

I bite the inside of my cheek. "I don't really know. I'm so confused and emotional and … and scared. I'm really scared."

He sits up and takes my hands in his, clear blue eyes locking with mine. "It scares me too, Lauren. But know I'm here for you—both of you." He leans in and gives me a quick kiss. "And I'm not saying this to get in your pants, but how is not sleeping together going to make it any less scary?"

I shake my head. "Sex is complicated."

Noah's eyebrows go up. "Who have you been having sex with? It's not that complicated."

"You know what I mean. And…" I can't say it, because saying it means I have to fully admit it to myself. As perfect as Noah has been over the last month, I'm terrified he's going to revert back to old ways, decide this baby-daddy thing isn't for him and leave me not just alone but broken hearted.

Because if he decided to walk away, it would break my heart. Hearts can only get broken when love is involved. I'm not in love with Noah, yet. But I'm starting to fall.

And that is terrifying.

"Hey," he says gently. "No rush, okay? Obviously, I'm ready when you are, but we'll take it slow."

Hearing him say that makes me want to rip off my clothes and throw him on the ground.

"Thank you, Noah."

"You don't have to thank me," he says softly. "I'm not doing this as a favor to you. I'm doing this because I want to, and making you happy makes me happy."

Tears bite at the corners of my eyes and I'm teetering even closer to the edge of falling.

"Don't look so surprised," Noah says softly and moves his face closer to mine. He brings his tattooed arms around me. "You have no idea how much I care, Lauren. I have for a while, longer than you know."

"Why?" I blurt.

He smiles. "You've been more to me than just my best friend's sister. You're different than anyone I know and I … I…" He looks away, unable to bring himself to say what he wants to say. Instead, he brings his face to mine and kisses me.

Time stops and I'm standing still as life swirls around us. Then Noah parts his lips and slips his tongue into my mouth. Suddenly I can't get close enough. I twist, wrapping my arms around Noah and straddling his lap.

It's crazy how one kiss can be the spark that ignites a fire of passion.

Noah pulls me to him with a desperation I didn't know he had. He flips me over and pins me between his body and the couch, kissing me like his life depends on it. I widen my legs, welcoming him closer. We continue kissing, and I feel his cock harden against me. It turns me on to know he wants me.

He moves his lips down to my neck, sucking and biting at my skin. My want is growing for him, getting hotter and wetter as each second passes. He runs a hand up under my shirt, fingers sweeping across the curve of my side then onto my breast. I moan when he slips his hand under my bra, fingers gently circling my nipple.

I let out another moan as he caresses me, and moves his mouth back to mine. He knows exactly what he's doing, and he's doing it better than anyone has ever done to me before. And we only just got started.

Holy fuck, Noah Wilson is hot.

He gets a little rougher and I can hardly stand it. I need him now. I reach down and pull up his shirt, running my hands along his muscular torso. I bring them down, finding the clasp of his belt. I try to get it undone when he sits up and yanks my shirt over my head. For a few seconds, 'he doesn't move. He just stares at me with hunger in his eyes.

"You are so fucking beautiful, Lauren," he whispers, deep voice sending tremors through me. Then he dives back down, picking back up where we left off. His hands go around me and my bra is off in two seconds flat. And I'm still fumbling with belt. I haven't even gotten to his pants yet, though his big cock is pushing so hard against the material it might rip it on its own and save me the work.

He takes both my hands in his and moves them above my head. Yes, I am so glad I insisted on shaving tonight. We're kissing again and now I'm feeling that same desperation. I don't just want Noah. I need him.

He pushes himself up just a bit and moves his bearded face down, taking one of my breasts in his mouth. He swirls his tongue around my nipple and I squirm underneath him.

Oh my god, that feels so good. My head falls to the side. His teeth gently bite down, then he lets up and works his tongue again. I rub myself against him, feeling close to coming already.

"Ohh," I say out loud. "That feels so—ow!"

Noah jerks away. "I hurt you?"

I hunch my shoulders forward. "No, not really, but yeah." I feel my cheeks flush from embarrassment and frustration. "Sensitive nipples. Ya know … another symptom." It was one of my first symptoms really I wrote off as PMS.

"Oh, uh, sorry. Want me to not do that?"

"No, I like it. It's just, um, super sensitive to any touch now." I let out a breath, mad at myself for ruining the passion-fueled moment. Again. Things are different now. I'm sharing my body with a teeny-tiny person. "So keep doing it. I think. Ugh. I don't know. I'm sorry, Noah."

He grins. "Don't be sorry. I've never fucked a pregnant chick before, so it'll be an experience for us both."

I put my hands on his waist and pull him back down to me. I put my lips close to his ear and whisper, "Who said I was going to let you fuck me?"

"I want you, Lauren," he growls. "I've wanted you for so long."

And I'm a goner. I put my lips to his and we are kissing again. I reach down and pop the button on his jeans—on my first try, I should add. I don't hesitate. I don't think things through. I push my hand inside his pants, feeling the full length and girth of his cock.

No wonder I was so sore the day after our one-night stand.

Noah lets out a groan, melting against my touch. I push his pants down, and they're not even over his ass when Noah impatiently sits up and kicks them off. My pants come off next, and Noah takes another few seconds to admire me.

I've never had anyone look at me like that before. There is lust and desire in his eyes, but there is also something else. Something deeper, and he's looking at me like he's just been given the one thing he's wanted but couldn't have.

I bring him closer and push my hand under the elastic waistband of his boxers, taking hold of his erection.

"Are you…" he kisses me. "Sure … this … isn't…" More kisses. "Too fast?"

Nothing is too fast right now. If anything, he needs to hurry up and finish undressing me.

"No," I pant. "I want this. I want you."

Noah lets out a growl, kisses me with more force than before, and scoops me up. I'm clinging to him, trying my best to keep kissing him, but let's face it. It looks easier in the movies than it actually is. We move down a hall and into his bedroom.

It's dark and I can't see anything around us. It's just his body against mine, our hearts racing in perfect rhythm. He lays me down on an unmade bed, cool silk sheets underneath me, and gets back on top, putting himself between my legs. I take his shirt off and run my hands over his chest, imagining the tattoos that mark his skin.

My legs wrap tightly around him, and it's just the thin layers of our undies keeping up apart. As if he can read my mind, Noah goes down, slowly rolling the sides of my panties off my hips and down my legs. His head goes between my thighs. His beard brushes against my skin, tickling and rough at the same time. He puts his mouth to me and flicks his tongue against my clit.

I gasp and tangle the sheets in my hands. He takes his time, and the soft wetness of his tongue against me contrasting with the gruff hair on his face is perfect. I'm so close to coming. My heart is racing and pleasure winds tight inside of me. My breath catches. I'm right there, teetering on the edge of orgasm. Noah starts to pull his head away.

"Don't you dare stop now," I order, letting go of the sheets to put both hands on his head. I slit my eyes open to see Noah grin before getting back to work. Only a minute later, my body goes rigid as I climax. Noah holds me against him, not letting up until I tremble, ears ringing from the force of the orgasm.

My head falls to the side, and I'm panting. He moves back on top of me, wiping his mouth before kissing my neck. I can't move yet even if I tried. My fingertips are numb and I can't feel anything but the after effects of coming.

Noah gently runs his fingers through my hair while he kisses my collarbone. My heart slows down to a normal rate and I can breathe again. I turn my head, cupping Noah's face in my hand. I kiss him, tasting myself on his lips, but don't care. I run my other hand down his back, squeezing his tight ass as I push him to me, letting him know I'm ready. I part my legs and he kisses my neck as he pushes into me.

"Fuck, you feel good," he moans and slowly pulls back then thrusts back in. He starts moving his hips faster and faster, and I think he's going to come already when he suddenly stops. "I'm not going to hurt the baby, right?"

"No," I say shortly. I was about ready to come again

too. "It's way up there."

"Are you sure it's safe?"

If I weren't on the brink of orgasm, I'd find his concern cute. But right now, not so much. "Yes. You can't hurt it."

"Even if I push in like this?" He pushes his cock deeper inside me and holy fuck that feels amazing. I lift my hips so he hits my g-spot.

"Fine. It's fine. It's way up there in my uterus. Out of reach."

"Okay. I don't want it coming out with a dent in its forehead or anything."

"Shut up and fuck me, Noah."

And damn, he does.

I come two more times before he finishes, pushing in and holding himself there. I run my nails down his back, feeling his cock pulse inside me. He lets out a breath and relaxes against me, then pulls out and rolls over, holding me against his chest. I trace his tattoos with my fingertips, still catching my breath.

"Do you regret that?" he asks quietly.

"Not at all." It's the truth. Physically, the sex was amazing. But it was so much more and I feel closer to Noah now, more like a real couple. Because real couples sleep together instead of abstaining solely to see if things can work. "Do you?"

"No. I don't regret doing it the first time either. Not that I wanted to knock you up, of course, but we wouldn't have this, whatever it is, between us. And I like this."

Those just might be the words that push me over. "I like this too."

NOAH

I SIT ON the bed, petting Vader and watching Lauren get dressed. She pulls on a blue dress. It's simple, yet still looks amazing on her. Her hair is in a braid over her shoulder, and she spent no more than five minutes doing her makeup.

I've never been with a woman like her. Hell, I haven't *been* with a woman in any sense other than horizontal (and vertical, or upside down…) in years. I dated Heather James for three months, and broke up with her the day after she told me she loved me. I didn't love her. I wanted to. I tried. But my heart belonged to another. It's belonged to another for years.

And the owner is standing in my bathroom, barefoot on the tile, brushing her teeth. After last night, things feel different. Different in a good way, that is. I didn't fuck Lauren, I made love to her. And trust me, there is a difference.

I don't let myself think too deep that often, but sometimes I wonder if I went for women the total opposite of Lauren to convince myself that's what I want. Don't get me wrong, I've had plenty of fun drinking and fucking, but there's always been a yearning in my heart for her, and it's dark and cold and even I cannot fool myself into thinking it had been filled. I didn't notice it most days, I've grown so accustomed to it.

But sitting here, looking at Lauren, the hole is closed up.

She turns the water off and turns around. I look down at my phone, pretending I wasn't watching her.

"Look," she says, putting her hands on her stomach. "I definitely look pregnant now. Kind of. Maybe?"

I smile and put my hands over hers. "Knowing that this wasn't there before, I say you do."

"So you're saying other people are just going to think I have a gut?"

"Pretty much." I shake my head and laugh. "Either way, I still find you to be fucking hot." I kiss her. "Want to take the dogs for a walk before we get lunch?" I ask, knowing Lauren worries the dogs get bored being in my apartment all day.

"That'd be really nice. It's beautiful outside for this time of year."

She grabs the leashes and I grab my camera. Lauren raises an eyebrow when she sees it in my hand.

"I have no pictures of you," I tell her. We have no pictures of us together, actually.

"I'm not photogenic," she says and clips Vader's leash onto his collar. "You can edit the pictures, right? Make me look good?"

I hang the camera over my shoulder and turn to Lauren, brushing hair out of her face. "You are beautiful, Lauren, in person and on film. It would be a shame to make any edits or changes."

"Whoa," she whispers, breath leaving her. "That's a good line."

I chuckle. "I wasn't trying to give you a line."

She tips her head. "Well, you did, and it worked."

"Worked enough for sex?" I ask hopefully.

"More than enough. But," she adds when she sees me raise my eyebrows and smile. "The dogs ... they're waiting."

"Fine, let's go."

"Good answer," she says, taking my hand, and we head out the door. There's a nature preserve across from the apartment complex, with several miles of trails. I keep a hold of Lauren's hand, and we walk in silence down the boardwalk that surrounds the lake. It stretches for a quarter mile then breaks away to a dirt path that winds through the trees.

"This is pretty," Lauren says. "I've never been here."

"It is. Peaceful too."

"You go for walks?"

"I run on the trails."

"Oh, right," she says dryly. "You and Colin are all into working out and all that lame shit."

I chuckle. "You really hate working out that much?"

She shrugs. "No. I mean, I like to stay in shape in case I happen to walk through a magical wardrobe that takes me to another land and go on adventures, but since the chance of that happening are pretty slim, I like my spare time spent on the couch. Preferably eating."

"At least you're honest. And a wardrobe?"

She turns, eyes wide. "You've never heard of Narnia?"

"That sounds familiar, but I don't know what it is."

She shakes her head. "It's a good thing I get to pick the next movie."

"Oh God," I say, amping up my horror. "Another

Disney movie?"

"What's wrong with Disney?"

"It's lame."

"No, it's not."

"Is too," I tease. "But really, why do you still like that stuff?"

She shrugs. "I like seeing good triumph over evil and seeing love always win. Real life doesn't always give our happily ever afters."

I just nod, hoping I can give Lauren the happy ending she deserves. We're two months into this dating thing, and I think I'm doing all right so far.

"So," I start. "Have you thought of names?"

"I have. Ethan, Peter, Jackson, and Aiden are my top boys names."

"Nope to Peter. He'd face a lifetime of dick jokes. Ethan, eh, not really a fan. Same with Aiden. Jackson is a yes, but that's because I like Sons of Anarchy."

"Jackson it is then."

"What about girl names?"

"I think it's a boy," she says.

I shake my head. "Nope. It's a girl."

"I hope it's a girl," she says and takes my hand again. "Is that horrible to admit?"

I slow and tip my head down to look into her eyes. "No, because I want a girl too."

"You do?"

"I want her to be like you."

Lauren's green eyes get a bit misty. Then she blinks and looks away. "Well, I'm not perfect. And hopefully this kid doesn't inherit my asthma. Or shellfish allergies. Or fear of heights and public speaking."

"You can't pass that stuff down, right?"

"Nah. Well, the allergies and asthma yeah, of course. But not the fears."

"If it's a girl, I hope she looks like you. But has my height, because you're kind of short." We both laugh and I lean over to kiss her. "But if it's a girl?"

"Ella. I've had my heart set on that forever."

"Ella Wilson … I can work with that."

"You want our kid to have your last name?"

Her question is like a sucker punch. A reminder that we're not actually *together*. A reminder that she doesn't love me. Not yet, at least.

"Noah!" someone calls.

I look up and see Melody slowing from a jog to a walk. She's wearing a bright-pink sports bra, with a pushup underneath. Not that she needs it with those big, fake tits. Her spandex shorts just barely cover her ass, and she's got a full face of makeup on. I turn to Lauren, eyes going to her belly. If I do end up with a daughter, I don't want her to alter her body for the sake of sex appeal.

"I haven't seen you in a while," Melody says, completely ignoring Lauren.

"I've been busy." I tighten my grip on Lauren's hand.

Melody blinks, looking at Lauren like she just appeared. "Oh, uh, hi. Who are you?"

"I'm Lauren. Nice to meet you."

"This is Melody," I say to Lauren. "She lives across from me."

Melody gives a tight smile. "How do you two know each other?"

The world "girlfriend" burns on the tip of my tongue. I want so bad to say it, but don't, afraid Lauren doesn't want to be it.

"We met in high school," Lauren says. "He's my brother's best friend."

I smirk. When she says it like that, it has a forbidden sexiness to it that turns me on. I slip my arm around Lauren.

"You got dogs?" Melody asks, eyeing Vader nervously. To be fair, the large dog stands protectively in front of Lauren, giving Melody a judgmental stare. "I saw you come in with them last night."

"They're not mine," I tell her. "We didn't want to leave them at Lauren's and have to go back in the morning." I reach down and pat Sasha's head. I've always liked dogs, and now I'm starting to *really* like these guys, almost as if they were mine.

"Oh, so you two are…"

"Dating?" I supply. "Yeah, we are."

"I thought you didn't date," Melody blurts.

I shrug. "I didn't, but I do now." I turn just in time to see Lauren smile.

Melody's face falls. "Oh, uh, that's nice." She inhales and regains her composure. "Well, good luck with him," she tells Lauren. "Enjoy it while it lasts. I hope you know what you're getting into."

"I'm well aware," Lauren retorts, not missing a beat. "Nice to meet you." Melody leaves in a huff, jogging away. Lauren faces me. "A bit of a heartbreaker, are you?"

"I can't help it."

"Really. So what's the story with her?"

Tell Lauren about my booty calls? Nope, that's not uncomfortable at all. "We hooked up."

"No shit."

136

I look down at Lauren, the shock apparent on my face.

"Noah, come on. I've known you for years. I know how you are—were—with the ladies."

"Oh, right. Melody and I had a no-strings arrangement and she got attached. That's all."

"You really think the whole no-strings thing ever works?"

"If done right."

She rolls her eyes. "Maybe. I've never tried."

I squeeze her hand. "I never would have guessed," I tease. We step off the boardwalk and start hiking through the woods. Vader stops and sniffs at everything, and Sasha pulls on her leash. I don't know which is more annoying.

"I'm going over to Colin's tonight for video games," I tell her.

"Is he still acting weird?"

"He glares a lot, but hasn't said anything. Other than that, things are normal. He's had a while to accept it by now."

I've lived a carefree life, not putting expectations on anyone or anything, but the few close friendships I've hung onto over the years mean something to me.

"I think he's more excited than he lets on. You two have had that bromance going on for over a decade, having you be part of the family has to make him happy." Lauren stops and makes Sasha sit, not walking again until the dog calms down. "He feels like he needs to play the protective older brother card, but we both know he's really a big ol' softy. But…"

"What?"

"Can I tell you a secret?"

I look behind me, locking eyes with her. "Of course."

"You might not want to know, because then you have to keep it from Colin, because he doesn't know I know, and if he knows I know and now you know, it could be bad."

"Huh?"

She presses her lips together and sighs. "Jenny told me they've been trying for a baby and not having luck."

"Oh, I knew that."

"Really? I thought I had top-secret information."

"Sorry to burst your bubble. I've known for a while. But why is that a big deal?"

"Because I'm pregnant and Jenny isn't and I think that hurts her."

"I guess I can see that, but it's not like we did this on purpose to spite her. It just happened."

Lauren nods, and I know she's not convinced. Actually, I can tell she feels guilty. She's too fucking nice. Too nice. Too pretty. Too good for me.

LAUREN

"I DON'T UNDERSTAND how something so little requires so much stuff." Noah looks down the aisle of baby toys and blinks. A week has passed since we slept together, and things have been pretty perfect. Though technically it wasn't our first time together, it felt like it.

And it was everything I wanted it to be.

Passionate, hot, and oh so satisfying. It was everything I imaged too, and I'd wondered from time to time how Noah was in bed. He definitely did not disappoint. Noah came over every day during the week, and we had sex every time. Sometimes more than once.

It's been a little over two months and I'm falling hard for him. Right now, he'll catch me, yet I still can't shake the fear that once the baby comes, he'll drop me. Hard.

I need to be fair. Noah has done nothing to make me think he'll be a bad father or will suddenly abandon me. He has been perfect, as in everything I want perfect. Too perfect? I believe in true love and fairy tale endings. Is it possible my Prince Charming has been right there in front of me the whole time?

"Where the hell do you put everything?" Noah asks.

"I was thinking the same thing. Maybe you switch it out?"

"Maybe." He picks up a box and looks at a rattle with

lights and sounds. "Whatever our kid needs, we'll get it. I don't want her to go without."

"If we have a boy, will you be disappointed?"

"Not at all. Honestly, I hope whatever we have is normal."

I raise an eyebrow. "Normal?"

"Yeah, a lot can go wrong. It kind of freaks me out when I think about it."

"So if we have an abnormal kid you won't love it?"

"That's not what I meant." He puts the box back. "And you've said it before: you hope for a healthy baby."

"Well, duh."

He playfully nudges me. "You're moody today."

He's right. "Sorry. I'm tired. I shouldn't have worked last night." I didn't end up clocking out until after eight on a Friday night.

"You shouldn't work so much."

"If I pick up more shifts now, I can take off more time later."

"I told you," he says softly. "Don't worry about money. I can help you."

I smile and nod, moving down the aisle and looking at play mats. I had a conversation with my parents about that just this morning. Noah paid for the first ultrasound I had when my insurance denied it and I didn't have the funds to cover the hefty bill. He gave me the money in cash, actually. It helped immensely and took the anxiety over not being able to afford it. And my parents agreed that letting Noah help cover the costs is more than fair since it's his kid too, but I shouldn't rely on it.

We're not married, after all. He has no obligation to cover my bills.

"I know, and thank you. I'll stick to my reg—oh my god, this is too cute!" I stop at a turtle-shaped play mat.

Noah stands close next to me, and he's smiling. "Want to get it?"

I bite my lip. "Yeah, but maybe it's too early? I don't want to jinx anything."

"Buying something isn't going to jinx anything, Lauren."

"You're right. So yeah, let's get it."

He takes it off the shelf and tucks it under his arm. He wraps his free arm around me. "I feel like real parents, buying shit we don't really need."

I laugh. "Then we need to go get some cute outfits too. And shoes to match."

"Do I need to turn in my man card by saying this is kind of fun?"

"Not at all. Actually, I think that, uh, increases it. There is something very hot about a man who loves his children."

"Ah, right. Taking a baby to the park to pick up chicks is better than taking a puppy."

I laugh and roll my eyes. "I'd go to the puppy. I know I'll love our child, but other people's children ... not so much."

We go down an aisle of strollers, then look at carseats and highchairs before emerging into the clothing section. I pick out a white and yellow onesie with ducks on it and a matching hat. It will work for a boy or a girl. Noah grabs a tiny pink dress.

"Ella can wear this when she comes home from the hospital," he teases.

I shake my head. "It'll be cold then. She'll need a

sweater and pants to go with that."

"Ah-hah! You agree it's a girl!"

"Hardly. But if it is, it'll need to be winterized."

"Fuck. I forgot about keeping a baby warm as we get her in and out of the car and shit. Do they make winter jackets small enough for babies?"

"Yeah, but you don't want them to wear it in the carseat. It's not safe because the material is too bulky and the straps won't tighten. It makes them at risk for being ejected."

"And now I feel like I know nothing about being a parent again."

"Join the club," I mutter. "It's a wonder people are able to keep their kids alive, really. There is so much I don't know."

Noah grabs lacy leggings and another frilly dress. "You know more than me."

"I look a lot up online. I have two baby apps on my phone and read books and magazines. You could read them too."

He makes a face then stops himself. "Okay. I'll start with the magazines. Less boring than books."

"Books aren't boring. I read at least one book a week." Or I did before I started going to bed at grandmother hours.

"I hate reading."

"That's sad. You don't know what you're missing."

"Nothing, I'm missing nothing."

"When was the last time you read a book?"

"For fun?" His blue eyes widen. "I don't know."

I'm reminded of how different we are. But opposites attract, right?

"Want to get lunch?" Noah asks me as he looks through another rack of newborn clothing. He's considering each teeny outfit he picks up, and it might be melting my heart.

"Yeah. I've been craving hot dogs all day."

We go to the registers, and Noah pays for everything before I even have time to dig into my purse and find my wallet. We get lunch, go back to my place, and Noah joins me for a walk around the block with the dogs. He says he has work to do and regretfully leaves. The goodbye takes ten minutes and involves lots of kissing and touching.

Once he's gone, I look at the baby stuff we bought. Are we going to have to buy two of everything? One for here and one for his house? Or do you pack up what you need and bring it with?

The logistics of this whole "having a baby and not being a couple" thing make my head hurt. Maybe for the first month or two, she can just stay here since she'll be so little and I'll be—dammit, Noah. You got me calling the baby "she."

I smile and look down at my stomach. Now that I've eaten, a small bump is definitely visible. I might not look pregnant to strangers, but anyone who knows me would know something is up. Is it weird I kind of like it?

My mind flashes to something Noah said a few weeks ago, about having sex with a baby belly. I know it's entirely possible to keep hooking up throughout the whole nine months, but *how* can we keep doing it? Positions seem pretty limited.

I go into the kitchen and grab a bag of chocolate chips, then get my laptop and come back into the living room, shooing the dogs away from my chocolate as I

Google "sex positions during pregnancy." I click on a site that includes photos, expecting them to be clothed couples or even drawings.

I'm not expecting porn.

And yet I don't click away. I look through the pictures, for research purposes, of course. I go to another site and find videos. The videos are just previews—I'm not paying for anything—and another two-minute clip starts as soon as one ends. I sit back, mostly curious, and watch. It's totally possible to have sex throughout pregnancy. And enjoy it too, by the sounds of the moaning and groaning. I bite my lip, considering calling Noah over to try some of these out. Practice makes perfect, right? I'm not that big yet. Better to try this out now.

The next video clip that plays showcases breastfeeding fetishes. I wrinkle my nose. "Sick." I go to click away when the doorbell rings, causing the dogs to rush into the foyer barking.

"Hey, Lauren!" my sister calls, stepping inside. "We were in town and thought we'd stop by and say hi."

"Hey!" I call back and get up to grab the dogs.

Soft moaning comes from the living room, followed by a woman's voice saying, "I'm so full for you, baby. Drink up. It's all for you, baby."

Oh shit. The computer.

"Uh, is this a bad time?" Katie asks, green eyes going wide the same time as her nose wrinkles in disgust. "You weren't masturbating or anything, were you? We can leave."

"No!" I exclaim, horribly embarrassed. "It's not what you think."

Katie can't look at me. "Yeah, explain that please. But

first turn whatever the hell you're watching off."

My cheeks are burning red as I slam my laptop shut. Now Katie and Jenny are laughing as they wait for me to explain.

"I was doing research."

"Research, really. Come on, Lauren, you can do better than that," Katie says.

"Not research on grown men drinking breastmilk! That video came up automatically. I might have been looking up sex positions that are safe during pregnancy." My hand settles on the small baby bump and my gaze stays steady on the floor, unable to face my sisters.

Jenny raises an eyebrow. "And why are you interested in that?"

Shit. Busted.

Katie laughs again. "Glad to see you stuck to your word about not sleeping with Noah."

"I said that like two months ago," I spit out. "Things change. He's changed."

The amusement vanishes from Katie's face. "You sure about that?"

With a sigh, I sink back onto the couch and wait for Jenny and Katie to take a seat before continuing. "Yes. Well, maybe he hasn't changed, but I'm seeing a different side of him. Yeah, he's made some really bad choices and put himself first before, but he's not like that now. When he's with me he's kind, and caring. As far as I know, he's been on his best behavior since I told him I'm pregnant."

"I hope it lasts," Katie says. "And I don't mean that as in insult to you, Lauren."

"I know." And I do know. Noah has been perfect the last two months, but what are months of being good compared to years of being the bad boy?

Is having his baby enough to change him? And am I enough to make him stay changed?

"So, how is it?" Katie asks.

"How's what?"

"The sex. I always assumed he was well versed with a woman's body."

I get a flash of his head between my legs. Maybe I will call him once my sisters leave. He'll come over for a booty call no matter what. "He's very well versed," I say with a smile.

"Well, good," Katie says. "So you're happy?"

"Yes," I reply without having to think about it. "As crazy and scary as this has been, things are good between Noah and I, and the baby's doing fine. This is still far from what I planned for my life, but I'm okay with it." The revelation hits me as the words leave my mouth. Just when did I become okay with this? Probably the same time Noah went from being that guy who knocked me up to something … more.

Someone more.

"I'm glad," Jenny starts. "Colin and I were really worried for a while. Noah doesn't play by the rules." I turn to look at her. Her eyes aren't on me, but are on the bags of baby stuff Noah and I got today from Babies R Us. She's sad, and I wonder if she's thinking it should be her instead.

Because I've thought that a few times before.

And it should be. Not that I'd trade my little baby for anything, but if I could shift everything to next year and let her have the first grandchild, I totally would.

Katie gets up to use the bathroom and tension grows

between Jenny and me. Do I need to say something? Let her know I'm sorry and don't mean to make her sad? Crap. I hate awkward situations like this.

"Jenny," I start, not able to look at her. "I'm sorry."

"It's okay, Lauren," she says, knowing exactly what I'm talking about.

"I know it's not fair, and I never meant to hurt you."

"Lauren, I know you didn't do this to hurt me," she spits.

I bite my lip and nod, forcing myself to look up. I expect her to look sad, not pissed. My eyes widen.

"Sorry," she says, shaking her head. "But it isn't fair. Why do you get to have a baby that you didn't try for and I can't get pregnant. But what makes it worse is him."

My heart is in my throat. I hate being yelled at in any way. "Him?"

"Noah. It's not fair he gets to have a kid, gets to be a dad. Do you know the strain he's put on my marriage? The time I've spent fighting with Colin because he was out late with Noah, or wants another motorcycle so they can ride together again? He's the last person who deserves a baby. And now he's going to be part of the family forever. Even if you two never speak again, I will be the aunt to Noah's kid."

Tears fill my eyes, shock mixing with hurt. I've never heard any sort of harsh words from Jenny before. It's like ice water has been dumped down my back.

Part of me agrees with her: Noah has caused a lot of trouble, and if anyone deserves to be a father when it comes to Noah and Colin, it's my brother. The other part of me thinks she's being dramatic and needs to get the fuck over it.

While I don't know what it's like to struggle with infertility, I do know how hard it is to see someone have something you desperately want. I feel guilty all over again.

"So," Katie says loudly from the hall, no doubt hearing part of our conversation. "Are you gonna call up Noah and act out that porn?"

I raise an eyebrow. "I'm not lactating yet. But maybe the other stuff … yeah, I'll try it."

Katie shakes her head. "It's so weird knowing you and Noah are hooking up. I always thought he was good looking when we were kids, but you know me. I don't date anyone younger than me."

"I never would have thought we'd end up together," I say. "Noah's not the type of guy I'd go for."

Katie gives me a small smile. "Just keep that in mind."

"I will," I promise. Maybe I'm getting ahead of myself, being too positive. But Noah has been playing the part of daddy-to-be perfectly. And that's exactly what worries me, what doesn't sit well in my stomach when I think hard about all this.

I'm falling for him, despite my best effort not to, and he's just playing. Eventually playtime ends.

NOAH

I BALL MY fists, muscles tense and ready for the fight. If you asked what we are fighting about, I couldn't tell you. I'm too drunk.

Fuck.

I went to The Roadhouse with every intention of letting Joey know I'm still alive and well, and that I'll be a dad in the winter. I had every intention of leaving after one drink.

Yet here I am, drunk and picking fights, just like before. Things aren't just like before. I know that, even as wasted as I am.

The first punch is thrown and I duck out of the way. There is still time to end this, to walk away and go home to Lauren. But I've never walked away from a fight. I can't do it now.

I hurl my arm forward, fist colliding with the side of the guy I'm fighting's face. His name isn't known; all I know is he did something to piss me off. Or maybe he hasn't.

I'd be lying if I said I wasn't on edge, if all this baby stuff hadn't rattled me. Because it has. Baby aside, the more time I spend with Lauren, the clearer it is to me that I'm more in love with her than I thought.

And that fucking terrifies me.

I don't want to mess this up. I don't want to hurt her. And I don't want to be a bad father, because that's the worst thing I can do to her, right? Let her down and not take care of our child.

I rarely ever know what the fuck I'm doing in life. I race through things at a hundred miles an hour, and, somehow, they work out. Well, most of the time. There have been bumps along the way.

But when I know what I want, I get it. I've never had expectations for anyone else. Expect nothing, invest nothing, lose nothing. It's been my philosophy for as long as I can remember. Have fun and fuck while I can. Live it up.

No expectations.

No rules.

No chance of getting hurt.

No chance of getting stuck in a loveless marriage with a child I didn't want, a child I don't want to be around. No chance of turning into my own father. A father whose emotions ranged from numb and drunk to angry and violent, with not much in between.

The guy stumbles back and crashes into a table, knocking beer bottles to the floor. Broken glass scatters along the ground. Fuck. Joey won't press charges against me for damaging the bar, but I can't avoid everything. Drunk and disorderly, public nuisance, the cops can get me for something.

I can't do that to Lauren. I can't do that to our baby.

Something inside of me protests as I whirl around and storm behind the bar. Something *else* inside of me trembles and I fear this is all for naught. I am completely in love with Lauren Winters, more so now than ever. If she

150

doesn't love me back, all this change will be for nothing.

But I'd be damned if I didn't try.

I grab a shot glass and a bottle of whiskey from behind the bar.

"I think that's enough." Joey's gruff voice is too loud in my ear. I blink, inhale, and turn around.

"What would you know?" I say to Joey. Or at least I think I said that. I'm swaying a bit on my feet, though hell if I admit that.

"Listen, kid," Joey says and slaps me on the back, turning me away from the bar. "I don't know what's going on, but we'll save that for another night. Find one of the stragglers, have her take you home and fuck you hard, then we'll talk, all right?"

I grumble in response. I never got around to telling him about Lauren before I started drinking. "Can't," I slur, looking at the few women left at the bar this close to closing on a weeknight. "Gotta get back to Lauren."

Joey raises an eyebrow. "You got someone steady?"

"In a way." She's not my girlfriend yet, but she will be.

He guides me to the bar to sit, then fills a plastic cup with water. "Have her come and get you."

"No." I shake my head. It's too late to have Lauren leave the house. I think. Fuck. What time is it? I put the cup to my mouth and take a sip. And why the fuck am I drinking water? I'm not drunk. I can drive to Lauren's. I want to see her. I need to see her.

I stand and pull my keys from my pocket.

"Where the hell do you think you're going?" Joey asks.

"Home. To Lauren."

Joey snatches the keys from my hand. He's too spry for someone his age. It's not fucking normal. Even drunk,

I know not to argue with him.

"Give me your phone," he says. I'm hit with tiredness as I pull my cell from my pocket. Maybe I am drunk after all. I put the phone in Joey's hand.

Joey just shakes his head and disappears into the backroom. I go around the bar and fill a glass with whiskey, slowly sipping it. A minute later, he comes back and hands me my phone.

"You better buy her some flowers, boy," he whispers. "Make it up to her. You don't want to lose this one."

No, I don't. I can't. Because it's her I love, her I need. It's always been her.

CHAPTER FIFTEEN

LAUREN

"HELLO?" I SAY, jerked into alertness the second I see Noah's name pop up on my phone. It's late. No one calls with good news this late. My heart instantly races.

"Is this Lauren?"

Uh, that's not Noah's voice. My mind gets ahead of me, and this is the coroner calling to tell me they found Noah's body on the side of the road after he crashed his motorcycle.

"Yes."

"This is Joey, from The Roadhouse. I got your man here trying to come see you. He's drunk as a skunk. Any chance you can come get him? Already took his keys."

"Yeah," I say, heart slowing down with relief. "I'll be right there."

I hang up and swing my legs out of bed, too shaken to be tired. I pull on a sweatshirt, go to the bathroom, then take off, having to program the address into my GPS on the way. I've only been there once, and I wasn't exactly in sound mind when I left.

Twenty-five minutes later, I pull into the gravel lot and text Noah. A minute goes by before he responds. Then it's another two minutes before I see him stumble out of the bar. Tiredness has set in, and now I'm just pissed. It's nearing three AM and I need to be at work at seven.

His face lights up when he sees me, and part of my anger melts away. He opens the passenger side door and gets in.

"You stink like smoke," I blurt when he leans in to kiss me. His lips taste like whiskey.

"Probably," he says and leans back into the seat. "You didn't have to come get me."

"You're drunk. How else where you going to get home?"

"I'll be fine in a little while."

I drive out of the parking lot. "I don't think so."

His eyes close and he doesn't respond. Just how much did he have to drink tonight? Neither of us speaks on the way back to my house. Noah follows me inside. The dogs take advantage of his drunk mind to lick him to death as he just sits there and takes it.

"Last time I was drunk at your house, we made a baby," he slurs as he struggles to his feet. He grabs me around the waist. "Want to make another?"

"We can't make another. And no, I want to go back to bed. I have to get up and go to work in a few hours."

He spreads his legs and pulls me closer. "Call off."

"I can't just call off for no reason."

He moves his mouth to my neck and good god, even drunk, that man can work his tongue and make me quiver. "I can give you a reason."

"As tempting as that is, I'm going to pass. Go take a shower, you smell."

His hand slips inside my pajama pants. "Don't go to work. Tell them you're sick. Love sick."

"That would be a lie." I smile and shake my head.

Noah pulls away and the hurt in his eyes is as shocking as a slap to the face. "I'm not sick," I say quickly. "Plus I get paid hourly. Missing twelve hours puts a dent in my paycheck." I take his hand and guide him through the house and into the small bathroom.

"I have lots of money." He leans against the sink as I strip him of his clothes. I'm not in the mood for sex. I'm annoyed and tired and dreading going through a freaking long-ass shift on little sleep. "You can not work and I'll pay for things. You can stay home and be a mom."

He doesn't know what he's talking about. He's too drunk. Because in order to be a stay-at-home mom while he provides for the family, we have to be a family first.

And he's not even my boyfriend.

"Take a shower, Noah." I help him step out of his pants. I keep my eyes up and my hands at my own side. I don't trust myself not to fall for his sex appeal, no matter how tired I am. "Then come to bed."

He nods and takes a step toward the shower. Then he stops and grabs me.

"You're too good to me, Lauren," he exhales, burying his head in my hair. I wrap my arms around him, taking in his warm skin and muscles.

"Oh trust me, I know."

"I don't deserve you." There is more emotion in those four words than I've heard in a lifetime of conversation with Noah Wilson. My breath catches in my chest and I'm suddenly cold, needing to be pressed closer to his naked skin for warmth. "You're too good for me."

I close my eyes and embrace him, feeling his heart beat against mine. "We can talk about it in the morning." *When you're sober.* He might not feel the same about me then.

EMILY GOODWIN

I hope he does.

And I didn't expect that.

"Take a shower then come cuddle with me?"

He pulls away and gives me a lopsided grin. "I can do that."

"Don't pass out in there," I warn, grinning back.

"I have to take a piss," he says suddenly and turns around to face the toilet. There goes the romance.

I get in bed, trying to hang onto Noah's words, trying to see how this *won't* become a pattern. Because Noah has changed. He doesn't get trashed and stay at the bar all hours of the night. It's not who he is anymore.

It can't be if this is going to work.

Tears pool in my eyes. I want this to work so badly. I want Noah in my life, in our lives. The fear of not having him is like a knife to the heart, more painful than I ever imagined. And now I know there is no use in denying it: I'm in love with Noah.

I'm almost asleep when Noah crawls under the covers next to me. He's wet, like he forgot to dry himself off, and he's naked of course. His skin is hot from the water, and his dick is hard.

Hard and pressing against my ass.

Fuck.

"Are you awake?" he whispers, lips brushing against my ear. For a split second, I consider not answering so he rolls over and goes to sleep. Because that's what I need to do.

Though, sleep will be elusive when my lady bits are tingling and getting wet at the thought of his cock.

"No," I whisper. "But I should be."

"I rarely do what I should."

156

I roll over and he moves on top of me. "I noticed."

He kisses me, heat spreading from his lips throughout my body. I brush his wet hair back and kiss him harder. Screw sleep. One night won't kill me. Because I want to screw Noah.

"Lauren," he says gruffly, but not gruff enough to hide his emotion. "You are entirely too good for me."

"That's not true." My voice is quiet as I look into his sky-blue eyes.

"It is," he says with certainty. "You always have been."

I lean up and kiss him, silencing any words that might spill out of his mouth. If he's going to tell me how he feels—really feels—I want him to remember it in the morning.

It doesn't take long before my clothing is removed, and he's spooning himself against me, stroking my clit as I squirm with pleasure. He waits until I come before sliding inside. I bend my legs and hook one over his, giving him access to my fun zone. He keeps working his fingers as he thrusts in and out.

Then he lowers his head and kisses the nape of my neck and, fuck, there is so much going on right now I almost can't handle it. I cry out as I come for the second time, body shuddering. The orgasm takes command of my body and my ears ring, toes and fingertips tingling. Noah pulls out and gets on top of me, fucking me as hard as he can.

So hard it would hurt if I wasn't still floating in bliss. He comes then collapses on top of me, his weight crushing my sensitive nipples against my chest and putting too much pressure on my abdomen. I push against him.

"Sorry," he pants and rolls off me. He lets out a deep

breath and puts one hand over his head.

My eyes flutter closed and I wait for the feeling to come back to my toes.

"Noah?" I push up and see that he's already passed out.

*

"You're moody."

I glare at Noah. "I'm tired."

"Don't take it out on me."

I stick my fork into my pasta and twirl the spaghetti around. "Who else can I take it out on? And besides, it's your fault I'm tired."

"You seemed to enjoy that last night."

I take a bite of food before I answer. "Maybe I faked it."

"You did not fake that. No one fakes it with me."

I respond by rolling my eyes. "And yes, the sex was good, but the whole getting you at two in the morning wasn't." I just got home from work a little while ago. Noah stayed here all day. He couldn't really leave since his bike was still at the bar, and I know he slept past noon.

Must be nice.

"Yeah ... sorry about that."

He called me when he got up and left a long voicemail, thanking me and apologizing. But this is the first time we got to actually talk since last night. I came home to dinner on the table, which almost made me forgive him.

"What happened last night?" I ask.

"You don't remember? You shouldn't be drinking, you know."

I roll my eyes, not amused. "I mean, why did you go to the bar and drink so much?"

Noah looks away and shrugs. "Just felt like hanging out with the guys. I didn't, uh, mean to drink so much. It just happened." He grinds his jaw, tense. What else isn't he telling me? His brow furrows. "Lauren?"

I bite my lip and look across the table from him. "Yeah?"

"I won't do it again. I promise."

I bite the inside of my cheek, considering each word carefully. "I don't care if you go to the bar to hang out with your friends. I don't care if you drink. But I do care about you doing something that could get you hurt because what you do affects me now. Affects *us*."

He lowers his head, looking guilty. "I know, and I feel awful. Last night I was thinking about..." he trails off and shakes his head. "It doesn't matter. It won't happen again."

He reaches across the table and takes my hand. "I don't want to let you down."

"You didn't let me down. You just made me tired." I give him a smirk. "Make it up with a back rub, okay?" My eyes lock with Noah's. *Fool me twice...*

"I like this, Lauren," he says softly. "Being with you, being together. Last night I ... never mind. But this, what we have, is nice."

I smile, finding it cute as he fumbles over his words. "I like this too, Noah. Things have been crazy and scary, and having you with me helps. Probably more than you know."

He holds my gaze steady and smiles. "Want to make things official? Do you want to be my girlfriend?"

"I do."

"Good. Because that would be really awkward if you didn't."

"And now I can at least say my boyfriend knocked me up."

Noah chuckles. "And I can say I got my girlfriend pregnant. Not just some random chick I took home from the bar."

"We're so classy."

"The classiest." We finish dinner then move into the living room. Noah starts rubbing my shoulders.

"That feels so good," I say. "My back has been hurting all day."

"This might be a stupid question, but is it from being pregnant? You don't have much of a belly yet at fourteen weeks."

"I think so, because it never hurt like this before. I can tell things are, uh, shifting around down there."

"Is it safe to keep working? I meant what I said last night." I flick my eyes to him. I wasn't sure if he remembered. "You don't have to work as much. You pull in a lot of hours."

"There are certain things I have to avoid, but I don't do more than the average person," I say. "Actually, when do *you* work? Shouldn't you have done something today?"

"I had a shoot scheduled."

"And you missed it?"

"It was an outdoor shoot and it rained. I got lucky."

"Yeah, you did."

He takes another few bites before going on to explain.

"I like to schedule stuff in clusters. Like do a shit ton of shoots one week then take some time off. I'm booked this weekend, actually."

"I thought you hated working weekends."

"I do, but a model I shot in the beginning of her career begged me to do her wedding. It's in Chicago, so it's not that far. Come with me. We can spend the night, make a weekend getaway out of it."

"That would be kind of fun." I shake my head. "But I can't just leave the dogs."

"Have your parents watch them. Say it's practice for when we drop off the kid so we can have sexy time."

"Yeah, I'll say just that to them."

Noah flashes a smile and damn, he's charming. "There's no use denying it at this point. They already know you're not a virgin."

"That doesn't mean I have to tell them the details of our personal life."

"Don't most grandparents assume that's why people want kid-free nights?"

"I don't know, maybe?" I wrinkle my nose. "I'd rather not think about it."

"You should. Because I'll want sexy time with you after the baby is born."

*

"I'm not getting any tonight, am I?" Noah asks me about two hours later. I just took him to pick up his bike at The Roadhouse.

"You got some last night."

"Yeah, but that was so long ago."

I laugh. "I won't rule it out. You know, since you're my boyfriend now and all."

He comes over to me as I take my shoes off and toss

them next to the door. He wraps his arms around me, hands landing on my ass. "It's hot hearing you say that."

"Boyfriend?"

"Yeah, that."

I look into his blue eyes and then he kisses me, stubble-covered face pressing hard against me, his soft lips crashing into mine. He picks me up and carries me to the couch, gently laying me down and moving on top of me, careful not to squish my abdomen.

"Lauren," he starts, brushing my hair off my shoulder and behind my back. He lowers his head and kisses my neck before looking into my eyes again. For a split second I think he's going to tell me he loves me.

My heart lurches in my chest.

I don't want him to, as much as I do.

I want him to because it's what should happen: two people in love, bringing a brand-new, innocent life into the world. I don't want him to because I'm scared.

Scared it won't last.

Scared he's just saying it because he thinks he should.

Scared he's going to mess up, get drunk again, and break my heart.

I close my eyes and pull him to me. I don't want to think. I just want to feel. He presses his lips to mine and I lose myself in his kiss. I don't waste any time. My fingers wrap around the hem of his shirt, pulling it up. Noah sits up and raises his arms. I take it off and throw it on the floor. I move my hands back to Noah, running them up his back, feeling every ridge of muscle underneath my fingertips.

Noah lets out a deep breath and sits up, unbuttoning my pants and sliding them off. His pants come off next, then my shirt, and now we're both naked on the couch. He's hard already, and the wet tip of his cock presses against me.

He puts his mouth to my neck and I swear that man has a magic tongue. Shivers run through me, bringing warmth to my core. He works his way down, kissing, biting, and sucking at my skin, until his head is between my legs. He tosses them over his shoulders and moves so that he's crouching on the ground and I'm sitting on the couch.

Fuck yes.

I put my hands on his head, tangling my fingers in his hair, pulling in rhythm with his tongue lashing against my clit. The muscles in my stomach tighten and I toss my head back, panting.

He slides his hands under my ass and lifts my hips, and holy shit that feels amazing. I let out a slow breath, wanting this to last. I could come right now but don't want it to end.

Fuck it. I can come again. And again.

I always do with Noah.

Desire ripples through me and I moan, the orgasm taking over. Noah presses his face harder against me and I squirm, so overcome with pleasure I think I might pass out.

Then I come for the second time.

He moves his head away and yanks me forward, rising up onto his knees. He keeps one hand on me, and grabs his cock with the other, guiding it into me.

He enters with no hesitation. I'm wet and ready for him, but it still catches me off-guard and I cry out, reaching for him, wanting to feel his skin against mine, to wrap my arms around him, and hold him close.

The angle he's fucking me is new, and it's hitting me in a way I've never experienced. It's almost too much.

Black dots float in my vision, and my ears are still ringing. Noah quickens his thrusts, pushing in harder and harder. My breasts bounce each time he rams into me, hurting so good.

"Nooo ... Noah," I pant, slitting my eyes open to look at him.

He slows his movements and leans forward. In a graceful sweep, he picks me up so we both lay on the couch. I wrap my legs around him and he kisses me. I run my hands through his hair, just as he puts his mouth on my neck again. Yes, he most definitely knows that's my weak spot.

I come for the third time, body going rigid and nails digging into his skin. His breath comes out in ragged huffs and I know he's holding out on his own orgasm, not wanting to stop fucking me yet.

I rake my nails up his back and he shudders, letting out a guttural moan. I love a man who isn't afraid to make noise in bed. There's something so hot about the animalistic sounds coming from sex. You can't hold back, can't keep quiet if you want to. It takes over in all aspects until you're screaming so loud it wakes the neighbors.

I run my nails over him again, pressing hard enough to leave red lines over his tattoos. His breathing gets heavier and heavier. I move my hands to his face, feeling his rough beard under the palm of my hands.

"Lauren," he grunts, putting his lips against mine. He pushes deep inside and lowers himself, letting out another moan as he comes. I kiss him, tasting myself on his lips.

He holds himself in me, cock pulsing, then slowly

pulls back.

"Told you I was getting some," he says, voice breathy. He flashes that famous grin, and I want to fuck him all over again.

"I never said no."

"Just admit you can't resist this." He sits up and motions to his body.

I laugh. "You know I can't. The second your shirt comes off, I'm a goner. Really, the power you hold over me isn't fair."

"Don't overdo it now," he teases. "I want to believe you."

"I think coming three times in ten minutes is evidence enough."

He grins again. "Yep. I'm good."

NOAH

I DON'T WANT to be the man Lauren expects. I want to be the man she deserves.

I'm on my way back from the studio, and I'm still feeling guilty about making her come and get me from The Roadhouse the other night. Though I was only half awake when she left this morning, I could see the dark circles under her eyes. She didn't say anything, not one complaint, as she quietly moved about the house so she wouldn't wake me.

I'm stepping it up. I'm not going to disappoint her again. And it's surprising how much disappointing her disappoints me. I can do better. I know I can.

For the first time in a while, I pull into the grocery store parking lot. I'm making Lauren dinner tonight. I just don't know what to make. I text Colin as I walk into the supermarket.

What's your sister's favorite food?

I should know this. She's the mother of my child, for fuck's sake. It takes until I'm pushing a cart down an aisle of vegetables to get a reply from Colin.

Which sister?

I roll my eyes at the screen. He's being an ass on purpose.

The one I slept with. So your guess is as good as mine.

He responds right away. *Not cool, dude. It's bad enough you actually did sleep with one. Lauren likes cheese.*

What can you make with cheese? Grilled cheese? I'd hope for something a bit … more … for tonight though. Fuck. I rarely got home cooked meals. Actually, ninety percent of any home-cooked, legit healthy meal I ate came from the Winters' house. No wonder Lauren is a good cook. She grew up like that.

And I want our kid to grow up like that too. Family dinners, all seated together and eating something that didn't come from a paper bag. My own mother was a fan of fast food, and then "fend for yourself" once I got old enough to drive.

It's not like she was a horrible mother, just an absent one. She took it hard when my dad left. She had to pick up the pieces of life, deal with the hell I raised, and still work to provide for us. She worked the evening shift as a nurse at a nursing home, and was gone by the time I got home from school and asleep when I left in the morning.

My mother was a hard worker—still is—but she put work first. I think it was her way of dealing with the divorce, of dealing with being cheated on and left with a child she didn't know how to raise.

But it was her dedication to work over me that caused me to drift away, and caused things to be awkward between us. She didn't want to be around me. I look like my father, after all. It hurt as a kid, but I'm over it now. She didn't try, and I sure as hell didn't either.

And it's not like I hate my mother. We're just not close. We talk on the phone on the important holidays. Once I graduated high school, she moved an hour away, saying she needed a fresh start. She never got over the divorce. Her untreated depression was almost contagious, and being around her brought me down, which is why I haven't told her she's going to be a grandma yet.

I know I need to. Even Lauren has been pestering me to. Ah, fuck. No better time as the present, right?

I pull up her number and press "call." Then I wonder if this is a good thing to talk about at the grocery store. Meh, I never did give a fuck about anyone else's opinion.

"Hey, Mom," I say when she answers.

"Noah. Is everything all right?"

"It is." I can't blame her. I never call. "I got some exciting news. You're going to be a grandma."

There's a minute of stunned silence. "You got a girl pregnant?"

"My girlfriend," I say so it sounds like this wasn't just some random hookup. It started that way, but it's not ending that way.

"It was only a matter of time," she replies. "I'm honestly surprised it didn't happen sooner."

I close my eyes in a long blink, trying to stay calm. "You, uh, might remember her. It's Colin's sister, Lauren."

"Your friend Colin? You're dating his sister? And he's okay with that?"

"Uh, kind of."

"How far along is she? Is everything going okay? Are you two living together? You were single at Christmas."

"She's four months, everything is fine, and we're not living together yet."

"This wasn't planned, was it? Not that there's anything wrong with that."

"No, it wasn't. We're working it out though. She's

excited."

"What about her family? I remember them being a bit uptight."

Strange how I take almost immediate offense to that. "It was a surprises for everyone. But now they're happy. Excited for a baby due around the holidays." I grab random produce and toss it in the cart. I make my way down the aisles, grabbing things that look good but having no idea what I can actually make with half these ingredients.

"Can I come over and meet her?" Mom asks.

"Yeah, of course. When do you want to?"

"I'm free this weekend."

"Ah, shit."

"Watch your mouth, Noah." Absent or not, that woman is my mother.

"Sorry. I have a photoshoot this weekend. I'll be out of town."

"I work next weekend, but the one after that I don't."

I take a mental note. "Yeah, come over then. Just call me first or something so we know to be home."

"Are you still in the same apartment?"

"Yep."

"Take care, see you in a while."

I end the call, dread building inside, and I can't figure out why until I'm putting groceries away at my own place. My life growing up was dysfunctional. Absent mother, no father … I'm worried that if Lauren is reminded of that, her faith in me will go out the window.

*

"I'm not going to have to break up any fights, am I?" Justin asks, eyeing Colin and me.

"Nah," I say, grabbing a beer and sinking onto the couch. We're over at Colin's for a video game party. "We're cool."

Colin nods. "As long as he doesn't fuck up. Again."

Justin laughs. "It's been, what, four months now and it's still so weird to me." His eyes go to me. "You fucked Colin's sister and you're going to be a dad."

"Shut up." I shake my head and turn on the PlayStation. Justin's been a mutual friend since college and has enjoyed every minute of heckling Colin and me about this. Though he hasn't had many chances to be an ass to both of us at the same time. Colin might have handled the news better than I thought, but things didn't go back to normal until recently. And it's a new normal. There's judgement in my best friend's eyes for the first time. And I get it: torn between your sister and your best friend. It's not a comfortable place to be. He shares the same doubts as the rest of the Winters family, that I'm going to fuck this up and hurt Lauren and abandon my child.

If he knew how much Lauren meant to me, he'd have no reason to worry, or he'd get pissed I'd been crushing on his little sister way back when.

"And you two are together now. Things are going good?" Justin asks me.

"They are," I say, deciding less is more right now, though they are. A month has passed since Lauren and I made things official, and I've never been happier. I spend most nights at her house, and I want to spend all my spare time with her. It's finally feeling like we're together because we want to be, not because we have to in order to raise our child. It's crazy when I think about it, and almost scares me that something bad is going to happen to mess this up.

And that thing is me.

Justin laughs. "So you're fucking Colin's sister on a regular basis now."

"You're such a shithead," Colin mumbles.

"Really though," Justin says. "Things are good with the pregnancy?"

"Doctor says everything is perfect and it's been pretty easy on Lauren."

"That's good. June had a rough pregnancy. Like bad enough to make us think twice about having another."

"Ah, yeah, I remember," I tell him, thinking back two years to when Justin and his wife had their baby girl. Seems like so long ago.

"We find out what we're having tomorrow," I say and trade my beer for a PlayStation controller. "I'm pretty excited."

"Yeah, that's a fun part. June did the whole lame gender reveal party thing. I wasn't even allowed to know what we were having until she opened the box with pink balloons."

"Lauren wants to do that too." I thought it was lame at first, and totally pointless, but now that Lauren's parents are 100% on board with having a grandchild, celebrating this milestone makes sense. Plus, Lauren seemed excited for a reason to eat cake.

"You wanna watch the birth?"

"I think so. I might stay by Lauren and hold her hand or something instead."

"You'll want to watch," Justin says. "I didn't think I'd

want to, but I'm glad I did. Seeing your kid come into the world isn't something you want to miss."

A door slams and Jenny hurries up the stairs. Ah, fuck. I remember what Lauren said about hurting Jenny's feelings. I don't know what if feels like to long for a child and not be able to have it, but if it's anything like longing for a lover you think you'll will never love you back, it fucking sucks.

I don't want to do that to anyone, let alone my best buddy's wife.

CHAPTER SEVENTEEN

LAUREN

I SIT BACK on the hard foam bed and pull my shirt up. The room is warm, probably since most women get some sort of naked in here. Right now it feels hot. Like boiling hot that makes me want to puke. I close my eyes and lean back, resting my head on the pillow that's covered with a paper case.

Noah stands next to me and takes my hand. He's more excited than nervous. Like I should be. But, being Worst Case Scenario Girl, I spent too many hours Googling birth defects found during a mid-pregnancy scan.

"Relax," he says softly when the ultrasound tech turns the overhead light off. He gives my hand a gently squeeze.

"This is so exciting!" my mom exclaims. She's sitting in a chair near the foot of the foam bed, already staring at the large TV screen mounted on the wall in front of us.

"Remember I'm booting you out at the end," I tell her with a smile. I turn to the tech, making sure she knows—again. I already said something when we first came in the room. "We don't want anyone to know the sex yet. Just us."

"I'll keep it secret." The ultrasound tech gives me a wink. She's nice and patient with me, thank God. She fires up the machines, tucks a large paper towel into the top of my pants, and smears gel over my stomach. Laying flat, I don't look very pregnant. But at twenty-two weeks, there's definitely something there when I stand. Or sit. And especially after I eat.

She puts the transducer to my stomach and I squeeze Noah's hand. A slew of things that are incredibly unlikely to happen go through my head, with the worst being finding no heartbeat and the soft movements I've been feeling are really just gas.

Right away, I can see our baby. And it looks like a baby this time, not a blob with a heartbeat. The head is big and round, and the cutest little legs in the entire world are kicking about.

"Can you feel that?" the tech asks.

"I think so," I say, getting choked up when I know for sure that fluttering feeling *is* my baby.

Noah squeezes my hand again, leaning forward. His blue eyes are wide and he's smiling.

"Oh my God!" Mom puts her hands to her face, blinking back tears. At least I'm not the only one getting emotional. "That's my grandbaby!"

I can't stop smiling, and I can't stop the tears from pooling in my eyes. Seeing our baby alive and healthy *and* having my mom just as excited is almost too much for this pregnant lady to handle. Noah keeps a steady hold of my hand, asking more questions than me, making sure everything is measuring all right.

It is. The tech says things look perfect. We're meeting with the doctor after this, who can go into more detail.

"All right, Grandma," the tech says and turns to my mom. "It's time for you to step out."

Mom stands, taking one more look at real-time images of our baby on the TV screen. "You know I'm good at keeping secrets."

"You are not," I laugh. "And you'll find out soon enough."

Mom gives me a pouty smile, then comes over to the head of the bed and gives me a kiss on the cheek. She hugs Noah goodbye and leaves. Noah widens his eyes and looks at me; Mom has never hugged him before. Seeing the baby affected her more than we thought.

"She's probably standing outside the door," Noah jokes.

That is something she would do. I laugh and shake my head, nerves bubbling in my stomach.

"Are you ready?" the tech asks.

I flick my eyes to Noah's. He takes my hand again and nods.

"I already know what it is," the tech goes on. "But your baby is showing off right now." She moves the transducer around on my stomach, pressing down a bit. It's pretty uncomfortable, really, but I don't care. The tech takes a picture of our baby's butt, presses a button, and the screen turns pink.

"It's a girl!"

I stare at the screen in disbelief. I'm smiling and tears leak from the corners of my eyes. "We're having a girl," I whisper.

"Ella." Noah's voice is soft. The tech switches back to live feed, and we watch our daughter move around.

Holy shit. Our *daughter*. I cannot stop smiling, and I'm already thinking about how to decorate the nursery.

The tech takes a few more measurements, prints us

several pictures to take home, and tells us congrats. We see the doctor after that, and she confirms that everything looks perfect. We leave elated.

"I told you it was a girl," Noah says once we're in his Charger. "And you said I shouldn't buy girl shit."

"I never said it wasn't. Are you happy, or did you want a boy?"

"Honestly," he starts and fires up the engine. "I wanted a girl. I feel like if I had a boy, he'd be a little shit like I was."

I laugh. "Let's hope this kid gets my karma."

*

"Is your mom coming?" Colin asks Noah. It's a question that wasn't meant to be overheard. I already know that Noah invited his mom and she canceled at the last minute.

"Nah, she's not into things like this." Noah brushes it off, but I wonder if it bothers him. I had that talk with Colin, and learned that Noah's mother wasn't necessarily a bad mom, just uninvolved. Colin said she was rarely home and seemed to care more about her job as a nurse than anything else.

No wonder Noah got in so much trouble as a youth, and that it carried over into adulthood. Though I can't say that now. We're standing here like proud parents, in the kitchen of my mom and dad's house, waiting for Katie and Wes to get here so we can cut into a pink and blue cake and reveal that we are having a girl.

We almost didn't get the cake. The lady behind the counter at the bakery took a very obvious look at my left hand when I ordered the cake after the ultrasound yesterday. Her eyes went from the non-ring on my finger, to my belly, to Noah, judgement growing with each second. It pissed Noah off and he was ready to leave and order a cake elsewhere.

And throw a fit.

He really doesn't like people upsetting me. I don't understand why strangers have to be such assholes. For all she knew we were getting our rings cleaned, didn't wear them, or followed a religion that didn't see the symbolism of wedding bands.

Stupid baker.

Noah kept his mouth shut for my sake. Not a lot of places can squeeze in a custom cake with just hours of notice. And whatever. It is what it is. No, we're not married and we won't be getting married until after the baby is born; well, if we end up married at all. People are going to judge and I can let it get to me or I can not give a shit. I opt for the latter, even though it's hard. So fucking hard.

"Finally!" my mom says when Katie walks through the door. "I was about ready to have her cut the cake without you!"

"I would never do that," I promise Katie when she comes in the kitchen. She gives me a hug.

"You look cute today."

"Thanks. My sundresses still fit and are pretty comfortable, actually." It's nearing the end of July and is hot as hell. I don't tolerate heat very well, and having a tiny person inside of me just makes it worse. I never knew how much I'd love these dresses. "You do too, of course."

"Thanks. And my guess is a girl. You know I don't

177

wear pink."

Just for fun, everyone dressed in either blue or pink to cast a vote as to what they thought we were having. Katie looks stylish in a white and blue halter dress and blue heels. Perks of owning your own clothing store, right? The majority of the votes are for a boy, which makes me happy that I'll be able to surprise everyone. Dad still insists it's a girl, and he told me Mom is secretly hoping for a granddaughter to play dress up with.

Jenny wore a green shirt and jeans. She said she couldn't make up her mind. We haven't spoken much since our talk in my living room. It just struck me when I saw her today that we really haven't seen each other or spoken since that day. I've been spending more and more time with Noah and less time with my sisters, but when I actually think about it, it feels like she's avoiding me.

And that makes me sad. Sad that it hurts her to see my belly growing and sad that I'm halfway through a pregnancy and she still doesn't have her own little baby growing inside of her. I only know they are still trying because Colin told Noah, who told me.

"Can we eat now?" Colin asks, though we've all been snacking.

"No, no." Mom grabs her camera. "Let's do the cake first!"

"She's been going crazy all day," my dad says. "Your grandmother too."

Nana, as I still call her, smiles guilty. She's my mom's mom and has been supportive since we told her. Well, once the shock wore off, that is. "It's my first great grandchild," she explains. "What else do you expect?"

Noah nudges me. "Let's do it now."

I smile, then feel a bit of embarrassment. I hate being the center of attention no matter the reason. "Okay."

"Ready, baby?" he whispers.

I nod and pick up the knife, having to go extra slow so my mom can snap pictures. I'm smiling again as I slice through the cake, making two careful cuts. Noah gets a plate for me to put the piece of cake on, then holds it up for everyone to see.

The kitchen erupts in a chorus of "it's a girl!" and I'm grinning even more. I look around at my close friends and family, all here to celebrate with me, and catch a glimpse of Jenny's forced smile. She's got her arms tightly wrapped around herself, and it's anything but cold in here. Mom and Dad aren't fans of turning on the air-conditioning until it's ninety degrees.

"Do you have a name picked out?" Mom's finally calm enough to speak. Dad was right; she was hoping for a granddaughter.

"Ella," Noah and I say in unison. His eyes meet mine. "Lauren picked it out before we knew."

"Oh, it's beautiful!" Mom wipes her eyes. "I'm going shopping tomorrow. Mom, come with me? Let's start spoiling this baby!"

My grandmother, who is in incredible shape for seventy-six, excitedly agrees. I take the cake from Noah and sit at the table, eating it while everyone else fills plates with the hamburgers Dad made on the grill. I'll have one too.

Just after my cake.

*

"So," Noah starts, lacing his fingers between mine. We're laying in my bed, both naked after sex. "We should start thinking about living arrangements after the baby is born."

"We should," I reply sleepily. And really, we should. After the gender reveal yesterday, my mom and grandma brought over enough clothes to fill Ella's closet already. I hung everything up, not wanting to divide and keep half here, half at Noah's house. I've brought it up a few times to Noah, and we've both skirted around the subject, knowing it isn't going to be easy to make a decision. "I want us both to live together. All three of us, I mean."

He leans forward and kisses me, then settles down, wrapping me in his arms. One hand settles on my stomach, waiting to feel movements. I swear Ella knows when it's his hand. She stops moving immediately.

"One of us should move in with the other."

"That's a huge step," I blurt and roll over to look into his blue eyes. Stubble covers his face, even though he shaved yesterday. His hair grows faster than anyone I know, and it's not fucking fair. "Too big?"

"I don't think so," he says without missing a beat. "I … I want us to be a family."

"I do too, Noah. I want Ella to grow up with her mom and dad."

"Then we'll have to pick a house and live in it. Together."

Together sounds nice. Together sounds right. And *together* is something we can do. They say you can't change someone, but someone can change for you.

Noah has. Not just for me, but for us.

"If I move in with you, I'd have to sell my house."

"Fuck." Noah takes a breath, not saying what we both are thinking. "Well, my lease is up at the end of the year," he starts and pulls me onto his chest. It takes a bit of creative rearranging to get my growing belly to fit against him, but we make it work. I run my nails up and down his arm, listening to his heart beat. It's steady, then gets faster and faster. "I want to be with you. I want to take care of you and Ella ... and even your dogs. Making you happy makes me happy. I've never felt that before, never realized that one person could impact me in such a way, but you do, and thinking about not having you there when I wake up in the mornings hurts. I want you in my life, Lauren."

"I want you in mine." Tears pool in my eyes. Hormones make me extra emotional right now, and damn, he is good with words.

"We don't need to make a decision now," he says, probably sensing my hesitation.

"I know. One thing we do need to make a decision on is what to put on our registry list for the baby shower."

"When is that?"

"I'm thinking have it around thirty weeks. It's a little early, according to the baby books, but you know me. I'd rather do it a bit earlier and have everything in place. I could go into labor early."

"I hope you don't," he says and puts his hand on my belly. "But I agree with you on being prepared. It won't hu—was that her kicking?"

"Yeah, that's her." With a smile on my face I put my hand over Noah's, feeling Ella's little kicks. I'm still smiling when I close my eyes. Maybe happy endings do exist.

*

"Noah and I talked about living arrangements post baby," I tell my mom and Katie the next weekend over lunch. Noah is out of town again this weekend, shooting another wedding. He says he hates it, but after seeing the invoice laying on his desk, I understand why he agreed to do it. He's making more this weekend in twelve hours than I do in three months.

No wonder he's always offering to buy me stuff.

"Oh." Mom's eyebrows go up "And?"

"He's going to live with us after Ella is born. Well, probably before too, actually. I don't want to deal with moving stuff and a newborn at the same time."

"Do you really want to do this, Lauren?" Mom asks.

"Yes. It'll be a million times easier to live together and raise a baby."

"You don't do something just because it's easy," Mom reminds me.

"I've seen Harry Potter enough to know 'easy' and 'right' aren't the same thing, Mom." I shake my head and look at Katie for support, but she looks just as unsure as our mother. "And he's moving in with me. If it doesn't work for some reason, he'll move back out. But I don't think that's gonna happen."

"Honey," Mom starts, "you made a poor choice the night you and Noah … you know." She waves her hand in the air. "You didn't mean to get pregnant. It was an accident—don't worry, you know that I support you and my grandbaby no matter what. But you don't accidentally move in with someone. You're young. Yes, you will have a child, but that doesn't stop you from living your life."

"What do you mean?" I ask.

"She means don't trap yourself with Noah," Katie says bluntly. "Single moms date people other than their baby daddy."

"Katie!" I exclaim, feeling betrayed. She gives Mom a sideways glance. Great, they've been talking about this without me. "Guys, I'm not selling my soul or anything. Yeah, I didn't mean to get pregnant. Obviously. But it happened and Noah and I decided to give things try and so far it's working."

"You said 'so far,' like you think it's not going to work." Katie pushes her salad around on her plate.

"Really? You're going to pick apart my words?" I set my fork down, abandoning my pasta, and rest my hands on my stomach. "I've been skeptical. Very skeptical. Come on, you know me. Who's better at coming up with the worst possible outcome of any situation than me?"

"She has a point," Katie says and gets a glare from my mother. "And even Colin says Noah's behaved since he found out."

"He has!" That one incident at The Roadhouse doesn't count, right? "I'm not going to deny Noah's bad behavior in the past, but it's in the past."

Mom nods. "Old habits die hard, honey."

"What, you don't think I'm good enough for him? You think he'll leave me for someone else?"

"Not at all," Mom says carefully, seeing the tears in my eyes. "I don't want you to get hurt, that's all. You're still my baby girl. You'll understand when you hold your own little one."

And now I'm close to crying again. Stupid hormones. I tip my head up and blink back the tears. "I know, and thanks for looking out for me. Just believe me when I say I want Noah to move in. Ella is his daughter too, and I really like being with him. There's more to him than I ever would have guessed, and I like all the extra stuff I'm seeing."

"He treats you well?" Mom questions.

"Very well. He makes me laugh, makes me feel pretty, even with this thing." I pat my belly.

"Just be careful," my sister says, eyes meeting mine. "I know how much you want a happily ever after. I don't want you to force it."

Doubt begins to creep over me. Am I forcing anything? "I'm not. Noah and I are taking things slow. We said from the start if being together as a couple didn't work, we wouldn't force it because neither of us want that."

Mom nods. "Consider all your options, Lauren."

I nod, take a deep breath, and reach for my lemonade. I guess I won't bring up Noah wanting Ella to have his last name just yet. "I am, and I will. In the end, I want what's best for Ella."

"You're a smart girl, Lauren. I know you'll do the right thing." Mom pats my hand and smiles. "Now, let's talk about the baby shower."

NOAH

THE KNOCK ON the door is most welcome, giving me a break from my work. I rub my eyes and look away from the computer. I've been editing for hours and still have at least a dozen more photos to go through. Stretching, I get up and make my way to the door, wondering why Lauren didn't use the key I gave her.

Does she not feel comfortable enough to let herself if? If so, isn't that a problem if we're going to be living together in a few months?

"You're not Lauren," I say when I open the door.

"Hardly," Melody replies.

I don't step aside and invite her in. "Can I help you with something?"

She smiles, dark-rimmed eyes narrowing ever so slightly. "I got locked out of my place. Can I wait here until the super brings up a spare key?"

"I'm leaving soon."

She leans forward and her tits almost fall out of her top. I want to look. Is that bad? "I call bullshit."

"I'm not bullshitting you. I'm leaving once my girlfriend gets here."

"You're still dating that chick with the dogs?"

"I am. Her name is Lauren."

Melody arches her eyebrows. "I'm surprised."

"And I'm surprised you still care."

"I don't care. What—or who—you do in your spare time is no concern of mine."

I roll my eyes. Yeah the fuck right. Why else would she be here? She takes a step closer.

"So you're really not going to let me in?"

"There's no point. I won't be here much longer."

She takes in a deep breath, pushing her tits out. The elevator at the end of the hall dings. I smile as soon as I see a few inches of Lauren's face, revealed as the metal doors slide open. Her eyes go from me to Melody, and her face falls.

Melody turns, and actually takes a step back in surprise when she sees Lauren.

"What the fuck?" Her hand flies to her mouth and she stifles a laugh. "You two … no way. No fucking way." She lets out a laugh. "No wonder you keep coming around."

"Bye, Melody," I say sternly. She takes a step back, allowing Lauren past. I shut the door as soon as Lauren is inside.

"What was she doing here?" Lauren asks, sliding her purse off her arm. She's wearing a black dress that's belted above her belly. Her hair is pulled back into a messy bun and she's wearing little makeup.

She's absolutely stunning.

"Nothing," I say and realize the one-word answer is the worst I could give. "She said she got locked out of her apartment and wanted to stay here until someone let her in. I told her no," I offer apologetically.

Lauren's jaw tenses and I wonder if she's thinking about how Melody and I used to fuck. Because I am, and not in a good way. I feel awkward now, having my girlfriend, mother of my child, and love of my life standing here in front of me. It reminds me how much I don't deserve her.

I'd take everything back if it meant being with Lauren sooner.

Her lower lip trembles and she looks down at herself. "I'm hideous and huge." A tear rolls down her face.

"Hey," I say and rush over, taking her in my arms. "You're not. Not at all."

"Yes, I am. Did you see the way she looked at me?" Lauren's voice is tight as she tries not to cry. I bring her to the couch and pull her into my lap.

"You are beautiful as always."

"No, I'm not."

I rub her belly. "You're carrying my child. What you're doing is amazing, and you look amazing. I promise. You know I find you hot as hell still. I can prove it to you." I wiggle my eyebrows. "Want to move this party into the bedroom?"

Lauren smiles. "Kind of. But I want to go shopping too."

"Then we'll shop first. Just know I'm going to ravish you when we get back." I cup her face and kiss her, tasting salty tears on her lips.

"Thanks, Noah." Her arms wrap around me and the words burn on my tongue. I want to tell her I love her—that I've loved her—so fucking much.

But I don't, because I'm scared. Scared she doesn't feel the same, that she'll tell me we're better off as friends, that she doesn't think I'm good enough for her and for Ella.

*

"Where do you put all this stuff?" I ask. "It's so much."

Lauren smiles. She's having fun registering items for the baby shower, and is going a little crazy with that scanner if you ask me. "Maybe we don't use it all at once? Like this play mat thing isn't until she's a little older."

"Right. She's going to sleep most the day for what, like a month?"

She scans another item. "That's what my baby book says, but from what I read online, they spend a lot of time crying too."

I force a smile, deciding to tell her I'm getting terrified to have something so small under my care later. I don't want to ruin her fun right now.

"Lovely." I follow her down the aisle.

"Maybe we'll get lucky and have a newborn that sleeps most of the night."

"Hopefully. It's kind of crazy to think you're in the third trimester already. Crazy, and a little scary." I pick up a pink and purple baby toy, subconsciously smiling down at it. "What about this?"

"Oh, that's cute!"

I flip it so Lauren can scan the barcode. She's twenty-eight weeks along now and getting bigger every week. I've never looked at a pregnant woman's body before, never taken the time to stop and think how incredible the whole thing is. Lauren says she feels like a whale, and I'm not ashamed to admit I'm looking forward to her having her body back, but I find her beautiful and sexy, baby bump and all. She's growing our child, after all. That's kind of a big deal.

I run my eyes over her and get hit with desire, brain flashing to her on top of me last night. I don't know how she doesn't see how beautiful she is. And now registering for baby stuff is taking way too long. She needs to be on me, under me, fuck, just touching me—now.

"What?" she asks, glancing up into my eyes.

"Nothing," I say, shaking my head. Nothing, just getting turned on in the middle of fucking Target. "We're almost done with the list."

"Good. I have to pee."

"You always have to pee."

"Hey, you try having a giant baby inside of you and see how long you can go without peeing."

I grab her around the waist. "Want another giant thing inside of you?"

She laughs and pushes me away. "Kind of. Yeah, I do. I think the answer will always be yes."

"It better be."

She rolls her eyes and laughs. "What's next?"

I look at the paper. "Bath supplies."

We head into the next aisle. "It's a shame your mom had to work and couldn't make it this weekend."

"Yeah, a shame." I don't even try to hide my sarcasm. Mom picked up an extra shift, and I can't help feel she did it on purpose to avoid seeing us—again. She sent me an Amazon gift card via email, which pissed me off even though I prefer it. It's convenient for the both of us, but that's how it is when you're mad at someone. Everything they do, no matter how innocent, pisses you the fuck off. Going to the store for a card and the gift card was too much work for her, which to me translates into how little she cares. How little she's always cared.

Lauren makes a face, one that's easy to read. She wants to ask me why I don't like my mother but doesn't want to offend me. Sometimes she's too fucking nice. I hate that she holds back on account of not wanting to risk ruffling feathers. Though on the other hand, I don't want to talk about it. Not now. Or ever.

"I really want a hot dog," Lauren says. "And a big pretzel with cheese. We need to stop at the cafe on the way out."

"That's doable. I haven't had a big pretzel in years. It sounds good."

"Doesn't it? I'm craving salty stuff bad right now."

"I got something salty for ya." I put my hands on her waist and she playfully shoves me away.

She takes the list from me, checking things off. I have to admit I admire her organizational skills. I've tried being organized before. It just doesn't happen and sometimes I have a hard time understand how anyone can keep their shit together like that.

"You're going to be a good mom," I tell her.

Lauren looks up from the list and smiles. "I hope so. I worry a lot about it. I don't want to let this kid down. It's bad enough I didn't take prenatal vitamins until I was over a month along."

"The doctor said that wasn't going to be an issue," I remind her. "And you seriously need to let that go and not beat yourself up over it. Ella is doing just fine." I put my hand on her belly.

"Thanks. And you're going to be a good dad." Her eyes meet mine and she smiles, honestly believing it.

I smile back, but feel like a fraud. She believes it, but I don't.

CHAPTER NINETEEN

LAUREN

"SHOULD YOU START bringing stuff over?" I ask Noah. It's Tuesday night and I just got off work. I'm exhausted. At thirty weeks pregnant, I don't see how I can get any bigger. And I still have ten weeks left.

"Probably. I hate packing." He makes a face and stands, taking both our empty dinner plates off the table to put in the dishwasher. "If I start now and slowly bring shit over it won't be that bad."

I nod. "What about your furniture? It won't all fit in here."

"Fuck. I hadn't thought about that. Is there room in your basement?"

"There is." With this house being older, the basement is dark and cold, making it feel more like a cellar. Plus, it's creepy. I keep the door closed and rarely go down there. "We can swap some stuff out. Your stuff is a bit nicer." Most of my furniture is a hand-me-down from my sister, parents, or grandma. But hey, it works.

"Whatever you want," he says. "But I am putting in my TV."

"It's going to take up the whole wall!"

"I know." He smiles. "Trust me, you'll learn to appreciate watching your princess movies on it."

"I probably will." I lean back, resting my hands on my belly, and yawn. "These twelves are killing me," I say then regret it. Noah worries too much about me working.

"You should cut back your hours. Or start your leave earlier."

"If I start earlier, then I'll have to come back sooner. Though, that is tempting." My back and feet scream in protest every morning when I get dressed. Noah comes over and helps me up, and we take our conversation into the living room. The dogs follow, squeezing onto the couch with us.

"You get off at four tomorrow, right?"

"I do. Why?"

His full lips pull into a smile. He shaved his beard off last week and it's coming in thick already. He looks good with and without it. "I booked you a prenatal massage."

My eyes light up. "Seriously? Oh my God, thank you!"

"I didn't know they were a thing, or else I would have done it sooner. A client told me about it yesterday. It's an hour massage then a pedicure. It's at four-thirty, so you can go right after work. Then come back here and I'll make dinner. And later you can thank me sexually, of course."

"Of course." Maybe I'll be in the mood after some pampering. Because right now, Ella is pressing down hard on my pelvis, making sex uncomfortable. So much for keeping romance alive the whole nine months.

My phone buzzes with a text message, and I reach to grab it off the coffee table.

"Yay! Rachel can make it to the shower this weekend!"

"Rachel Brown, right?" Noah asks. Should I be impressed he remembers her? She was over at our house just as much as he was when we were kids. I guess it's not that surprising.

"Yes. She wasn't sure if she could get off work Monday. She lives in New York now. I haven't seen her in ages."

"I'm glad she's coming then." He pulls me close and kisses me.

My heart feels so full right now, sitting there with Noah. He's been so thoughtful, so caring and attentive. Thirty weeks ago, my life changed forever. And right now, I'm thinking those changes are for the better.

*

I get home from work Thursday, ready for a nap already. I go inside, change out of my scrubs, let the dogs out, and get the mail. Afraid of getting another bill insurance won't cover, I cringe every time I open my mailbox. Half the time there's nothing in there since I get everything via email now.

Today, there is one large white envelope. My heart drops into my stomach when I see it.

"Holy shit," I mumble and flip the envelope over. With everything else that's gone on, I totally forgot about this. Now my hands are shaking. I start to open the letter but stop and rush inside, grabbing my phone. I call Noah, get his voicemail, and hang up.

I can't wait any longer. I rip open the envelope and unfold the letter, eyes scanning like mad. My hand flies over my mouth and excitement rushes through me. Holy fucking shit.

"I got in!" I scream. I have to read the acceptance

194

letter one more time to believe that I got into vet school. Ella flips around, excited with me. "I got in, little girl!"

Then it hits me: I can't go away to Purdue University in the fall.

I can't leave Ella.

My excitement dies and I sink back onto the couch, unsure of how to feel. I'm incredibly disappointed ... but I shouldn't feel that way, right? I've worked so hard the years to get this far, and now I'm in. I got into vet school. And I can't go.

My phone rings, and I get up to get it, moving on autopilot. "Hello?" I say to Noah.

"Hey, baby. I'm still at the studio. A shoot took longer than I expected. I'll be home soon."

"Good."

"How was your day?"

"Fine. Hurry, because we need to talk."

"Is something wrong?" he asks, a little panicked.

"Yes," I say without thinking. "Well, maybe. I don't know."

"Are you and El—"

"We're fine. Sorry," I sigh. "I didn't mean to freak you out. It just ... I got accepted into vet school."

"Correct me if I'm wrong, but that's fucking awesome, not bad."

"It is awesome. It's everything I ever wanted, only now I can't go."

"Why can't you go?"

"Seriously?"

"Yeah, seriously," he says. "Why can't you go?"

"Because I'll have a baby then!" I snap. I'm upset, but not with Noah. I shouldn't take it out on him.

"Lots of people with kids go to school."

"Not vet school. I can't go. I'll never go. Might as well give up."

"Lauren, calm down. It'll be okay."

He means well, but I'm too emotional. "Stop acting like it's not a big deal. Do you know how hard I've worked for this?" Tears run down my cheeks.

"You have worked incredibly hard. That's why you'll go. We'll figure it out. I promise."

I inhale, feeling guilty again. I run my hand over my face, the conflicting emotions starting to confuse me.

"I'll leave soon and bring home something for dinner. Lay down and rest. It'll be okay."

I take a deep breath. "Thank you, Noah."

"You don't have to thank me. I want to help you. I'll see you soon."

I hang up and debate calling my mom. Though I almost would rather tell her I didn't get in than to make her get excited and disappointed like I am.

"I'm not mad at you," I tell Ella. "Not at all. Things … things are complicated." I rub my belly and lean back on the couch. "We'll figure it out somehow, little girl."

An hour later, Noah comes home with Chinese takeout and a box of cupcakes. I so need this right now. He sets the food down on the coffee table, shoos away the dogs, and sits next to me. His arms wrap around me, pulling me in. I rest my head on his shoulder, inhaling deep, loving the way he smells like cologne and leather from his motorcycle jacket.

"I should be happy. Am I being dramatic?"

"You're allowed to be dramatic right now," he says with a chuckle. "And you're not. It's kind of complicated.

Can you apply to vet school again next year?"

"I can, but there's no promise I'll get in again."

"What about taking just one easy class your first semester."

"It doesn't work that way." I pull away and open the cupcakes, sighing. "Everything I want is happening, just not in the right order. I had a plan, you know."

Noah's blue eyes meet mine. "Life doesn't go according to plan."

"You can say that again." I peel the wrapper off the cupcake. "I honestly didn't think I'd get in. Only like seventy people get into this program, you know."

"Seriously, that's it? You're going then. If that's what you want, we'll find a way."

I bite my lip. Dammit, I'm having second thoughts and already dread leaving Ella. Noah takes notice puts his hand on my thigh.

"Hey, you don't have to make a decision right now."

I bury my head against him. "I know."

"I asked you before, but let me verify. You like your job now, right?"

"I do."

"And part of why you wanted to be a vet was to make a better living."

Is it horrible to admit that's true? "Yes. But that's not the only reason. I've always wanted to be a vet. Always, Noah." I close my eyes, feeling something weird shifting around inside me … and no, it's not Ella. It's my priorities, what I hold dearest to me. "But right now I don't know if I can do it."

"School?"

"Leave Ella. And you."

197

"Who said you'd have to leave us?" He beams down at me. I can't speak. I can only kiss him.

NOAH

IF I EVER had a purpose in life, it's to make Lauren happy. Making her happy makes me happy. I never believed in true love before, mostly because the one person I truly loved was someone I thought I could never have. But now that she's here in my arms—literally most of the time—I know it to be true.

She's still upset from yesterday, when she got her acceptance letter. I'll admit it's a weird situation. Getting into Purdue University's vet program is a huge accomplishment. We should be celebrating right now, and she should be fucking proud of herself.

But she's right: it's going to be damn hard to do that and have a baby. We went over the schedule of classes, and that shit is intense. Though if anyone can do it, it's Lauren. I don't want her to give up on her dream of being a vet.

It was one of the first things she ever said to me.

We will make it work. I look around my office in the back of the studio. I like this place, love the location … but it's not necessary. I *could* move. Easily. If not leaving Ella—and hopefully me—is Lauren's main concern, she doesn't need to worry.

We'll eventually end up back here. She told me her

boss said she'd hire her in a heartbeat to be part of the practice, and I know Lauren wants to be near her family. Yeah, those four years she's in school will be rough, but she can do it. *We* can do it.

She said she doesn't want to think about it too much this weekend. We have the shower, after all.

I turn off my computer and pack up my camera. It's Friday night and Lauren and I are going out to dinner. I plan to spend tomorrow packing up some stuff to move into Lauren's house while she hangs out with her friend Rachel.

Reservations for dinner made, I get up and text Lauren to let her know I'm leaving. She'll be out of work soon too. I lock up the studio, leaving through the back. A man gets out of a black pickup that's parked next to my motorcycle. His eyes fall on me and my first instinct is to ignore him, not wanting to talk to anyone at the moment. I just want to get home to Lauren.

I can still feel his stare after a few paces, so I cast my gaze up. My eyes meet his and a shock of familiarity goes through me. It takes a second, but I recognize him as soon as he says my name.

"What the fuck are you doing here?" I spit out, staring down my father.

He smiles, lines forming around his mouth. I freeze, mind racing with how to react. I've grown up to look like him, and it pisses me off. There is gray peppering his dark hair, and there's a fucking wedding band on his left hand. Of course the bastard got remarried. Probably had a few kids too, completely forgetting about his firstborn.

"I guess I deserve that greeting." He steps closer. "It's been a while, Noah. Wow, you've grown." He looks me up and down, nostalgia on his face.

I recoil. "What the fuck are you doing here?" I repeat.

"Heather—I mean your mother—called. She told me the happy news that I'm going to be a grandfather. Congrats, son."

"I'm not your fucking son," I retort, anger rising with each beat of my heart. My mom fucking called this asshole? After I specifically said I didn't want him to know about Ella.

"Noah," he says, frowning. "I see you haven't changed."

"How the hell would you know?" I want to punch him. *Lauren, think of Lauren.* I clench my fists and keep walking. "Do me a favor and never talk to me again." I take a step toward my car.

My father reaches out, hand landing on my shoulder. "Noah, come on now—"

"I have things to do."

"This isn't just about you anymore."

I stop, whirling around. "It's certainly not about you."

"And what if your daughter wants to know her grandfather?"

I shrug. "I'll tell her he's dead. Because you are dead to me. You died when you left Mom and I for broke. You died when you got arrested for a DUI and I had to spend my eighth birthday at the police station. Get it? You dug your grave. Now leave me alone."

He lets his arm fall. "You're going to regret this one day."

"Yep, go ahead with the threats. Just like old times. Might as well get drunk and hit Mom too."

Without another word, I get onto my bike, rev the

engine, and speed away. I'm seething with anger, nearly shaking I'm so fucking pissed. Just seeing Gerald's face brings it all back: the disappointment, the hurt. Thinking everything was my fault, believing the lies he told me, hearing him say I was a burden and didn't care.

It was so long ago, and yet it feels like that shit just happened. It freaks me out that parents can fuck up their kids' lives years after they move out. What if I do the same?

Wind hits my face and I twist the throttle, pushing the bike over the speed limit. I'm not going to be like my asshole father. But, fuck, what if I am even if I don't mean to be? What if I let Ella down, can't be who she needs me to be? I don't know how to be a parent when my own parents sucked. And look how it's still affecting me.

*

"I checked the registry list and almost everything has been purchased," Lauren gushes at dinner. We're seated outside at a Mexican restaurant, taking advantage of what could possibly be one of the few warm nights in October. "So that means we can set up the nursery completely Monday!" She smiles and pats her belly. "Ella is moving so much right now. I'm getting excited about the birth. Excited and terrified. The doctor asked if I had a birth plan, by the way. I don't, other than 'don't die.' That's still my biggest fear. Well, second biggest. First is something bad happening to Ella."

"Yeah," I mumble, watching beads of condensation roll down my beer. I felt kind of bad ordering alcohol when Lauren can't drink, but fuck, I need it right now. I'm still mad as fuck about seeing my father and I'm trying to let it go.

For now, at least.

Lauren's excitement for the shower is temporarily blocking her anxiety over vet school, and I don't want to do anything to hinder that. So I don't say anything. And even if the whole school thing wasn't an issue, why upset her? Making Lauren happy is a top priority. Telling her about my shitty childhood will only upset her.

She's still talking about the nursery, something about paint maybe? I can't concentrate on her words. I'm not sure who I'm more pissed at right now: my father for all the shit he did in the past, or my mother for using my own daughter as a reason to call that prick up. Because she doesn't care about him being involved in his grandchild's life. She's so desperate to get him back, even after all these years.

It's fucking pathetic if you ask me. The man pushed her around, hitting her more than once, and did a lifetime of emotional damage and she still wants him back. I don't want Ella around her, now that I think about it. Talk about a bad role model, right?

"Noah, are you listening?" Lauren asks.

"Uh, yeah. What?"

Lauren lets out a breath. "Never mind." She finishes her lemonade, then gets up to use the bathroom. I look around the patio, eyes falling on a couple with a baby and a toddler. The mom nurses the infant while she eats, and the toddler sits on his father's lap, stealing food off his plate.

Could that be us someday? Enjoying dinner with the kids, handling it like it's no big deal? I swallow and drain the rest of my beer, then flag down the waiter to order another. I feel like a fraud, thinking I can be a good dad. I didn't have a good dad. It's like saying you're a doctor without going to medical school, right? I'm not qualified to do this.

Our food arrives soon after Lauren gets back to the table. She's talkative, telling me about birth stories and what to expect during labor. I smile and nod along, trying to share in her excitement.

She is so beautiful. So kind, so strong. She's going to be the perfect mother, and she will be the perfect wife … a wife I don't deserve. Because I can't give back what she gives to me. I'm feeling all sorts of shitty about myself and my ability to make her happy.

"You're quiet," she observes. "Everything okay?"

"Yeah, tired." I force a smile and take her hand. The moment her skin touches mine, I relax. I can do this, right? Her green eyes meet mine and I give her hand a squeeze. Three words burn on my tongue, yet I don't say them. Not now. Lauren likes fairytales and happily ever after. This isn't the right setting to tell her I love her.

Maybe after the shower when the nursery is set up? Yeah, that seems about right. I see it now, standing behind her, arms wrapped around Lauren with hands resting on top of her belly. We'll have just set everything up picture perfect the way she wants it. Then I'll tell her. And then we'll have sex of course.

I keep that vision in my head for the rest of dinner. It helps keep me from getting pissed, and it helps me from feeling like I'm going to completely fail at this parenting thing.

"Are you sure you're okay?" she asks when we sitting on the couch back at her place. "You don't seem like yourself."

"I'm fine," I snap without meaning to. Fuck. I put my arm around her, and she doesn't immediately melt into me like usual. "I'm just feeling a little overwhelmed." It's not exactly a lie. "But it's okay. And I'm glad you're excited."

"Yeah, me too." She doesn't sound convinced. "Want to watch a movie?"

"Sure."

"Do you care which one?"

"No."

Lauren sighs and flips through Netflix, finding an older Cinderella-ish movie. Halfway through, she's dozing off and says she's going to lay down in bed. I mean to join her shortly, but end up staying up. If I went and laid down, I'd be bombarded with self-destructive thoughts, which will only further cement how fucking scary it is that a parent can fuck up their kid's life.

I don't want to fuck up Ella's. Suddenly I'm terrified of messing her up for life.

At three AM, Lauren comes out. "Noah? Are you coming to bed?"

I look up from the Adam Sandler comedy I'm watching. "Yeah. Once this is over."

"Come to bed now? I don't sleep as well without you next to me and I'm tired."

"If you're tired, go to bed."

She stands in the hall for a minute before turning and padding back into the bedroom. Immediately, I feel bad. Taking my frustrations out on her is taking a page from my own father's book.

Am I damned to be like him?

"No," I say to Vader, who is sleeping on the floor in

front of me. I get up and slip under the covers, spooning myself around Lauren.

"I like when you hold me like this," she mumbles, already falling back asleep. I smile and kiss the back of her neck. I'm holding her, but really, she's holding me.

LAUREN

"RACHEL AND I are going to a movie. You don't mind, do you?" I ask Noah over the phone.

"Not at all. Go and have fun."

"Thanks. Can you let the dogs out too?"

"Already did."

"Thanks again, Noah. Are you and Colin still hanging out?"

"No, he had to cancel. Something about Jenny wanting to renovate their living room."

"Ohhhh, right. They're tearing out the carpet for hardwood."

"Yeah, that's it."

Is it weird I feel bad about going out when Noah is at home with the dogs? "Go to the bar or something. See your other friends."

"You're telling me to go to the bar?"

"Yeah. I trust you. Just be home when I'm home because I need a back rub."

"By back rub, you mean sex, right?"

I laugh. "Possibly." But not really. My pelvis is all kinds of sore and swollen tonight. The joys of pregnancy, right? "I miss you."

"I miss you too, baby. Have fun."

"You too."

I hang up and put my phone in my purse. Rachel and I went to lunch, then shopping, and now are going to see a Nicolas Sparks movie that I know Noah wouldn't enjoy. We arrive early, get popcorn, and prime seats in the back.

"You are seriously the cutest preggo ever," Rachel tells me when I rest the bucket of popcorn on my belly.

"I don't believe you but thanks."

"Really, I mean it!" she laughs. We've been friends since eighth grade, and though we don't get to see each other very often anymore, things are the same between us. I'm as comfortable around her now as I was then.

"What's your man doing tonight?"

"Hanging around the house. Roles have been reversed tonight," I laugh. "I'm usually the one at home on weekends, though he's been at home with me pretty much since we found out."

"It's still weird to see him like this. We both had huge crushes on him, remember?"

"Didn't most girls have crushes on him in high school?"

"Very true. I'm glad it's working out like it is though."

"Me too. Because this went from a clusterfuck to pretty much working out. Even with the whole vet school mess." I sigh. It's been eating me alive since I got that letter, but Noah is trying so damn hard to make me feel okay about it, I decided to drop it.

"Don't take offense," she starts and pushes her short blonde hair back behind her ear. "But I know you remember the same Noah I do. I'm glad he was able to go cold turkey on the drinking and partying."

I nod. "Honestly, I didn't have faith in him." I shake

my head. "I have a confession, actually. I haven't told anyone either. When he asked me out on our first date, I agreed because I thought it would be a disaster."

Rachel hikes an eyebrow. "You have the weirdest sense of logic. Maybe you got used to all those horrible first dates people set you up on or something."

"I mean I expected it to be a disaster and for that disaster to prove to me he wasn't fit to be a dad so I could cross off us ending up together. I feel bad now, since he's been the total opposite."

Rachel nods. "Makes sense. And you should have just asked me. Of course it would have worked out. Don't you know my best friend is awesome? Noah would be a fool to *not* be with you. You're fucking hot, even when pregnant."

I smile and shake my head. "We need to hang out more often."

*

I pull my knees up and roll over, trying to get comfortable. Three pillows are in use around me, holding up my stomach, under my back, and under my head. I reach over and grab Noah's. He's not using it anyway. It's one-thirty and he's not home yet, nor is he answering his phone.

I'm not worried. Not yet at least. I told him to go to the bar. I told him to have fun with his friends. And that's what he's doing.

I also told him I trusted him.

And I do.

But each minute that ticks by and he's not calling me, saying he's coming back, makes me question that trust. I don't think he'd cheat on me. Even before, Noah wasn't that kind of person. It was one of the reasons he never settled down, he told me. I don't know much about his parents' divorce, but I do know several affairs took place before they split.

I doze off, waking at three. I grab my phone, certain I'll see a missed call or text from Noah. My background image of Vader looks back at me. What the hell, Noah? Where are you? I call him, get his voicemail, then call right back. Voicemail again.

Unease grows and now I'm thinking he's dead on the side of the road. Stupid, dangerous motorcycle.

I flop back down, getting a little pissed. I was up late last night after dinner, and now I'm up late again and need to get up early tomorrow for the shower. And so does Noah, because he said he wanted to go with me.

Five whole minutes go by before I call him again. If he's not dead already, he's going to be when he gets home. Voicemail again. I turn on the TV, unable to sleep. Exhaustion hits me around three-thirty, yet I can't turn my brain off to sleep. I call Noah again, and he answers, but all I hear is background noise. Loud music, muffled voices.

"Noah?" No reply. "Noah!"

I'm fairly positive I hear his voice before the line goes dead. At least he's alive, right? Well, alive for now, because I'm pretty sure I'm going to fucking kill him in his sleep tonight. If he ever comes home.

I lay down, trying to take solace in the fact he's alive and still at the bar, but it doesn't work. I'm mad he made me worry, mad he didn't come home to spend time with me, and mad I'm going to be tired in the morning. I've been constantly tired since I got knocked up, and this isn't helping.

I close my eyes and the phone rings. It's Noah.

"Hello?"

"Hi, Lauren, it's Joey. Again. Your man is drunk as a skunk. Again."

I sigh. "I'll be there to get him."

Joey gives a grunt in reply and hangs up. I toss my head back against the pillow, not wanting to get out of bed. I throw on a T-shirt and yoga pants, and step into flip-flops. I get super tired as I drive to the bar, which only enhances my anger.

Pregnant lady rage is a real thing.

I park in front of the bar and call Noah but get no answer. I cut the engine and wait. There are still quite a few cars here. What the hell do people do at bars for that long? Don't they have lives to get back to? And how much money is wasted buying drink after drink for hours on end?

I should have opened a biker bar and not had to worry about school and student loans.

Five minutes and eight calls later, Noah still isn't out. Angrily muttering to myself, I get out of the car and walk into the bar. I can smell the cigarette smoke already and take one last deep breath before pulling the door open and stepping inside.

Noah is sitting on a barstool, eyes fluttering, talking to some guy who looks just as drunk. He blinks when he sees me then gets up, stumbling. He's fucking wasted.

I grab his hand and pull him outside.

"Hey, baby," he slurs. "I missed you."

"Yeah, yeah. Get in the damn car."

"Want me to take you out back and rock your world?"

I shake my head. "I'll pass."

"Oh, come on."

"Car. Now."

He makes a face and trips over his own feet. *This* is the Noah Wilson I remember from our youth. It takes him more than one attempt to buckle himself in. Tired and cranky, I don't talk on the way home. Noah wobbles his way inside and falls onto the couch.

"Get up and shower. You smell like an ashtray."

He grumbles in response and doesn't move. I cross my arms. "Noah, get up!" I tug on his arm. "This is pointless."

He groans. "I don't feel good."

"Of course you don't."

"I think I'm gonna puke."

Oh god. That's another thing I do not want to deal with. I go to him and help him up, practically dragging him to the bathroom just in time for him to heave into the toilet. He slumps against it, retching. I'm fucking pissed, but I can't leave him like that, not when he could choke.

It takes great effort, but I get him stripped from his stinky clothes, and drape a blanket around his shoulders. He throws up once more then lays on the bathroom floor. I get into bed but can't sleep out of worry I'll wake up and find Noah dead of alcohol poisoning or something.

He's passed the fuck out when I check on him. Finally feeling he's okay, I get back into bed for a few hours of sleep.

*

"Where is Noah?" Mom asks the next day. People are

just starting to arrive for the baby shower that she's hosting at her house. *Our* baby shower. That Noah isn't at because I couldn't get him to wake up this morning. He swatted his hand in the air and mumbled something incoherent. I gave up and left in tears, fixing my eye makeup in the car.

"He's not feeling well," I say, feeling like it's a lie. Noah isn't feeling well, but it's because he for some reason got wasted last night. "He said it feels like the flu so he's staying away and will be here later if he feels better. He's napping now." Dammit. I'm a horrible liar. I tend to overcomplicate things.

"Do you think you're coming down with it? You look a little ragged today. Ragged, but beautiful." Mom puts her hand on my stomach. "The flu is no fun when you're pregnant. I got it twice when I was pregnant with Katie."

"I think I'll be all right." I only look ragged because I'm tired. I text Noah to see how he's doing and to tell him to get his butt over here. His mom will be here soon and I don't want to lie to her, because she'll probably know it's a lie. Noah is her son, after all. She might not have been the best mother, but she knows him.

The shower starts, and I'm temporarily distracted. Then it's time to open gifts, and I'm missing him. I don't like sitting in front of people, opening presents. It's awkward. What if I don't like what someone got and they can see it on my face?

I send him another text and actually get a reply. He's waking up and will be on his way. Thank goodness. I just need to stall for about fifteen minutes and I won't have to open presents alone. How can I buy time? I can spend at least five in the bathroom, maybe? I don't want people to think I'm pooping. That's just as awkward as the gifts.

"Are you okay?" Rachel asks me when I sneak away from the living room into the laundry room. "What are you doing in here?"

"Uh, taking a minute." It's the truth. I plan to take at least ten of these minutes. "Just feeling overwhelmed with everything." Another truth, but it feels so wrong to blame my unease on Ella.

"It's a lot to take in, isn't it? Seeing all the baby stuff makes it that much more real, I bet."

"Yes, that's it. I just need like five minutes to chill."

"Take the time you need. I'll tell Katie and she'll distract the crowd."

I smile at my best friend. "Thank you." She gives me a hug and leaves to find my sister, who's able to stall for ten minutes. I text Noah again, and he doesn't reply. Maybe because he's on his way? I can only hope.

Another ten minutes go by and I can't get out of presents any longer. I sit on the couch and open them one by one, holding everything up for my guests to see. It takes forever to open everything. And Noah still isn't here.

The party dies down, until only Rachel and my sisters are left to help clean up. Jenny hasn't said one word to me but I'm just too tired to worry about it right now.

"Sit down," Mom tells me when I help toss paper plates. "Put your feet up. You look tired, sweetie."

"Thanks, Mom." I go into the living room and lay on the couch, feeling like I'm to the point of exhaustion where I just want to cry myself to sleep.

*

Once the house is clean, Mom and Dad help load stuff into my Jeep. Ella is sitting low in my ute and I'm waddling as I walk, carrying bags of clothes to the door for Dad to grab. The last parcel is in my Jeep when Colin pulls in the driveway, here to pick up Jenny and eat whatever is left over. Noah is in the passenger seat. Oh, right. His bike is at the bar and his Charger is still parked at his apartment. I wonder what he told Colin when he picked him up.

I stand in the threshold of the door, waiting for Noah to get in the house.

"Your mother already left, and you missed the baby shower." I say each word slow and quiet as soon as Noah is in earshot.

"I know. I'm sorry," he says and tries to hug me. I might be acting childish, but I turn and walk away.

"Oh, Noah!" Mom says. "Glad you're feeling better. Lauren said you thought you had the flu."

"Yeah … the flu," he mumbles and comes inside. "Do you need help with anything?"

"No," I snap. "We got it all without you."

Katie narrows her eyes, watching and noticing something is off. Dammit, she's too observant. I make myself appear relaxed, and take Noah's hand. Yes, I'm pissed at him. So incredibly pissed. But I don't want the others to know. Not yet at least.

We stay and talk about babies and parenting with my family for a bit, then leave when Rachel does.

"You told everyone I had the flu?" Noah questions, getting into the driver's side of the Jeep.

"What else was I supposed to say? The truth? You were shit-faced drunk, puking in the bathroom all night."

"I'm sorry," he says slowly. "And thanks for not

215

telling them."

"Oh, you're welcome."

Noah lowers his head, sighing, and pulls onto the street. A few minutes pass before he speaks. "I only got drunk because I was stressing about you and Ella."

"Like that's supposed to make me feel better? I'm exhausted, Noah. You have no idea how bad my back hurts every day. I cannot do this. I can't work and deal with pregnancy symptoms, try to have a life, and take care of you. There's no way I can go back to school with two people to take care of. I was up worrying you were going to choke to death on your own vomit. You promised me this wouldn't happen again, and here we are—again. Fool me once, shame on you, fool me twice…" I look away, tears in my eyes. Why can't he see this is the last thing I need? "You missed our baby shower. Don't you care? If not about being there for me, then for Ella?"

I put my hand over my stomach, feeling our baby kick up a storm. I don't think she likes hearing her parents arguing, even if she has no idea what is going on.

I hate it.

I hate feeling like we're not enough. I hate being afraid to raise my daughter on my own. I close my eyes, pushing out tears that roll down my cheeks. It'll be better in the end. Yeah, it's going to suck and be hard as hell, but I'd rather be a single mom for as long as it takes than be in a relationship that's full of disappointment and hurt. Ella deserves better than that. She deserves to see her mom happy, to see what a healthy relationship looks like.

Noah parks in front of my house. We unload the gifts in silence, putting everything in the living room.

"I can help organize the nursery," Noah offers.

"No," I say shortly. "I just want to lay down. Please go."

"Lauren," he starts.

"Stop," I say, holding up my hand. I can't hear what he has to say, because I might cave. My heart is threatening to overrule my head right now, and I can't have that. My worst fears about Noah have surfaced, and this proves how much he isn't ready to be a father. "Please go, Noah."

Noah looks at me, brow furrowed with hurt. His jaw tenses. "We don't have to—"

"No!" I turn away, tears streaming down my face. "Go. I'll call you when I'm in labor. Just leave."

I can feel his eyes on me, waiting for me to say something. I want to. I want to tell him it's okay and he can have a second chance. I want him to hold me, kiss me, tell me he's sorry and it won't happen again.

But he already said that. And here we are. Again.

He takes a breath and turns to leave. "Bye, Vader," he says softly and pats the German Shepherd on the head. My heart breaks as I look at Noah, knowing that there is no way this is going to work.

CHAPTER TWENTY TWO

NOAH

I'M GOING TO make things work. I can't lose Lauren. The thought of not having her next to me in the morning takes my breath away and replaces my heart with a cold, empty ball of ice. Life without Lauren isn't living. It's surviving, going day by day because I have to, not because I want to.

And life without Lauren means life without my daughter. Not on a daily basis, that is. I want us, all three of us, to be together for the rest of our lives, happy and together. My heart broke when she told me to leave, shattering into a million pieces when I walked out the door. I don't want to think I'll never walk in again.

But I don't think I will.

Not as I did before.

She's mad now. Tired, hormonal. Lauren is level-headed. Lauren is kind. Will she forgive me?

If I tell her the truth, she'll see everything in a different light. But open up about my asshole father ... I've never said anything to anyone before. Not even Colin knows about the shit my dad put me through.

Oh, fuck. Colin.

I didn't just lose the love of my life. I lost my best friend. Because Colin won't forgive me for hurting his sister, and ultimately his niece. My mind flashes to the future, to holidays and birthdays. Will we have to do everything separately like a divorced couple?

Stop. Lauren could still forgive me. But why should she? I'll probably fuck up again. I don't know how to be a dad. Maybe Ella is better off without me too. It hurts, thinking I won't be in her life, but if it's for the best, then that's what I want.

*

It's been three days since I last saw Lauren, and I'm terrified that might have been the last. I know I'll see her again, as in literally see her, but that's not the same. I stay at the studio late that Wednesday night, later than I need to. Going home to my apartment by myself isn't something I want to do. I stayed late at the studio Monday and Tuesday too, trying to keep busy.

I called Lauren Monday, thinking she'd cool off and we'd make up after a day. But she didn't answer. I texted her that night and didn't get a reply. Tuesday came and passed with nothing, and today I've stared at my phone more than I looked at the photos I'm supposed to be editing. I'm broken without her, and I don't know how to make things right.

I die a little more each day that passes and I haven't heard from her.

Lauren has no obligation to be with me, to keep me informed. But she'd tell me if something was wrong with her or with Ella. Maybe? My fist comes down hard on the desk. Fuck. I don't know.

And Ella? She's better off without me, because I'll

probably fuck up being a dad too. My heart hurts and I want to go to The Roadhouse tonight and drown my sorrows in a bottle of whiskey.

I won't, because that's exactly what started this mess. My head drops and I'm suddenly so ashamed, so incredibly pissed at myself.

I've become my father.

The asshole who ran to the bar whenever shit hit the fan. Who spent more time on a barstool than at the dinner table with his family. He didn't know how to be a father because he never tried. He never put effort into our relationship, didn't give a shit about me.

I was so fucking terrified of becoming him, I pushed Lauren away. And I don't blame her. Really, I'm glad she did. Because what I did was wrong. What I did will never happen again. I will not be my father. I will not let Lauren down. I will not let Ella grow up without her daddy.

I sit up and turn off my computer, chair scooting loudly as I stand. I've been in love with Lauren since the day we met, and there is no moving on from there. She's been in my heart for years, and I don't see her leaving anytime soon. Or ever. How can you move on when you can't let go?

I will do whatever it takes to win her back.

*

I sit back on the couch only to get up again, too pissed and too restless to stay in one place. I'm mad at myself. I fucked things up. I lost the love of my life, and consequently lost being in my daughter's life the way I want to. I grab my leather jacket and the keys to my bike and storm out the door.

I peel out of the parking lot, feeling the anger melt off me as the wind and rain hits my face. The rain is coming down in sheets, but I ignore it. It's almost like I deserve it for messing everything up.

On autopilot, I head toward The Roadhouse. Fuck. I can't go back to having that be my escape. I'm not going to be the dad that runs to the bar the minute shit hits the fan. I'm not going to be like my father.

I twist the throttle, going a good thirty over the speed limit. Lightning flashes above me and I'm getting pissed all over again. I fucking blew it, and I've been so focused on how awful I feel, I didn't even think about Lauren and how hard this must be for her too. I grit my teeth, not knowing how else to calm the fuck down. It hits me as I speed through a red light.

Lauren.

She's all I need. I miss her, and right now I need her. I've never told anyone about my asshole father, never let on how much it hurt me when he walked out. That I'm terrified I'll be a shitty dad like he was because it's in my blood. Because I don't know what a father is supposed to do.

The more I think about it, the more enraged I become. Not just at the man who was supposed to be a dad, but at my mother. She shut me out when he left us. Buried herself in work. Left me to raise myself. I convinced the world—and myself most of the time—that it didn't bother me, that the nights at home alone, heating up a shitty dinner in the microwave, and eating by myself at the empty kitchen table were fine.

My mind flashes to Lauren, exhausted after work,

sitting next to a highchair, feeding Ella. They're alone.

I'm not leaving them.

I'm not abandoning my daughter.

I'm never going to hurt Lauren again.

The rain comes down harder, making it difficult to see. But I don't stop. I let out a breath, thinking of Lauren.

Her smile.

Her lips.

The way she sees the good in everything.

Her smooth legs, wrapping around me.

How good it feels when she's holding me.

Her.

I let off the throttle, and the bike loses speed. My mind is on Lauren as I coast down, and I don't notice it until it's too late. Thank the fucking Lord I'm not going fast anymore. My tires slip on loose gravel. Time stops.

Everything happens in slow motion, yet passes too quickly for me to react.

I'm falling, body sideways just inches from the road. I hit the road. I'm skidding along, skin tearing, clothing ripping. I can't stop. Can't move. Can't do anything but wait until it's over and think of her.

Her smile. Her lips. Her kiss.

My vision starts to go black and pain takes over, deep inside my head. And I can't help but think I will never feel those things again.

CHAPTER TWENTY THREE

LAUREN

"YOU LOOK EXHAUSTED," Julia says as we go into work Monday morning. "Did the shower yesterday wipe you out?"

I force a smile. "Something like that." Really, I was up all night crying. My heart is broken. It's only been about twelve hours since I last saw Noah's gorgeous face, and I miss him so much. So, so fucking much. Hell, I missed him this much only seconds after he walked out the door. It's not the length of time passing between us, it's knowing that this is how it's going to be.

Me. A single mom. A working mom. Trying to figure it all out on my own. I'm not the first to do it, and I certainly won't be the last. But that doesn't make me feel any better. And right now I'm not sure I can do it. I'm not sure I can provide everything for Ella.

And really, that's what matters.

My broken heart can heal. I can learn to sleep alone again. But Ella … I can't even think of her wanting, of her needing something I can't get her without crying.

I start the day, blaming the exhaustion on the pregnancy. The lie is bought with no question. The clock moves so slowly sometimes I swear it's going backwards.

But I keep pushing, because that's all I can do. The current is against me, but I won't drown.

I can't drown. I won't drown. Because I have Ella.

"Lauren," Dr. Banfield calls when I walk past her office after going to the bathroom for the millionth time that day. "Any news from Purdue? I know letters are going out around this time."

The words are like a slap to the face and I can't help the tears that spring to my eyes.

"Oh, I'm so sorry." Dr. Banfield gets up from her desk. She's an older woman with her eyes set on retirement. All her employees love her. "I honestly assumed you'd get in. You're so smart and such a hard worker."

"I did get in," I squeak out.

Dr. Banfield raises an eyebrow. "So are those tears of joy?"

My head falls and emotions take over, turning me into The Incredibly Pregnant Hulk. "I got in but can't go because I got drunk and slept with my brother's best friend and got pregnant and now he's gone and I'll be alone forever." I have no control over myself at that point. I break down in tears.

Dr. Banfield is a wise, older woman, but she's not emotional by any means. Reserved at all times, she awkwardly hugs me then calls Julia in into the office.

"Honey, what's wrong?" Julia asks, wrapping me in an embrace. I hiccup and sniff back my tears.

"I got into vet school and can't go because of Ella," I say through tears.

"Oh, honey." Julia gives me another hug, then the three of us sit around Dr. Banfield's desk. Julia gives me a tissue.

"I went to school during a completely different time," Dr. Banfield starts, trying to console me. "But there were parents in there with me. It's possible."

"Thanks," I say and wipe my eyes. *Parents* are different. Parents are plural.

"What about Noah? Can't he help?" Julia asks and suddenly I'm embarrassed. No, Noah can't help because he's not ready to be a dad, nor does he want to be. He made it quite clear when he missed our baby shower.

"Maybe," I mumble. "Purdue is hours away. I just don't see how it'll work."

"There's always next year," Julia offers. "You got in once, you could get in again."

I nod. "I could."

"And don't rule out other schools," Dr. Banfield adds. "You know I'm a fan of MSU." She points to her degree on the wall. "And that's a lot closer."

I nod again. Talking it out makes things seem so easy. My heart needs to believe it is that easy, because it can't take any more pain. It's beating for two right now. I have to protect it.

But it's not that easy. Ella will be older, but I'll still have to find a way to pay for daycare and then find someone to help me in the evenings so I could study and do homework. Paying for daycare on my salary right now is damn near impossible; there is no way I could pay for daycare *and* school. Oh, and still squeeze in time to work. Because I'll have to pay for shit somehow.

I smile, tell my boss and my friend thank you regardless. Nobody likes a wallower, so I'll wallow in sorrow at home by myself. Because there really is no way for me to go to vet school.

I've been told that the best laid plans sometimes fail, but I think it goes farther than that. The more you plan, the more you try to get things just right, the more off course you go. And then the clear path you were counting on disappears beneath your feet and suddenly you're alone in the forest, unable to see a way out.

*

I get home from work Tuesday exhausted, sore, and sad. The temperature has dropped, and gray clouds have moved across the October sky. Not feeling like making dinner, I get a bowl of ice cream, a big glass of lemonade, and plop on the couch, crying as I eat.

I miss Noah. I want him back. I want Ella to grow up with her father, and I want her father to be *good*. You can't have your cake and eat it too, right?

Life doesn't work that way.

Instead of watching one of my cherished Disney movies, I search Netflix for something more violent. Because right now I'm feeling like the fairytale endings are even more unrealistic than wild animals cleaning the house.

My phone rings, and my heart jumps. Noah has called more than once, and I've watched his calls go to voicemail each time. I'm not strong enough to talk to him, not yet. If I hear his voice I'll cave. And I can't. I have to be strong for Ella.

"Hello," I say to my mother, more disappointed than relieved it wasn't Noah calling.

"Hey, honey. I didn't hear from you yesterday. How

are you feeling?"

I open my mouth, wanting to tell my mom everything. She'll come over and I'll have a good cry session, and when she's leaves I'll feel better, even if it's just for the night. "I'm fine," I lie before I have time to think about it. Maybe I'm not ready to face the fact that Noah really isn't coming back into my life the way I want him to. Saying it out loud makes it more real. "Just tired from work."

"Have you thought about cutting down on your hours yet?"

"Uh…" Yeah. I had. And was going to, back when I thought I could count on Noah for financial support. I'm sure glad I dodged that bullet, even though it feels like it hit me. Right in the heart. "Yeah, I will soon. Everyone at work babies me." I consider telling her about vet school too, but chose not to solely because I'm too tired to bring up those emotions. Again.

I chat with my mom for a few more minutes, hating lying to her the whole time. I end up falling asleep on the couch and wake up stiff. A hot shower helps loosen my muscles, then I'm off to work again. We're busy with surgeries and two walk-in emergencies Wednesday, and the day actually goes by pretty fast, thankfully. I'm limited in what I can do now, which often leads to boredom, and boredom leads to my mind wondering.

I take the dogs to the dog park after work, leaving them there while I go grocery shopping. I keep myself busy and distracted enough that I don't feel like I'm dying from a broken heart.

I go to bed early, hoping I can sleep away some of the pain, but I'm woken by my phone ringing at eleven PM.

It's Colin.

What the fuck? He rarely calls, let alone this late. My hand shakes when I pick up the phone, scared something happened to my family.

"Hello?"

"Hey, Lauren. Are you at home?"

"Yes, what's wrong?"

"Nothing," he says and hesitates.

"Then why did you call and wake me up."

He inhales but doesn't speak.

"Colin!" I exclaim. If nothing is wrong, then I'm pissed for being woken up. "Are you drunk dialing me or something?"

"I wish. Noah got in an accident."

It feels like I've been dunked in ice water. "Is he okay?"

"Yeah. He's pretty banged up and needed a few stitches, but he'll be fine. I just took him home. He said you guys got in a fight and he didn't think you'd come get him, but I know you. You could hate the guy and you'd still go, and you'd probably spend the night just to make sure he's okay. That's all he would say. What the hell did he do?"

Tears run down my cheeks. I would go get him. I would stay and make sure he wasn't in pain, make sure he knew how to clean and care for whatever injuries he had.

"He's just not ready to be a dad." I take in a shaky breath. "Are you still with him?"

"Yeah. I'm about ready to leave. He got a shot of morphine and is passed out."

"Stay there. I'm coming over." I don't have to think about it. Noah is hurt. I'm going to him.

"Okay. Drive safe."

"I always do."

I hang up, and gather up everything I need in a mad run. I forget dog food, and run my pregnant ass back into the house, spilling kibble all over the floor in my haste. Then I'm speeding through the dark to get to Noah.

The drive takes forever. I don't even turn on the radio. Finally I pull into the parking lot, grab my bag and the dogs, and rush inside, texting Colin that I'm here and to buzz me in.

"You brought the dogs?" my brother asks as soon as we bustle through the door.

"I'm leaving for work at seven. I kinda had to. Plus Noah likes them." And now my heart is breaking all over again. Tears fill my eyes and I don't want to cry in front of Colin. He'll hate Noah for hurting me. Colin crouches down to greet the dogs while I run (okay...waddle at this point) through the apartment and into Noah's room.

It's dark, and the first thing I see is rumpled sheets. I'm hit with the memory of the first time we made love. I have to bit my lip to keep from breaking down.

"Noah?" I whisper, voice tight. "Are you awake?"

I dig my phone out of my coat pocket and use it as a flashlight. He's lying on his back, and shadows merge with bruises on his face. His shirt is off, and a blanket is pulled up to his chest. His left arm is bent, resting on his stomach. It's wrapped in gauze.

As a vet tech, I see a lot of nasty things. Infected wounds, horrible injuries...it doesn't faze me. But seeing Noah like this makes my stomach hurt. Tears run down my cheeks. I wipe them away and gently kneel on the bed, bending over to kiss Noah. The second my lips touch his, my heart breaks into a million pieces.

This is out last kiss.

Noah takes a deep breath and his eyes flutter open for a split second. "Lauren," he mumbles.

"I'm here," I say through my tears. I lace my fingers through his. "I'm here, Noah. It's okay."

"Lauren," he says again. "I'm sorry."

No matter how hard I try, I can't stop from crying. I cover my mouth with my hand, hoping to muffle the sounds of sobbing enough from Colin. A few minutes pass and I'm able to get myself under control. I mop my face with the bottom of my pajama shirt, and then go back into the living room with Colin and the dogs.

"Do you want me to stay?" Colin asks. I didn't do a very good job covering up the fact I was crying, apparently.

"No, it's okay. Jenny probably wants you home."

"She's not home; she got stuck doing a double."

"Oh, okay. You don't need to stay. I'm gonna sit in there with him and make sure he's okay, but I'll probably fall asleep soon anyway."

Colin nods. "Are you two really done?"

"I don't know." My voice breaks. "Probably."

"If that's what you want," Colin says and I know he's confused since neither Noah or I offered an explanation. I don't want to ruin Colin's friendship.

"It's not what I want, it's what I need. I don't want to think I can count on him when really I can't."

"I won't tell you what to do," Colin starts. "But I will say I've never seen Noah like that."

"Injured?"

"No, I've seen that plenty of times. I mean sad."

I close my eyes and fat tears roll out.

"I don't know what happened," Colin goes on. "But I do know he cares."

That's the best and worst thing to hear right now. It's making my resolve waver.

"Thanks for picking him up, Colin."

"Yeah … let me know what's going on, okay? And if I have to throw a few punches, I'll at least wait until Noah's stitches are healed."

"Thanks." I step forward and give my brother a hug. I lock the door behind him when he leaves and turn around, leaning on it. I suck in a breath, jaw trembling.

I hate this. My head hurts, though not as badly as my heart, and I know I need to get some sleep since I have to be up early for work in the morning. Sleep won't come easy, and I don't know where to sleep. Next to Noah? He's injured…but we broke up. Being here is hard enough. Being in bed next to him…I'm not strong enough.

Ella has to come first.

If I lay down next to him, wake up to his arms around me, I might go back on everything. I can't. Instead, I set food and water up for the dogs, check on Noah, then take a pillow from his bed and move onto the couch. Physically, I'm exhausted. Mentally, my brain won't shut the fuck up. And Ella is right there with it, kicking and pushing on my bladder, making me get up to pee every few minutes.

Finally, I fall asleep, only to be woken up by someone gently poking my cheek. I open my eyes, to see Noah standing next to the couch.

"Am I dead?" he asks.

"What?" I push up. "No, you're not dead. What's wrong?"

He blinks, and I notice his eyes are super dilated. He's still heavy under the influence of pain medication. "Are you sure I'm not dead? I woke up with the dogs. And now you're here."

"Why would that make you think you're dead?"

"Because this is what I want. You, with me."

Damn you, drugged up Noah. Nine little words, like nine little bullets. I burst into tears, thank you hormones.

"Well, if I was dead I wouldn't make you cry," Noah says.

"It's okay," I hiccup. "Are you hurting?"

"I've been hurting since you said goodbye."

I can't handle that right now. Or ever. "Come here," I say and heft myself off the couch. "Let me see."

"Okay," he says softly and follows me into the kitchen. I have him sit on a barstool so I can inspect his wounds. I don't take care of people, but stitches are stitches. He has five stitches on his left arm. The skin around it is in bad shape from road rash, and I can see bruises all over the left side of his body.

Colin summed it up perfectly: Noah is beat to hell but will be okay. I believed my brother, but seeing it first hand offers relief. Noah and I might not be together, but I didn't stop caring about him. I don't think I'll ever stop caring.

"They look good," I say, putting the gauze back over the cut on his arm. "Make sure you keep it clean and dry."

"I will."

"Do you have anything to take for pain later?" I can't look at him when I talk.

"I do. Lauren…thanks for coming over."

"You don't have to thank me."

"Yes I do."

I turn and he catches my wrist. His skin against mine causes a ripple in my soul.

"Lauren."

"Noah, I can't." Tears are running down my face.

He gives my arm a gentle tug. "I miss you."

I pull my arm back, breaking his grasp. "You need to rest, Noah."

He nods, and through my blurry vision, I see the heartbreak on his face. He stays there for another few seconds, looking at me, before going back into his room.

I cry myself to sleep.

My alarm goes off too soon. I wake up tired. This is going to be a great fucking day. I stiffly sit up; sleeping on the couch with a pregnant belly is not comfortable. Sasha is on the floor near me and Vader is nowhere to be seen. He must be in with Noah.

After using the bathroom, I duck into Noah's room. Vader is snuggled up with him, head pressed against Noah's chest. It's sad and it's sweet and if I keep staring, I'm going to start crying again. So I turn and get ready for work. I make a sandwich for Noah and put it in the fridge. I know he'll be hungry when he wakes up and won't want to cook anything. He came home with extra dressings for his wounds. I go through the discharge instructions, rewriting it in simpler, easy-to-follow steps, and lay out what he'll need to keep his stitches from getting infected on the counter.

I'm dressed and ready to get the dogs and leave. Yet here I am, sitting in the kitchen. When I walk out that door, I won't ever come back here. At least not in a way that's enjoyable. I hug my stomach, thinking of the little girl who's inside.

It's for you, baby.

I don't try to hold back the tears. They will come eventually anyway. I am sad. I am broken hearted. And that's okay. What's not okay is giving in and letting myself get hurt again.

I get up, and go into Noah's room, stopping in the doorway. My heart aches as I gaze upon him. I miss him so much.

"Goodbye, Noah," I whisper.

I'm sobbing when I get into my Jeep. I want to rush back in, hold Noah, and never let go.

CHAPTER Twenty Four

NOAH

MY BODY HURTS. I'm stiff and sore and every step is agony. But it's nothing compared to the heartache.

Lauren was here.

She came over last night, took care of me. Knowing she still cares just makes it that much worse. It would be easier if she hated me, if she yelled at me and cursed my name.

Why does she have to be so *good?*

It only makes me feel that much worse about myself. I'm such a fuck up. Maybe my father was right all along in avoiding me. He could see how worthless it all was.

I hate myself for hurting someone as beautiful as Lauren. I hate myself for messing up the chance to be with the only person I've ever loved. Most of the time, no matter how deep of shit I'd gotten myself into, I can find a way out. I rarely feel hopeless, rarely think I'm stuck with a shitty situation.

I get up, mouth dry, and limp into the kitchen. The blanket is neatly folded on the couch. I stare at it a moment too long, heart hurting.

Fuck, I want Lauren back.

Then I see the note on the counter and I'm about to

completely lose it. I've never been this torn up before. Can I even handle reading what Lauren has to say? For sure I can't handle *not* knowing. I pick up the paper.

Noah-

Leave the dressings over your stitches for 24 hours. You can gently wash it with soap and water. Pat dry and put antibiotic ointment on. Cover with gauze and keep area clean and dry. Don't go to the gym for at least a week. Go back to get the stitches out in ten days. Call the doc right away if you see redness, swelling, or feel an increase in pain.

Take care.

-Lauren

That's it? I blink and look down again, hoping I missed some sort of hidden message where she confessed her undying love for me and need to be back together.

I know she cares. She has to. Why else would she have gone to the trouble of coming over? I crumple the paper and throw it across the room, mad at myself, not at Lauren.

It's nine-thirty; Lauren is at work. I call her anyway, but hang up when I get her voicemail, mind suddenly blanking. I want so badly to tell her everything, to hold her, to feel Ella's little feet kicking away.

My phone vibrates and my heart jumps out of my chest. It's not Lauren; it's Colin asking how I'm doing. I respond with a quick "sore but okay" and press send.

I set the phone down and open the fridge to get something to eat. There's a turkey sandwich in a plastic baggie, made by Lauren. She's the most fucking considerate person on the planet.

Someone like Lauren doesn't happen twice. She didn't walk into my life. She ran. And though we collided, only one of us got hit.

CHAPTER TWENTY FIVE

LAUREN

"LAUREN W."

I stand when the nurse calls my name and walk across the waiting room.

"Hi, how are you?" she asks cheerfully.

"I'm good," I lie. I haven't been good since the baby shower eight days ago. Add in knowing Noah was in an accident, and I've been a ball of anxiety and nerves. "Tired, of course."

She laughs. "At almost thirty-two weeks, you're really feeling it."

"Sometimes I don't think I can make it another eight weeks."

We stop at a scale. I step on, not even phased by the weight gain anymore. "You're getting into the home stretch now."

"Thank goodness." After getting weighed, I go in to the bathroom, give a sample of pee in a cup, and join the nurse in the exam room. It's nearing five o'clock on a Monday night. I'm pretty sure I have the last appointment before the office closes.

"How are you feeling?" the nurse asks.

"Uh, sore along with tired," I say, downplaying how awful I've felt since Noah and I broke up. After getting his text Thursday afternoon, I hadn't heard from him. Colin let me know that Noah really was okay, but as the weekend came to a close, I wondered if he maybe he finally let go and is trying to move on.

"But it's probably just normal," I go on. "I worked this weekend and I usually don't." Now that I'll be on my own, I need the extra money, and being busy keeps my mind off of Noah.

Father material or not, I miss him. The breakup might have been my doing, but that doesn't mean it didn't hurt. Because it did.

Hell, it still does just as much as it did when he walked out that door.

As hard as I tried, I fell for Noah. And now I have to get over him, put my own heart behind my head and do what's best for Ella.

And that's not Noah Wilson.

I wanted a happily ever after, to find my Prince Charming and have him ride me off into the sunset. Real life doesn't work that way.

"Where are you sore?"

"My back mostly. And I feel a lot of pressure in my pelvis, almost like she's gonna fall out if I stand too long."

The nurse enters my symptoms into the computer, and then grabs the doppler. Ella is moving around so much it's hard to get a good read of her heartbeat. Little stinker.

Next, she gets out the blood pressure cuff. I smooth out the fabric of my long-sleeved T-shirt and extend my arm. I yawn again, feeling the dull headache that I've had for the last few days to come back. Too much stress does this to me. Dammit. I can't take anything else for pain for another four hours.

The nurse takes my blood pressure, makes a face, then takes it again. I can tell by her expression something isn't right. She puts the equipment away, smiles, and says the doc will be right in, just like normal.

But this isn't normal.

"It'll be okay, little girl." I put my hands on my stomach, feeling scared. I wish Noah was here.

Only a minute later the doctor comes in. Yep, this is bad.

"Hi, Lauren," Dr. Linn says. "How are you feeling?"

"I'm okay," I say.

She pulls up my file on the computer. "Your blood pressure is high. Are you having any headaches or blurred vision?"

"I have a headache," I tell her, nerves on fire. Is Ella okay?

"How long have you had it?"

"Uh, since like Thursday. But it's been on and off."

"Have you tried taking anything for it?"

I nod. "Tylenol. It helps for about an hour."

She moves to me and motions for me to lay back so she can check Ella's positioning. "Her head is down," she tells me. "And she's low. I bet you're feeling lots of pressure." She helps me sit up. "I'm going to send you over to the labor and delivery floor for blood work and monitoring, just to make sure baby is doing okay. Your blood pressure has gone up quite a bit since last time."

I feel like throwing up.

"Are you able to go over there now?"

My head moves up and down. The OB office is attached to the hospital. It's just a walk away.

"Okay then. I'll have one of the nurses assist you." She pats my hand. "We're gonna take care of you and baby." She leaves and a minute later a nurse comes in with a wheelchair. I tell her I can walk, but it's a policy and I have to be pushed.

My heart is hammering as the nurse pushes me down the hall and into an elevator. I pull my phone from my leather purse and bring up my contacts. I need to call Mom and let her know, but I hesitate. There is someone else who deserves to know just as much, and I want him there with me more than anyone else.

I pull up Noah's last text message and reread what he wrote.

Tears prick the corners of my eyes, heart hurting. I miss Noah so fucking much. What do I even say? I start typing, then delete what I wrote and try again.

Are you busy?

The elevator doors shut and we go up two floors. I stare at my phone, waiting for a reply. Only a minute later, Noah sends me a text.

Noah: *I'm not. Are you okay?*

Me: *I don't know yet. My blood pressure is high. Doctor is sending me to the hospital for monitoring. Can you meet me here? I'm scared.*

Noah: *I'm on my way.*

I get checked into the labor and delivery floor and hooked up to machines. The nurse, JoAnna, does her initial assessment, then says she'll be back in a few to check on me. She can read the monitors from the nurses' station as well.

So now I sit in a hospital bed, belts and monitors around my belly, alone and scared. I grab my phone to call

Mom then stop. I should wait until I get some answers before I make her worry and speed over.

The door to the room opens and I look up, expecting to see the nurse come back. But it's Noah. His sky-blue eyes meet mine and everything comes rushing back.

How good it feels to have his arms around me. His lips crashing into mine. The way he makes me laugh, makes me feel beautiful.

The way he makes me feel loved.

"Lauren." Noah crosses the room. I push up and he throws his arms around me. I bend my head, pressing my face into his neck, and break down in tears. "It's okay," he soothes, gently running his fingers through my hair. "It'll be okay."

He pulls back just enough to look at me. I don't waste any time. My hands fly up, landing on either side of his face, feeling his beard beneath my skin, and bring his face to mine.

"I missed you," I whisper, tears freely falling down my cheeks. Noah wipes them away.

"I missed you too. So fucking much." He kisses me again then brings me to him. The belts slide out of position, making an alarm sound. "What's going on? Is everything okay?" I've never seen him so concerned.

"Yeah." I push the belt back up to where it used to be, but it doesn't silence the alarm. "It moved." I motion to the belt. "Thanks for coming."

"Don't thank me," he says. "I should thank you for telling me what's going on."

My bottom lip trembles. "You were the first person I wanted with me. I miss you, Noah. I miss everything we had."

His jaw tenses and emotion takes over his face. "Lauren I—"

JoAnn comes back into the room, readjusting the monitors on my belly and turning off the alarm.

"Is she okay?" Noah asks, not moving away from me.

"So far everything looks good on the monitors," JoAnn tells us. "No contractions and baby's heart rate looks good." I relax a bit.

"But Lauren's blood pressure is still high?"

"Yes, it's elevated."

"Why?"

"There could be a number of things, and once we get the results from the blood work back we'll know more. Has the lab come in yet?" she asks me.

"Not yet."

"They should be here soon." She gives us a smile. "Do you want anything?"

"Some water would be nice," I say. She gets me a cup then tells us to relax while we wait.

"Easier said than done," Noah mumbles and pulls a chair up close to the bed and takes my hand. I close my eyes and link my fingers through his. It feels just like how it used to be, despite not speaking for over a week.

"Are you okay?" I ask.

"I'm fine, and I get my stitches out in a few days." He rolls up the sleeve of his shirt, showing me a two-inch line on his bicep. "I thought about you, about Ella, as the bike was going down. All I wanted was another chance to see you."

"I'm glad you got it." I blink back tears.

"How has everything else been?" Noah asks.

"Same as before, really."

"Is Ella moving a lot? I miss feeling her little feet."

I smile to cover my guilt of making Noah miss out on that. "She moves all the time. What about you, well, other than the accident?"

"Same too. Just trying to stay busy and keep my mind off of you."

I close my eyes. "I don't want to do this," I whisper.

He takes his hand back. "Do you want me to leave?"

"No. Not at all. I mean, I don't want to not be together. I want things to go back to how it was before."

"Me too. Lauren," he says, voice heavy with longing. "I would do anything to redo things."

I turn, looking at his handsome face. "I would too."

"Is that your way of saying you forgive me?"

I give him a half smile. "Kind of. I want us to be together." Ella kicks me hard, causing me to flinch.

"Then we should."

I close my eyes, trying not to cry … and I can't look at Noah when I say this. I don't want to see the hurt on his face. "Sometimes what I want isn't what I need. I can't take care of a baby and have you getting drunk, so drunk you're passing out and puking. And I can even forgive special occasions, like you overdo it at a New Year's Eve party or something. But for no reason … I don't want Ella growing up around that."

Noah inhales then slowly lets his breath out. "I know. And I agree."

I open my eyes, looking right at him.

"I don't want to be that dad. I don't want Ella thinking I'll run out when times get tough. I don't want to be like my own father. And, Lauren … that's why I drank that night."

"What?"

"My dad. He showed up outside the studio Friday before the shower. I'll just say it brought up a lot of bad memories and old feelings I didn't know I still had. It freaked me out. My dad left when I was just a kid, and it still gets to me, still hurts. I … I don't want to be a bad dad too. I don't want to let you down or ruin Ella's life."

I take his hand again. "That's why you were acting weird Friday night."

"Yeah," he admits.

A few beats pass in silence. I trace a tattoo on the inside of his wrist. "Why didn't you tell me?"

"You had enough going on. I didn't want to add to it."

"Noah, you have to tell me these things. If we want to be a couple—a family—then we can't keep things from each other like that."

"I know now."

"You know what will ruin Ella's life?" I start. "Bottling up your feelings and drinking away the pain. Not trusting me enough to help."

"It's not that," he says definitely. "I do trust you, more than anyone, Lauren. I didn't tell you because there's no need for you to know how I spent my eighth birthday at the police station because my dad got arrested for a DUI on the way to the football game he was taking me to." He shakes his head, looking at the floor. "But the real kicker? My own mother used Ella as an excuse to call that asshole, even after I said I don't want anything to do with him. He doesn't deserve to meet Ella, and Ella doesn't need to be anywhere near someone like that. Bad parenting, a life of disappointment and hurt, it's in my blood."

"That's not true."

245

"It's all I know, and I'm damned to repeat it. I did the best I could for you, and it wasn't good enough."

"That's not true either. Why didn't you just ask me? Noah, what we had was perfect. This started as a nightmare, as the worst thing that could possibly happen besides dying, and we made it into something beautiful. I was really happy."

"Was," he mumbles. "I'm sorry, Lauren. If I could do it over, I would."

"You can't rewrite the beginning, but you can create a new ending."

"I want that ending to be a happily ever after for you. You deserve it, even if it's not from me." Each word hurts him, every syllable tearing his heart bit by bit. The pain is obvious on his face.

I've never felt stronger for him than I do right now.

"I want it to be you." And I do. I want Noah not just because he's Ella's father, but because I've fallen for him, hard. There is more to him than motorcycles and tattoos.

Noah moves forward, cupping my face in his hands, bringing my lips to his in a kiss.

"I love you," he says, lips hovering over mine. "I've been in love with you for years. Ever since the first time I saw you, when you came into Mrs. Jefferson's office to protest against dissecting the cats in biology."

"You remember that?"

"I remember that you were wearing a pink and white dress. I remember how you smelled like strawberries. And I remember how crushed I was when I found out you were Colin's sister. I thought I'd get over you. It was just a stupid teenage crush, but I didn't, and the more I got to know you, the harder I fell. And then that night when you walked into the bar and I took you home … I thought one night with you would be the closet I would ever get. But then in a bizarre twist of fate, you got pregnant and gave me a chance. And then I was so scared of losing you, of letting you and Ella down, that I fucked it all up, and you deserve better."

Tears are streaming down my face. I open my mouth only to close it again. The words soak into me, deep inside my heart, healing the hurt. All this time, he's loved me. All this time he's cared.

"I love you too, Noah."

We kiss again, then Noah rests his forehead against mine. "Now what?"

"I don't know."

"I'll fight for you. For our *family*. I'll do whatever it takes to prove to you this can work."

"Noah," I squeak out, unable to talk without crying.

"Can we start by being together and you be my girlfriend again?"

"Yes." I close my eyes and press my lips to his. "But only if you make me a promise."

"Anything."

"Tell me when something upsets you. Let me help you and share the burden."

"I hate doing anything to make you upset—"

"Noah," I stop him right there. "Not telling me makes me a whole lot more upset. Obviously."

Noah closes his eyes. "Fuck, I'm an idiot. I should have told you and this wouldn't have happened."

"Live and learn, right?"

Someone knocks on the door; it's someone from the lab to take my blood.

"Do you feel sick?" Noah asks me when the phlebotomist leaves.

"I'm tired and have had an on and off headache for the last few days," I admit. "But I've been stressed."

I regret the words the moment they leave my mouth, Noah looks so guilty.

"I'm so sorry, Lauren. And I understand if you decide not to do this."

"I want to, and people fight and make up." I give him a smile. "But it's different when a kid is involved. Ella has to come first, no matter what."

He nods. "And right now, taking care of Ella means taking care of you. I will do whatever it takes, Lauren."

I look into his eyes, finally seeing past the walls he's put up all these years. "I know you will."

*

"Does your mom know I'm here?" Noah asks, sitting on the couch next to me at my house. He puts his arm around my shoulders.

"I didn't tell her, but it's not because I didn't want to. She kinda freaked out when I said I had signs of pre-eclampsia."

"Do they know what happened?"

"Yes and no. They know we broke up, but not the fine details." I rest my head against him. "I didn't want them to be mad at you. Even if we weren't together as a couple, they'd still see you sometimes. Ella's both of ours. And I didn't want Colin to completely hate you."

"That's very considerate."

"Well, you two have been friends for a long time. I

don't want to break you guys up too."

"Fuck, I love you." He kisses the top of my head. "You have no idea how good it feels to finally say that to you, and to hear it said back."

"I've felt this way for a while, Noah. Really. I tried not to fall for you, but…"

"I told you, I'm hard to resist."

I smile. "Most of the time."

He brings me in closer and rests a hand on my belly. "Things can't go back to how they were, can they? We can't pretend this never happened and move on like normal?"

"I wish we could. I meant what I said: it's different now. It's not just my heart on the line. Ella's is too."

He turns and locks eyes with me. "That's what scares me. I don't want to hurt her like my father hurt me."

"Knowing you're scared of being a bad father makes me think you won't be."

He shakes his head. "That doesn't make sense."

"Do you think your dad worried about being a good dad?"

"Hell no. Oh, I get what you mean now." He leans back with a sigh. "I won't let you down again. And I'll never let Ella down."

Am I a fool for believing him? "Did you ever think about telling me how you felt before?"

"Many times."

"Why didn't you?"

He runs his fingers up and down my arm. "I didn't want to piss Colin off. But mostly because I didn't think I had a chance with you."

"I had a crush on you too."

"Seriously?"

I laugh. "I think the entire female population of that high school did. Some of the popular girls tried being friends with me because they knew you stayed the night at my house a lot."

"Should I apologize for that?"

"Nah, it's not your fault. It must have been hard to be so good looking and popular as a teen."

"It was just horrible." Noah snakes his arm around me and leans over until his lips touch mine. I missed his kisses so fucking much.

The dogs run to the door a second before the bell rings. I make a move to get up.

"I'll get it," Noah says. "You're on strict orders to rest."

I nod and settle back, watching Noah wrangle my super well-behaved dogs from bombarding my mother.

"Oh, Noah … hi." She bustles past, too concerned to question things now. Though really, even if Noah and I were done forever, the well-being of Ella is still his concern. "Pre-eclampsia," Mom starts. "That can be serious. Are you okay? Is the baby okay? Should you be in the hospital?"

I flick my eyes to Noah, having warned him that she would act this way. "We'll be fine," I say. "I go back to the doctor weekly now and I'm on partial bedrest."

"Partial? What does that mean?"

"I'm allowed to get up, but have to limit what I'm doing."

"You're not working anymore then, right?" Mom asks.

"Well…"

Noah's eyes widen. "Don't even think about it,

Lauren. It's not worth it to risk your health or Ella's. Whatever you need, I'll pay for."

Mom looks at Noah for a few second before saying, "He's right. And if you need help, your father and I are more than willing. I can buy you groceries."

"Thanks, but you don't have to," I say and run my hands through my hair. "I'll figure it out."

"That's what family is for," Mom says and hugs me. "You just take care of yourself and keep growing that baby. It's too soon for her to make an appearance. Let us take care of you."

"Okay." I rest against the back of the couch again, tired. This has been one of the longest days.

"Do you need anything?" Mom asks.

"Not right now. Noah got me ice cream and the tacos I was craving on the way home. I'm just ready for bed now."

"Is he staying tonight?"

Noah looks at me from across the room, hopeful.

"Yes," I say. "He is."

"And you two are…" Mom starts.

"We're back together," I say with certainty.

Mom nods but doesn't look convinced. "I'll let you get some sleep, and we can talk later. Call us if you need anything. We're only a short drive away."

Noah walks her to the door, and ends up going outside along with my mother. Ten minutes pass before he comes back in.

"What was that about?" I ask.

He shakes his head and smiles. "Nothing. Just talking about how much we both care about you. And Ella." He sinks down next to me and pulls me into his lap. "How are you feeling?"

"Okay, just tired."

"I mean, mentally."

"Oh. Stressed. Really stressed and worried. I feel like my body is a failure to Ella."

"It's not. There is nothing you could have done. The doctor said this can happen to the healthiest person."

"I know. Still, not being able to work scares me."

"You can apply for short-term disability," he reminds me. "And I can cover everything else. I want to. I've wanted to, you know that."

I let out a breath. "It helps. Thank you." My eyes close and the emotions from today weigh heavily on me. Noah and I move into the bedroom; he rubs my back and I'm asleep in minutes.

*

"You survived your first week of bedrest," Noah says as he sets the table, like he has all week. He hasn't left my side other than to go to work since I got home from the hospital. Things between us are back to how they were, only better since he tells me he loves me every chance he gets.

"It wasn't so bad," I say and fill two glasses with water, placing them at our spots at the table. I take a seat and wait for the potpie to finish cooling enough for us to eat. "I caught up on all the reading I missed from being too tired after work. Time is going by slow, though."

"You're doing great. And Ella is okay."

"Thankfully." I had to go for more testing today. My condition hasn't worsened, but it hasn't gotten much better. My blood pressure went down a little, but not enough to be out of the woods just yet. If I can stay pregnant for three more weeks, I'll be happy. Thirty-six weeks is still a ways from my original goal of thirty-nine, but I'll take what I can get.

I don't know how I would have gotten through this without Noah. We're not officially living together like we had planned, but he's here more than he's at his own place, and I think a majority of his clothes are at my house right now. He might as well get his own key, because he's not going anywhere. I won't let him.

He said he'd fight for me, do anything to prove to me this can work, and he has.

NOAH

"CAN WE GO over everything one more time?" Lauren asks.

"We've gone over it twice," I say.

"Please?"

I can't say no when I look into her sea-green eyes. My heart softens, knowing her compulsion is out of nervousness.

"Of course."

She swings her feet over the side of the bed and extends her hand for me to take and help her up. She's thirty-eight weeks along today and is being induced in just a few hours.

"We have diapers and wipes," I say with smile. "That's pretty much all we'll need. Just keep Ella clean and fed and she'll be good."

"Hah-hah, not funny." She slowly makes her way into the nursery, hands on her large baby belly, and stops in the middle of the room, looking around.

And I look at her.

She gave me a chance to prove myself—again—and I won't ever let her or Ella down. I never thought I could feel any stronger toward Lauren but this last month proved me wrong. I'd never opened up to anyone before. Making the promise not to bottle shit up and let it slowly fester and eat me up has made us closer than I ever thought possible.

Being honest with Lauren means being honest with myself, and that's a new thing. A good new thing.

"Okay," Lauren mumble to herself as she goes around the room. "Diapers, wipes, clothes arranged by color and size ... first aid kit ... books and toys ... swaddle blankets, burp cloths ... all the bath stuff is in the bathroom." She nods. "I think I'm good here. I just need to check the diaper bag and my hospital bag one more time."

"Then let's rest for a few hours before we have to head in. Maybe even get a little sexy time in there."

Lauren raises an eyebrow. "Don't hold your breath. I have a seven-pound baby pressing on my cervix. I don't want anything else inside me."

"Fine. It'll be the last time we get to have sex for a while."

She makes a face. "I'm scared I'm going to tear."

I'm scared she will too. "It'll be fine, I'm sure."

"And as long as Ella is okay, it doesn't matter, right?"

"Right." I take her hand and help her check the bags one more time, then pretty much have to drag her into the bedroom so we can lay down.

"The next time we're in here, we'll be a family of three," she says. "It'll be weird. A good weird. But weird."

"Definitely good." I spoon my body around her; she's laying on her side with a big pillow under her belly ... pretty much the only way she can sleep now. Ella hasn't been born yet and I'm already feeling like the luckiest man in the world.

*

"All right, it's time," the nurse says after checking Lauren. "She's pretty far down. I think it'll only take a couple of pushes and she'll be out."

"I'm scared," Lauren tells me. "What if I can't do it? What if she gets stuck?"

"Deep breath," I say, leaning over the bed to kiss her. "You can do this. You've been amazing this whole time." Ten hours ago, she got induced and hasn't complained about anything the whole time. Her mom and Katie are here with us, but stepped out for the actual birth.

"I can't feel anything. I shouldn't have gotten the epidural. What if I push wrong?"

"There's no wrong way to push," the nurse says. "And you did great with the practice pushes. Are you ready?"

Lauren looks at me, green eyes full of fear. "I think so."

"I'll get the doctor."

"Noah," Lauren says as soon as the nurse leaves the room. "I'm scared."

"I know you are. But you're going to do fine. Our baby is almost here. You can do this."

She closes her eyes and lets out a shaky breath. "I hope you're right."

"I know I'm right."

The doctor comes in, and just a few minutes later I'm holding onto Lauren's leg, watching our baby come into the world. She's tiny and wrinkly and covered in goo, but she's the most beautiful thing I have ever laid eyes on.

She's perfect.

Then she opens her mouth and lets out a little scream, followed by a cry. I'm hit in the heart with emotion.

That is my daughter.

That teeny tiny little thing is mine. She gets to come home with us, make us a family.

The nurse puts a blanket over Ella then puts her on Lauren's chest.

"Oh my god," Lauren whispers, tears running down her face. "Ella." Carefully she wraps her arms around the little bundle and kisses Ella's head, which is full of hair, dark like Lauren's.

I move to the head of the bed and put my hand over Lauren's. Ella's cries quiet, soothed by the touch of her mother.

"Dad," the nurse calls a bit later. "Time to cut the cord."

I don't want to step away from Ella. It takes me a few seconds to tear away and cut the thick cord. Then I'm right back up there with Lauren and Ella.

"Hi, sweetie," Lauren says softly. "I'm your mommy, and this is your daddy. We love you very much already." She closes her eyes, nuzzling her face against Ella. "Is she okay?" she asks the nurse.

"She's prefect."

"Told you," I say with a smile, looking down at our baby. I lean over and kiss Lauren. "Good job, Mama."

"Do you want to hold her?" Lauren asks.

"Yeah. How do I pick her up?"

The nurse comes over and helps, tucking the blanket around Ella's little body. She opens her deep-blue eyes and looks around, taking in the new world. She's so light in my arms, like a feather. It's crazy how something so little, something I've only seen for mere minutes, can make me feel so much love.

I look down at Ella, then at Lauren. "We did this."

*

I sit in an uncomfortable chair next to a hospital bed, holding a sleeping baby. It's been four hours since Lauren gave birth. We're in a different room now, and her parents—and my mother—are all crowded in to see Ella. Everything went as smooth as we could hope, and Ella is perfect.

"It's my turn to hold that baby," Mrs. Winters says. I carefully stand and hand her Ella. I move to the bed, sitting on the edge next to Lauren.

"Are you doing okay?" I ask.

"I'm sore," she says. "The epidural is completely worn off now."

"Want me to call the nurse? She said you can have pain medicine."

"Yeah. And I have to pee. Help me up?"

I take her hand and slowly help her to her feet. She winces when she takes a step. She did end up tearing and needing stitches.

"Can you fill this with warm water?" she asks, sitting on the toilet.

"Sure, but, why?" I take a squirt bottle from her and move to the sink.

"I can't wipe."

"Oh." I turn the water on. "Birth is a lot more, uh, messy than I thought."

"Are you glad you watched it or do you wish you

hadn't?"

"No, I'm glad I did. Yeah, it's messy but it was kind of amazing."

She smiles. "I'm glad you were there. I'm glad *we* were there."

I know what she means. We were there together, as a couple. "*We* will always be there."

"And we just had a moment while I'm on the toilet," she chuckles.

I fill up the bottle. "I didn't even realize that. Spoken like a real couple, right?"

"Right."

I help her back into bed.

"She looks just like you," my mom tells me. "I'll find your baby pictures when I get back home and send them over."

Our parents stay for a while longer, then leave so Lauren can sleep. But right after they leave, the nurse comes in to check on Lauren and Ella, then sticks around to help Lauren with breastfeeding. Ella is sleepy and not wanting to latch.

I thought pushing out the baby was the hard part.

Twenty minutes later, I'm able to take Ella and Lauren lays down. Not five minutes later, someone knocks on the door, asking about insurance. By the time they leave, the nurse has to come back and take vitals.

And now I remember why I hate hospitals.

"You're never going to get any sleep at this rate," I say, taking Ella out of Lauren's arms after a feeding again. "Try to rest now."

"I know," she sighs. "I'll sleep tonight. Well, probably not." She looks at Ella and smiles.

"I'll stay and hold her."

"You don't have to. That chair looks super uncomfortable."

"It is, but I feel like I shouldn't complain. I didn't get my nether regions ripped just hours ago."

She shudders. "I asked the doctor to stitch me up extra tight."

I laugh. "It'll feel like your first time, baby."

"We have at least six weeks until we attempt anything again. That's probably the longest you've gone without sex since we started dating isn't it?"

I look down at Ella, heart still so full. "It's not, actually."

She raises an eyebrow. "Really?"

"There was a time, recently. I haven't been with anyone else but you since that night."

"Since the night we got drunk and made a baby?"

I nod.

She smiles, but looks confused. "I'm glad to hear that, but you didn't know I was pregnant—hell, I didn't know—for like two months after that. It just seems out of character for you. The former you, I mean."

"I wanted to be with you for so long. Then I finally was and couldn't remember anything. It was worse than putting food out of a starving man's reach. It was letting him taste it but not eat it. I had you, had what I wanted, but blew it. I would have given anything to have that chance again and remember it. Because I knew being with you would be different."

"Noah," she says softly, looking at me with so much love in her eyes.

"I love you, Lauren. I always have, and I always will."

CHAPTER TWENTY SEVEN

LAUREN

"AM I HURTING her? I'm hurting her!"

"You're not hurting her," Noah says, somehow calm.

"Then why is she crying?" I scoop Ella up out of the carseat, feeling like I'm fumbling with the world's most precious football.

"Because she's a baby?"

"Shhh," I soothe, gently swaying Ella. It takes a few seconds, but she stops crying. "See? I don't think she likes the carseat."

Noah puts his hand on my shoulder, steps in, and kisses me. "Want to wait until the nurse comes back?"

"Yeah." I cradle Ella to my chest and sit, cringing when my ass hits the mattress.

"Are you hurting?" Noah sits next to me and slips his arm around my waist. I'm still in my pajamas. The cute going-home outfit I had packed for myself—leggings and a sweater—isn't working. I can't breastfeed in the sweater, and feel dumb for not thinking about that when I picked it out. And the leggings are too revealing for the mesh undies and giant pads needed after pushing out a seven-pound babe.

Live and learn?

"Yeah. I think this is worse than labor."

"You'll heal and forget all about the pain."

"Hah, maybe." I bend my head down and kiss Ella. She's in her cute going-home outfit at least. She looks like a little wrinkled peanut, but she's the cutest little wrinkled peanut that ever existed.

Noah's mom said she looks like him as a baby, and texted over pictures from his baby book. There is no denying this is his child.

The nurse comes back in with our discharge papers, and helps up get Ella into the carseat. She cries for her too, which is a little reassuring. At least it's not just me. The nurse is young and pretty and it's probably the huge hormone shift and lack of sleep that makes me think she's hitting on Noah. Not that I can blame her.

Everything is loaded and ready to go home. I'm excited to leave the hospital and get back to my own house, but scared not to have help at the call of a button.

Noah clicks the carseat in place and helps me into the back. Ella's fast asleep, looking peaceful and adorable in a little pink dress with striped leggings and a matching bow.

"Are you warm enough?" Noah asks, slowly pulling out of the parking lot. It's misting and cold out today, typical for the end of November.

"We're good." I look up and meet his eyes in the rearview mirror. We are good. Noah, Ella, and myself. *Good.* Right now, life is pretty damn good.

*

"Lay down, Lauren," Noah tells me. "I got her."

We've been home as a family of three for

approximately two hours and I'm already having a panic attack. I grind my teeth together and nod, but don't even attempt to move out of the living room.

"Lauren," Noah repeats, a little stern. "You need sleep."

"I know. I'm just … anxious."

"Everything is fine. You just fed her; she'll be good for two hours and if she wakes up I'll bring her to you."

I nod, staring at the wonderful man across from me. His sky-blue eyes light up when he looks down at our daughter, smiling without even thinking about it. Ella, so small in his tattooed muscular arms, is wrapped in a soft purple blanket, snuggled and sound asleep.

"Go rest," he orders again. "Your parents will be over in three hours with dinner. Sleep until then."

I blink, and some sense comes to me. "Okay. Thanks, Noah."

"No need to thank me. I want some daddy-daughter time." He flicks his eyes to me, still smiling. "She'll be okay, I promise."

I nod again, and slowly turn and go into my bedroom. The dogs follow me, and I close them in with me. Just one less thing to worry about. Though they've been fine. Vader got a little pushy wanting to sniff everything, but after both him and Sasha did their initial investigating, they lost interest in the little crying thing in Mommy's arms.

Noah has been surprisingly calm. Well, maybe it's only a surprise compared to me freaking out. I assumed I'd be nervous, but I didn't expect to feel so much panic and have every possible bad situation run through my head at a million miles per hour.

I tuck myself in bed, irrationally thinking of ways Ella

could drown and worrying about it. Vader jumps up next to me, and I carefully snuggle up next to him. It still hurts to move and I'm terrified of ripping out my stitches. I worry away an hour of sleep, then finally pass out from sheer exhaustion.

When I wake, it's dark outside. I sit up in a panic, listening for signs of life. I hear nothing, then realize the dogs aren't with me anymore yet the bedroom door is shut. I check my phone; I've been asleep for about three-and-a-half hours. I feel a world better, but panic rises in my chest and I get out of bed quickly.

Too quickly and I feel a painful pull in my vag. Wincing, I limp my way into the living room. Noah is sitting in the recliner holding Ella. Both dogs are at his feet, chewing on bones, and my parents are sitting on the couch. The TV is on, and my dad and Noah are discussing football in low voices. My heart settles back into my chest.

"Hey," Noah says, looking up at me. His eyes sparkle and something passes through me, something that tells me things will be okay. For real. "I was just about to get you."

"How's Ella?" I cross the room and Noah stands.

"She's been a sound sleeper this whole time. She woke up when I changed her diaper about an hour ago then she fell back asleep." He carefully hands me our little girl. I try to keep her awake to nurse while my mom heats up dinner.

After we eat, my parents order Noah and me to shower and nap. Noah falls asleep right away and I get another hour and a half of shut-eye in before my parents leave, and then it's just us.

We sit up in bed until we're both too tired to stay awake any longer. Then comes the moment of truth: trying to sleep while Ella sleeps. I lay her in the bassinet next to the bed, checking to make sure her swaddler is tight enough three times before putting my head on the pillow. We get four hours before Ella wakes up fussing. Not too bad for our first night home.

*

"We kept her alive for a week," Noah says, sitting down at the table. "I say we're doing this parenting thing right."

"I think so." I brush my hair back and fix my dress after nursing Ella. I've worn nothing but pajamas up until tonight. My stitches aren't healed yet, and I'm still sore when I walk, move, think about it … pretty much all the time. But after being cooped up for days, Noah suggested we go out, and I have to admit it feels good to put makeup and join the real world.

"I'm still trying to figure out how to do anything productive though." I smile down at our one-week-old. "It's hard to put her down. She's growing too fast."

"Fast enough to make you want to have another," Noah jokes. Or maybe he's not joking.

"Oh, I'll definitely be wanting another."

"With me?"

I look up, expecting to see a smile on his face. His genuine concern makes me laugh. "Of course, dummy. Well, unless I decide to get drunk and have a one-night stand again."

"Just checking. Sometimes none of this seems real. Me and you, together." He looks down and shakes his head. Emotional Noah doesn't come around too often, but I like it when he does. "And now add the perfect baby. Almost seems too good to be true."

I'm smiling as big as I can, looking from our daughter to Noah and back again.

"It does. But it's not." I cradle Ella against me, kissing the top of her head. The story of my life had some major plot twists thrown in, some so big and gnarly I didn't think they'd ever straighten out. And though this story is far from over, I know it will end with a happily ever after.

LAUREN
Four years later...

I YAWN, QUIETLY getting out of bed as not to wake Noah. Early-morning light sneaks through the curtains and I'd do anything to get back under the covers and go to sleep. At least today is the last day of my work week. I shuffle downstairs and into the kitchen, firing up the coffee pot.

"Hey, old man," I say to Vader. He wags his tail and slowly gets up, old bones creaking and cracking with every step. We go together outside; he needs help getting up and down the stairs now.

It's late in April and actually warm out already. I fill a Cinderella mug with coffee and sit on the back deck, waiting for Vader to get done so I can help him inside. I start to doze off and groan when I force myself to stand. I'm really not wanting to go to work today.

"Hey," I say softly, seeing Noah in the kitchen. "What are you doing up?"

He runs a hand over his face, wiping the sleep away. He's still just as tatted and muscular as he was when we first got together, and actually he's added a few more tattoos since then.

"Was gonna help you with the dog," he mumbles, still

half asleep. "You shouldn't be lifting him."

I put my empty coffee mug in the sink. "He helps. It's not like I'm carrying him completely. But thanks. That's sweet of you."

Noah steps behind me and wraps his arms around my waist, hands landing on my belly. "You're already carrying enough."

I put my hands on top of his, leaning back against him. "Charlotte is a chunk. She's going to be bigger than her sister, I'm sure."

Noah kisses my neck and I'm hit with desire. My libido has been crazy high this whole pregnancy. Even now, at thirty-two weeks, I'm jumping Noah's bones every chance I get.

He doesn't mind one bit.

It's crazy how different the two pregnancies have been. I threw up every day for thirteen weeks this time around, but was able to drink all the coffee I wanted. I've been sore pretty much since conception this time, but haven't had any blood pressure issues.

Noah worries, of course, and has gone above and beyond to make sure I'm not stressed, which is hard to do considering this is my last year of vet school. These last four years have been fucking hard, and I worked my ass off to get to where I am now. But this time, I wasn't just doing it for myself. I was doing it for my family.

I didn't go to Purdue like I wanted. Noah tried coming up with every solution he could think of, including moving down to central Indiana with me.

But that took Ella away from her grandparents, and took the extra help away from us. And we needed the help to get me through school. Instead, I took a chance and applied at MSU and, by some miracle, got in. It took a lot of time, energy, and tears to get to this point, but we made it, and my last semester is an externship at the clinic I worked at before.

Looking back, I don't know how I survived. I was getting used to having a young kid my first year. Noah proposed my second year, and between classes and raising Ella, I planned our wedding. We got married the third year of school, and conceived our second child at the beginning of this last year.

This time around, the timing is perfect. I'll graduate a few weeks before my due date, take some time off, then go back to work at the clinic as an official doctor of veterinary medicine. I'll be working part time, just two days a week, until the new baby is older.

"I don't want to go to work," I groan. "I have a paper to write this weekend too."

"You're almost done," Noah says. "Then I can start saying I'm married to a doctor."

I laugh. "I'm making everyone call me Dr. Wilson. I think I've earned it, right?"

"More than earned it." He kisses my neck again. I whirl around in his arms, big belly pushing against him, and hook my hands around his neck. "Do you still want to go to dinner with Colin and Jenny? We can stay home instead."

"No, we can go. Ella is looking forward to playing with her cousin tonight at my parents."

Three months after Ella was born, Jenny finally got pregnant. She and Colin had a baby girl as well, named Hannah. She and Ella get along great.

"As long as you're okay with it," Noah says. "You've

been working so hard lately. You know I'm proud of you, right?"

My lips meet his. "I'm proud of you too. For taking such good care of us."

"You're my girls." He smiles and shakes his head. "I'm seriously outnumbered here." We kiss again. "But I wouldn't have it any other way."

ABOUT THE AUTHOR

Emily Goodwin is the author of the twice banned dark romance, STAY, as well as over a dozen other titles. Emily writes all types of romance, from love stories set in the zombie apocalypse to contemporary romances taking place on a western horse ranch. Emily lives in Indiana with her husband, children, and many pets, including a German Shepherd named Vader. When she isn't writing, Emily can be found riding her horses, designing and making costumes, and sitting outside with a good book.

STALK ME

www.emilygoodwinbooks.com
www.facebook.com/emilygoodwinbooks
Instagram: authoremilygoodwin
Email: authoremilygoodwin@gmail.com

52981802R00155

Made in the USA
Lexington, KY
17 June 2016